THORNY SECRETS
&
PINOT NOIR

Other Books by this Author

PATRICIA STEELE

Non-Fiction
Living with Cystic Fibrosis (MyHealth Magazine)

Memoirs
A Roundabout Passage to Venice
Mind the Gap in Zip It Socks
Fairydust to Daffodils

Novels
Tangled like Music, More than a Love Story
Cloisonné, It was never about the jewels
Slutty Memories

The Callinda Beauvais Mystery Series:
Shoot the Moon, Book 1
Wine, Vines and Picasso, Book 2
Thorny Secrets & Pinot Noir, Book 3
Flamenco Strings Uncorked, Book 4

PATRICIA RUIZ STEELE
Genealogy ~ Spanish Pearls Series
The Girl Immigrant
Seeking Duende in America

Touching Spanish Soil
Spain Calling
A Spanish Haven

Silván Leaves – A Family History Book
Ruiz Legacies – A Family History Book

Thank you for taking the time to read Thorny Secrets & Pinot Noir. This is a work of fiction. Names, characters, businesses, places, events, and incidents are either the products of the author's imagination or used in a fictitious manner. Any resemblance to actual persons or actual events is purely coincidental. If there are mistakes in the story, they are my mistakes. However, the life lessons and values are real. I learned them from many people who have graced my life. Some, I still miss every day. Others are still touching my life with a smile.

Plumeria Press
Printed in the United States of America
ISBN: 9798288153495

www.patriciabbsteele.com
www.facebook.com/patriciabbsteele.com

Table of Contents

DEDICATION

To J.D. Steele
1935-2015

My husband passed away just before Christmas during the final stages of this writing. Though my heart was broken, he would have been happy to know I eventually finished it.

This book is also dedicated to men and women who think they know all the secrets their spouse or significant other holds within their hearts. It reminds us that we all carry those small secrets that we hold close for various reasons.

    Everyone has a story.

    Everyone has a secret.

But remember, too, that everyone is human and should be treated accordingly. Just because the secret isn't shared does not diminish their love for you.

THORNY SECRETS
&
PINOT NOIR

A Callinda Beauvais Mystery, Book Three

By
Patricia Steele

A standalone sequel to *Wine, Vines and Picasso*

CHAPTER 1

Her stomach lurched, so she munched her last piece of chocolate candy, anxious for her new life to begin in…She glanced at her watch. Fifteen minutes. As the Delta jet swooped out of cloudy skies to touch down at Portland International Airport, Callinda Beauvais studied the tree-lined Columbia River. And her lips lifted in the semblance of a smile. Portland held so many sad memories for her that, compared to the past few weeks in France, she admitted this town was no longer her home. She'd ticked off the things that waited for her, mainly packing boxes and preparing to sell both houses so she could move on to share a life with Jules Armand.

The plane glided over fir trees and several cement pads as it dropped its wheels to slide onto the tarmac and stand on solid ground. She chuckled. She hadn't stood on solid ground for a long time, not since François died. And now she was finally ready to get on with her life.

A disembodied voice barked, "Please do not remove your seat belts until the captain has turned off the seat belt sign."

Beside Callie, the woman's fingers gripped both armrests before she smiled, still fidgeting. "Don't worry, I don't intend to." Her black ponytail swished as trees skimmed past Callie's airplane window.

Callie patted the woman's hand. "Don't be nervous. Over the past six hours, we've solved the world's problems, you beat me at Gin Rummy, and we've shared photos from home. Landing now should be easy."

Her seatmate grinned at her and opened the piece of chocolate candy Callie had given her a few minutes earlier. When Callie saw the girl's knuckles begin to turn pink again, she lay her head back and closed her eyes.

She'd just begun dreaming in French again and smiled at the thought of moving back to Provence. As their plane taxied up to the gate, she could hardly wait to get her hands on her belongings, toss some, save some, and donate the rest before the sale. She glanced down at her list. Call Alexis at the Albertina Estate office. Two houses, two sales.

Callie twisted the colorful scarf around her neck that Veronique had given her when she left the south of France. Her fingers threaded around the long fabric circling her neck, and she smiled. One would think that finding a child nobody knew existed would knock her socks off, and it did. Not only was the young woman delightful, but she added a layer of excitement, a bit of intrigue, and a lot of love to Callie's life, something she could never have imagined just a month earlier.

Her chest tightened against the anger that swelled there, thinking about the man she'd married and his secrets. To believe that François could hide this beautiful daughter was so astounding, it made her mind stumble. She'd finally come to terms with most of her anger after his childhood friend, Jules Armand, reminded her that "François was just human. Someone once said it is hard to look forward when you keep looking behind you."

Now, Callie had closed that door to look ahead.

Gripping her roller bag and briefcase, she inched off the plane with the other travelers, anxious to see her best friend waiting outside. Her mind was awhirl with her to-do list as she skimmed by shops, restaurants, bookstores, and coffee stalls on her way to baggage claim. She'd miss this place, this time, and the people she cared for. But her life was finally on an even keel again, and France was where she needed to be.

As promised, Olivia Phillips-Carle waited at the curb. She nearly knocked Callie's breath out when she threw her arms around her in a fierce hug before tossing the bags in the trunk. "You look good. Did Jules put that rosiness on your cheeks, or was it from jogging down the concourse?" Olivia teased her as she eased her car toward I-84, which would take them to Callie's house in southwest Portland.

Callie laughed.

"Your wedding at Beauvais Vineyards seems much longer than just three weeks ago, Livvy. I've missed you. It was a fairytale wedding among the grapevines."

Olivia laughed deep in her throat. "And I'll not forget all that flowing champagne amidst laughter and dreams...soon it will be your turn."

"Mm…hmmmm," Callie murmured, and her face warmed. It was challenging to hold down her excitement when she thought about Jules, a man who showed her how to open her mind and park her doubts.

"Shall we stop by the office to say hello before heading toward the house? I'm yours the rest of the day either way."

Callie's brow furrowed for a moment. "Let's go straight home. I'm not ready to face Nate yet after breaking our engagement. He's such a good guy; I hated hurting him."

Olivia raised her eyebrows when she glanced toward Callie.

"It's your call, but you have to see him one day soon. You know that."

Callie nodded grimly and turned her head to watch the streaming traffic and MAX, the light rail train, running the rails beside them. She refused to dwell on Nate. Not yet. She had to finish creating the Dear John letter inside her head before she talked with him. It was a conversation she dreaded. One thing at a time, she argued.

After Olivia swung her car into the driveway, Callie stared at her house before turning toward her friend. The paint was a pale yellow trimmed in white, set apart from its neighbors who chose bright colors and brick. "I'm right, you know. I have always loved this house and the lake house, but they both belong in another time. I'm still angry at François. I haven't quite let it go. I know it will be hell pawing through all the memories waiting inside. I've danced around the hidden crannies for three years, and it's time to pull everything out. But knowing Jules is waiting at the other end makes it much easier."

Olivia grinned. "Well, let's get started then, Cal. Your new life awaits." She reached into the back seat to pull out a bright green, cloth shopping bag and winked. "Wine and food. We can't work on an empty stomach, can we?"

The women's laughter accompanied them to her brightly-colored front porch. Bits of debris littered the wooden portico, and the wind picked up as Callie rolled her bag up to the perky, blue door. After turning the key in the lock, she swung it open. And stared. The women stood in the doorway, both speechless. The room looked like an avalanche had moved everything; chair cushions were on the floor, table lamps were lying beside the couch, and her table ornaments lay in pieces.

"What in the world...?" Callie moved into the room. "Oh my god, I've been burgled. What a mess." She pushed past the couch, dropped her bags, and rushed into her kitchen.

Olivia pulled her cell phone to her ear and dialed the police. While Olivia told the man on the other end of the phone what happened, she was assured a police car would arrive soon.

"Look at my kitchen. The dishes are broken, glasses in the sink, and furniture tossed around in the sitting room, too." Both women headed down the hallway. When they stood in the doorway to her office, Callie sagged against the door frame.

Her desktop was bare. Everything that sat on it when she'd left for France a few weeks earlier lay on the floor like debris. She twisted Veronique's scarf around her neck and yanked on both ends before dropping into her office chair. It was the only piece of furniture that didn't lie on its side in the overall mess. Papers were strewn about like confetti. Her bookshelf was emptied and bare, the books tossed from hell to breakfast.

Her stormy eyes lifted to Olivia.

"Oh, hon, I am so sorry."

The room groaned with chaos. "It's crazy. Dammit. Things were returning to the normal I'd missed for so long." She glanced around her. "Someone was looking for something. I don't think a random thief was looking for expensive items to sell. This looks different...They didn't take my computer, but they broke the keyboard."

The doorbell interrupted their conversation. Both women returned to the living room, where two patrolmen stood at the open front door. After Callie let the men inside to see the damage, she saw them study each window, door, and the mess.

"Since you've been gone for over two months, it's hard to pinpoint when this happened, so it's doubtful we'll find the vandals who did this." His face held a note of impatience and a lot of disgust.

Callie signed their paperwork and stared around the corners of her living room. Shaking her head at the debris, she kicked through everything on her way to the door. Olivia trailed behind her.

"I wish I could give you hope of finding these people, Ms. Beauvais, but I really can't." The officer handed Callie his card and tipped his hat toward her before she shut the door behind them.

As the police car's tail lights disappeared around the corner, Olivia opened her bag. "Wine. Glad they didn't break everything. The creeps left a couple of your wine glasses intact. …"

"How comforting." Callie looked at her surroundings and shook her head in disbelief. Thinking back to all the scenarios she'd conjured inside her head, returning to Oregon to pack up her old life to prepare for her new, this particular image certainly wasn't one of them. Accepting the wine, she fought the small lump in her throat and tried to keep her lips from trembling.

Despite her anger, Callie plopped down her empty glass. "Okay, since I have you for the rest of the day, our job is just a bit nastier than I'd envisioned. Do you want the kitchen mess or the sitting room? I'll save the office and my bedroom for last."

"Are you sure you don't want to rest after the long flight? You must be exhausted."

Callie stared at Olivia. "That's the reason I'm here. This isn't home anymore. Forrest Gump said, 'My Mama always said you've got to put the past behind you before you can move on,' and that's what I'm doing. I slept on the plane, Livvy. I'm glad you were here when I walked into this mess."

Hours slipped by as the women put the rooms to rights, pulling boxes from the garage, taping them, and filling them up afterwards. A pile of damaged glassware, ornaments, and other items stuffed into a garbage bag sat beside three others in the cold garage. The heavy plastic bulged and slumped toward the lawnmower and tools, as if they were tired.

When she heard Olivia's cell phone ring as she pushed torn pillows into another bag, Callie's shoulders slumped. How would she ever get this stuff organized? Her electronics were still in the house. Why didn't they steal them? What were they looking for? She stood at the kitchen sink, peeling an orange, and popped a slice in her mouth. She had a fleeting thought as she wiped the dripping juices from her chin. Her cleaning lady, Maria, came on Wednesday. This was Friday. So, the house must have been trashed between Wednesday evening and this morning. *Did someone know I was coming home today?* She tossed the last piece of orange into her mouth, savoring its sweetness with her tongue.

"Callie, Bram's bringing us a salad and those yummy bread sticks from the Olive Garden about seven. I told him to bring wine too. He wants you to stay with us tonight after what happened." Olivia said, optimistically.

"Good idea," Callie whispered. She pulled more boxes from the garage to drag into her office. Inching through debris, she stumbled over the pile of books that littered the floor behind her desk. The room wasn't that large, about ten by twelve. The desk swung around to fill most of the room, framed by built-in bookshelves that she and François had stuffed with their favorite books and photographs.

Callie glanced down at a broken picture frame, its glass ground into the carpet beneath her feet. She picked up the small frame, carefully removed the remaining glass, and stared at the photograph of her and François. Their arms were entwined around each other, and happiness flowed from their eyes. It had been taken at Lost Lake on their first camping trip. He'd promised her she'd like sleeping under the stars.

She didn't. She'd disliked the lumpy ground and mosquitoes. After he'd placed an inflated mattress beneath her sleeping bag, she'd kissed him for it. When she'd asked him where the toilets were located, he'd laughed that special laugh, head thrown back and mouth wide open. No, she hadn't liked camping, but that day--- with the blue sky smiling above them, a hiker had come by and snapped this photo.

She'd loved this man so much. Her finger slid across his face, now devoid of glass, and she sighed heavily. She pulled the photo from the broken frame and slipped it into her pocket for safekeeping. She'd do something with it later.

She could hear Olivia vacuuming in the other room as she balanced several books on her chest. She upturned the lamp, piled the desktop with books and broken picture frames, and grimaced. "Why would someone do this?" She reached down for the last of the books from the floor.

Olivia stood in the doorway holding up a broken lampshade. "Do you want to keep the lamp and get a new shade or just put the whole damn thing with the furniture for the estate sale?"

"Just throw it away, but save the lamp base. At least it isn't broken. I bought that in Napa when Mom and I went antiquing years ago. I may take it to France with me." Her sad eyes looked at Olivia, and she blew out a breath. As she turned, her toe stumbled over an Oregon Duck's paperweight that François had loved. She burst into tears when the books flew out of her arms to land in a heap.

Olivia put down the lamp and sat on the edge of the desk, swinging her leg and shaking her head sadly.

Callie's face turned stony. "I will survive. It's just another bleep in the road. I want to clean up this mess and get out. Going home with you and Bram is a good idea for tonight. I'm not sure I'm up to staying alone, wondering if the vandals are still around. But they won't beat me. I've struggled with much worse."

Olivia grinned. "You're certainly right about that, my friend."

When she left Callie to continue juggling items in the other room, Callie squatted down to pick up the remaining books. Seeing François' favorite book, *To Kill a Mockingbird* by Harper Lee, she held it against her cheek. She would take it to France and give it to his daughter, Veronique. She slipped it inside the box of other keepers. As she jammed it in to fit with the others, a piece of paper protruded from between its pages like a bookmark.

Curious, she yanked the book back out of the box and pulled out a small envelope about the size of a note card, addressed to François. *Huh. No return address, but stamped in Portland.* She squinted, trying to read the date. One month before François died?

Sitting in the chair again, she slid her finger under the flap and pulled out a card with pansies encircling the words, thank you. Slipping a finger inside to open it wider, she was perplexed after reading the words.

> *Dear François,*
>
> *Thank you for Lily's money. It surprised me because we thought the first check was the amount we settled on. I'm happy Lily won't have to face this again. She's having a difficult time. This money means so much. I never imagined we'd receive this enormous amount of money.*
>
> *Big hugs from both of us,*
> *Mae Haydon*

Callie's hands shook so badly, she dropped the note as her thoughts ran dark. Could this money be the same money François got after selling his shares of Jules' company out from under him?

As another one of her husband's secrets bloomed inside Callie's head, her anger rose incrementally as more questions filled her mind. She jumped up to flip through the lateral file beside her desk. Her finger skimmed the pages when she found their bank statement from three years earlier. No date matched a withdrawal to Mae's note. Nothing was listed in François' old checkbook either. She closed her eyes. What am I missing? It must have been a bundle of money for this woman to be so shocked.

Will another one of François' secrets push me over the edge? But if I don't find out the truth, I may never get another good night's sleep again. She read the handwritten note one more time. Her jaw was clenched so hard, she wondered if she'd need a crowbar to open her mouth to eat dinner. What should she do now? Ignore it? Look beyond the words? She sighed and hesitated. Blinking back tears, she put the note on the desk and stood. A sob rose in her throat.

"Who is May Haydon, and why did François pay her that money?

CHAPTER 2

"I found something!" Callie's voice sailed down the hallway. In seconds, Olivia's anxious face filled the doorway. Callie pulled a side chair to the desk for her friend, sat down in her own, and lifted the note. Placing her elbows on the desktop, she propped her chin in her hands, waiting for Olivia's reaction.

Olivia read the words twice. When she glanced up with a question on her face, she slid the note onto the desk and sighed heavily.

"I want to leave this alone... just forget it."

"It may be completely innocent," Olivia said quietly.

"Will his secrets never end? My life is so good right now!" Callie stomped her foot against the leg of her desk.

"This may be nothing." Olivia tapped her fingers on the desk.

Callie bit her lip so hard that blood rose to the surface. "I wonder who Lily is." She slapped the note against the desk. "I didn't want to find any more of François's secrets after the mind-blowing one in France. Good god, first I find he had a daughter twenty years ago, and now this!"

Olivia placed her hand over the note. "But Callie, can you begin a new life with Jules... always wondering what this is about?" Olivia's face showed concern, and she shook her head.

"I don't know," Callie blurted in dazed exasperation.

There was tension in the air, a kind of spellbinding anticipation, like how things felt before a roiling storm. Callie closed her eyes and began taking slow, deep breaths, seeking the calm that had filled her when she had boarded the plane in Marseille, her lips still warm from Jules' kiss. The note brought back waves of distrust again. Why did her husband give this woman money? Olivia was probably right. But was she strong enough for the possibility that Lily might be another illegitimate daughter? She demanded answers, but Callie's usually clear-eyed outlook about life now whispered an ominous silence.

~

Tucked away in Olivia's guest room later that night, she called Jules. "Good morning." Closing her eyes, Callie visualized Jules holding a cup of steaming coffee in his strong hands. It was nine hours ahead in France.

"Bonjour, ma belle. I miss you already."

Jules' warm voice soothed Callie, who leaned into the phone. "I had a bit of excitement when I got here."

"Oh? A welcome party?"

She chuckled, enjoying his laid-back charm. "More like an unwelcome party. My house was trashed. Everything on the floor, a lot of things are broken. The police doubt they'll find who did it. I'm now lying on Livvy and Bram's guestroom bed because I didn't want to stay at the house alone yet."

"I am sorry to hear this. They robbed you of important things?" Jules' voice rose an octave.

"No, I don't think so.   That's the strange thing, Jules. Everything seems to be there. I think they were looking for something. They left my computer, my television, and my CD player. I can't figure it out. Olivia and I packed a few boxes and have trash bags stacked in the garage. The estate sale takes place in two weeks. I have to organize the lake house, too." Suddenly, Callie felt overwhelmed with the idea of what lay ahead. She leaned back on her pillow and closed her eyes to stifle unwanted tears.

"Do you want me to come to you, *ma chère*? I can be there soon."

 Callie smiled at his words. "No, I'll be returning to France before you know it. I do miss you, Jules." She clutched the blankets and pulled them to her chin, almost feeling his warm arms around her.

"I wish I were there with you right now." His voice was like velvet.

She felt her body heat up as she tried to push the intriguing vision from her mind. A few short words later, Callie hung up and stared at the ceiling for a long time. Between the jet lag and the uneasiness that quaked through her body, she doubted she'd snooze at all.

It was dawn before she fell asleep.

Monday morning, Callie dialed Bryan Martos' number. He was running the law firm on his own now, and she wondered why he hadn't replaced François with another law partner yet. When she heard his voice, she hesitated for a heartbeat.

"Hello, Bryan. This is Callie Beauvais."

"Callie," he answered quickly. "So nice to hear from you after all this time... You're doing well?" His voice was warm and cordial.

"Yes, thank you for asking. I could use your help."

"Sure. What do you need?" His voice sounded cautious.

"Do you recognize the name, Mae Haydon?"

His sharp intake of breath was only a blip in the conversation, but Callie didn't miss it. "The name doesn't sound familiar. Why are you interested in this woman?" His voice turned a bit cool.

"I found a note while packing up the house, Bryan. I'm selling everything and moving to France soon…the note was strange and I wondered who she was."

"Well, can't think who she is. What did the note say?" His voice held a slight tinge of probing. "If it's important, I'll look in the files, but I'm swamped now with a big case. Can it wait? I doubt it was very important since it's been a few years since..."

Callie's brow creased when she heard the timber in his voice change from friendliness to something else. She thanked him before hanging up and couldn't shake a twinge of disappointment. Bryan had never been one of her favorite people, but he had always been friendly and forthcoming. Today, not so much. She wasn't sure why she hadn't told him the note's contents, and he hadn't asked her again.

She tried to shake the panic that was rioting within her. Why was it so important? And wasn't it odd that Bryan wouldn't know the woman? Their firm had not been large, and she knew they often shared their cases and brainstormed over the phone at night. This one, François had evidently kept secret from his partner. Maybe that should make her feel better?

The next few days, Callie worked in a blur of activity. Boxes were strewn all over her house, the debris from the break-in was long gone, but packing papers and bubble wrap still filled the corners of each room. She'd procrastinated about looking for Mae Haydon to learn who Lily was. However, she knew she couldn't put off going to the office to say her goodbyes and see Nate Leander. He'd been an essential part of her life as he'd helped her get past her grief after losing François. He showed her she could love again. It just wouldn't be with Nate, and she was sorry because she thought a lot of him and his family. She blew her nose, fighting the tears that wanted to escape. He deserved more. But then she'd found Jules.

A few boxes were set aside in the garage with France boldly written on each one. The others sat for Alexis' estate agents to go through, tag, and prepare for the sale set for ten days from now. The plan was set to finish at the lake house the following week.

WHO WAS LILY?

Her ordered life was in quicksand again, and she didn't like it. Maybe Olivia was right, and it didn't mean anything. But, perhaps it did, and Callie knew there was no ignoring it. Words scrambled around in her head like marbles, and she kept hearing, 'Who was Lily?' over and over again. Pressing her hands over her ears, as if to stop the questions ripping through her brain, she sank into a chair filled with packing debris.

Refusing to believe Lily might be someone important in François's life, she turned to thinking about other scenarios instead. A friend? A client? Someone's sister? She was driving herself nuts, and she couldn't stop herself. Who would know about these people? Mae Haydon must be a local resident, and once she spoke with her, she could clear up the gloom, and then Callie could finish packing, sell the houses, and get back to France. The obvious person to call had been Bryan Martos, the old partner at the firm. She was stumped when he didn't recognize the name, so maybe the woman wasn't a client at all? There she was, back again, to the furtive, unspoken fear that Lily was more to François than an acquaintance. He'd done it before, and they say the first time is the easiest when you start hiding secrets from your wife.

She thought of her friend, Valerie Blume, the paralegal who worked with François in the Beauvais Martos Law Firm. She might know who Mae and Lily were. Why hadn't she thought of her before?

They'd been friends for years. They'd lost track of one another, and Callie had missed her.

Arguing with herself about the note for a few days as she stuffed boxes and pulled items off shelves she hadn't thought of in years, she decided to call Valerie. Callie admitted to herself that she wasn't sure if she wanted to know the answers. She'd already gotten past the secrets in France. Did she really want to face more secrets in America? Ultimately, she needed to decide because the constant barrage of arguments between herself and her alter ego kept blasting through her head day and night.

Before she changed her mind, she dialed.

"Val. It's Callie."

"Oh my god, it's so good to hear from you. I've been busier than a two-headed chicken working on a huge project. I've thought of you, often wondered what you were up to since that big prescription drug war you were involved in last year. Quite the Headline Queen, lady."

"Ha *ha*. It was wild, but we won. That's what counted. I'm sorry I haven't been in touch with you. I think the last time I saw you was when Nate and I ate dinner at Alexander's." Callie's voice slowed down.

"That good-looking guy only had eyes for you if I remember right. Are you still a couple?"

"Uh…no. A lot has happened since then. I've been running in a hundred directions since then, went to France, found old brandy bottles, met a new man…let's get together for lunch and catch up. There's something I want to throw at you and hope you can help me."

"Now, that sounds very interesting. What's it about? We could meet at Jake's Grill. It's always fun to walk into that place and see all the stained glass; everyone is so friendly. Food's good. Can you meet me tomorrow at one? I'm on the phones during the regular lunch hour."

"Perfect. I don't want to go into it now, but I found something while packing…something François evidently didn't want me to see."

"Packing? Are you going somewhere again?"

"No, I'm leaving Oregon. Moving to France."

Valerie gasped. "Wow. But I'm not surprised. You and François always loved Provence. So, you hope I can fill in some blanks or something? It's been a long time since I worked for François, Callie. I will try to help you, but I'm unsure what you are looking for." Valerie's voice turned oddly apprehensive.

"It will be a treat to catch up on news, too. My life is in an uproar, but each day is moving me toward France. Thanks for meeting me, Val."

Valerie made a humming sound in response.

Callie loved Jake's; she and Olivia enjoyed Happy Hour over wine and two-dollar hamburgers. She knew she couldn't put off stopping by the Larkspur Insurance offices, though. Nate must know she was back in Portland by now. Her replacement was one of her top agents, and Callie wanted to stop by her old office, too. As she lifted the phone to call Olivia to make sure she'd be there the next morning, her mind wandered back to what she now called the 'Lily note.' Then, her thoughts switched to Valerie. Maybe she'd knock loose some of her memories during her tenure with the law firm before François died. Maybe. Maybe. Maybe.

When Olivia picked up the phone, Callie almost forgot why she was calling.

CHAPTER 3

CAllie looked at her watch. In another hour, she needed to be at Jake's Grill to meet Valerie. She almost dreaded what she might learn from her. She had worked closely with François, but she was also a friend. Callie wasn't enthusiastic about putting a pinprick into the past, but had no choice. Maybe if she could learn enough to settle her nerves, she would feel less tormented over the stupid note. Hearing reticence in her friend's voice over the phone had given Callie a feeling of apprehension, but she pushed it away. Surely, she'd help Callie solve this little mystery.

When Callie stepped off the elevator Wednesday morning at Larkspur Insurance, she came face to face with Lana Potts, Olivia's secretary. The women grinned broadly at one another before hugging tightly and heading toward Olivia's office.

"Well, you are a sight for sore eyes, Callie. I heard you found a special someone in France? I'll miss you. My stomach hit the floor when Olivia said you weren't returning. The boys will miss you, as well. I want you to be happy…but France is so far away!" Lana's reddish hair bounced as she chattered to Callie along the hallway.

"Well, you and the boys will have a place to stay if you holiday in Europe. You know that you're always welcome."

Lana grinned and whispered, "That sounds like a dream. I'd like to hear about your new man. Maybe we can get together just the two of us…well, with the boys, of course," she said with a laugh. And then the smile left her face. "Have you talked with Nate yet, Callie?"

The expression on Callie's face answered the question.

"Look who I found loitering in the hallway, Olivia." Lana spread her arms wide to pull Callie into the room and left discreetly.

Olivia Phillips's office was simple yet elegant. Large windows overlooked a heliport pad on the adjacent building, a view that kept her sane when the work issues were anything but. Callie watched her friend run fingers through her short blonde hair before turning to her with a warm smile. She knew she would miss this woman.

Olivia got up for a quick hug before she grasped Callie's shoulders to stare into her friend's face. "Did you see Nate yet?"

"No. I came directly to you, Livvy. I'll see him on my way out because our conversation will be too emotional for me to see anyone else. I'm meeting Valerie Blume at Jake's in about an hour about that note I found lost between the pages of François's book. I know I should probably ignore it… but dammit, for some reason, it's pulling me in. Guess I have nose trouble, as usual."

Olivia laughed. "Nose trouble? Nosy, you mean?"

"Ha *ha*." Callie nodded, enjoying the camaraderie they always shared. Her life was in an earthquake of flux, and she wondered if she was ready for all the changes. Then Jules' face glimmered in her mind, and she knew everything would find its way… in all the right spots.

The next half hour was filled with farewell hugs and tears. She wanted to run down the stairs and avoid Nate altogether. But of course, she couldn't. Her feet slowed as she turned down the last hallway near the elevator, and a large lump formed in her throat.

Nate's assistant stared at his computer as if it were speaking to him. When he looked up and saw Callie, his face first reflected excitement and then caution. "Hey, Callie. Nice to see you. I'm sorry to hear you're leaving Larkspur…" His eyes flicked behind him into Nate's office before darting back toward Callie, unsure of what to do.

Callie smiled and nodded toward Nate's door before peeking in and seeing him standing and gazing out his office window. He was good-looking, about 5'9" and built solid. The man exuded confidence and had a quick smile. He must have realized he was no longer alone because he turned his head, letting dark, curly hair fall over his forehead. His mouth formed an O as Callie walked into the room.

She wasn't sure how he would respond to her, but she knew she needed to walk into his arms and hold him tightly. And that's exactly what she did. His arms came around her automatically, then slightly fell, and he stepped away. Callie noticed his gray-green eyes turn misty as she slid into the chair opposite his desk.

"Callie." He whispered her name before taking a huge breath.

"Nate. Please forgive me for the decisions I've made that affect both our lives. I had to talk with you in person…You are so special to me and…"

"Special? But you aren't in love with me as you'd led me to believe. Just a hot-tub one-night stand?" His voice turned cool.

Callie's face turned pink. "It wasn't like that, Nate, and you know it. I was vulnerable, and you were the amazing person who helped me open a part of my heart that I thought would remain closed forever. I will never, ever forget you. Please forgive me, Nate. Please," she implored. Tears threatened to spill over, but she held them back for both their sakes, looking at him sadly. Her hands shook so badly that she had to sit on them.

"Oh, Callie, I wanted so much for us. I want you to be happy, there's that. And I'm jealous as hell you found some Frenchman to take my place. It just isn't fair, dammit." He took a deep breath and turned toward his office window again when his voice broke.

When he turned around, her chair was empty.

Callie stood in the doorway and lifted her hand toward him. She couldn't remember feeling so desolate; it felt as if she'd buried one of her best friends. Since she couldn't trust herself to speak another word, she walked to the elevator and punched the button. When her mind sped to Jules and the way he made her sing inside, she knew she'd made the right choice but damn, it hurt.

Callie was glad to leave Larkspur and all its complications behind. She hurried along the pavement toward Jake's Grill at Tenth and Alder Streets, her breath vaporizing in the chill of February air. She hugged her purse beneath her arm and pushed her wayward, silvery bangs from her forehead. Then, she shoved her gloved hands deeper into her coat pockets, seeking the last warmth from her body.

She was drawn to the familiar green awning of the granite and brick building. Her steps quickened as she entered the foyer. To her left, an archway led to the bar, which resonated with laughter and the soft clinking of glasses as patrons smoothed out the wrinkles of another day.

She had always loved the place, and meeting Valerie there would help her overcome the awful tears she kept swallowing with each step away from Nate. Jake's was already filled with people, even though it was past the busy lunch hour. Noise filled the foyer. Lucy raised her eyebrows as Callie walked in. She had been the friendly greeter for longer than she could remember.

"Hey, Callie. So nice to see you." Lucy gave her a swift hug.

"Good to be here. I'm meeting a tall blonde with green eyes."

"Ah, Valerie." She pointed to the corner table. "She said her friend liked that area best. If I'd known she was talking about you, I would have already ordered your Crème Brûlée..." Lucy chuckled.

Callie saw Valerie wave and hurried toward her. They reached for each other's hands and squeezed hello.

"You look great. Sorry, I haven't kept in touch much since..." She blew out a breath. Freckles stood out on her face, and the lipstick she'd hastily put on her lips was long gone.

Callie patted her hand. "I know, but it feels like yesterday." She smiled at her friend, understanding how difficult it was for her to discuss François. The woman had worked for him for over ten years and had spent more time with him than she had. Callie tightened her fingers around the strap of her purse where the note was stashed.

"Tell me how you've been and why you're leaving us."

"Wonderful, and Provence. I'm selling my houses, and moving next month. I met a man." A warm glow flowed through her.

"Wow – guess that pretty much answers my question. What a move for you...closer to François' family by the vineyard? And I want to know all about him." Valerie's face softened into a smile.

"Yes, close to them, and Jules is a big part of the change. There's more, but first... let's order something to eat. I'm starved."

While the women forked their Ahi Salads and sipped iced tea, Callie pulled the note from her purse and slid it across the table toward Valerie. She wasn't sure how to broach the subject, so she'd let the note do the talking. The wooden privacy panel closed in on her, and the other patrons' voices made it difficult to talk.

Valerie was perplexed a moment before picking it up and looking across at Callie with a question on her face. "What's this?"

"I'm hoping you can tell me, Val. I found this between one of the pages of François's books while packing up the house a few days ago. He may have saved it for a good reason...but this person's name is unfamiliar. I hope you can shed light on it. Can you tell me why he gave this woman money?" Callie's eyes urged her to read the note while her heart thumped hard in her chest. She knew it was ridiculous, but she felt torn between the knowing and the secret it might hold.

Callie noticed a slight tremor in Valerie's hand as she read the note. Valerie smiled sadly before sipping her tea. Her finger tapped against the floating lemon slice, playing a rhythm on the ice cube. Her fair hair fell across her freckled face as she stared into her glass.

Callie saw her hesitation and looked at her shrewdly. "Well?"

"Yes, I know who Mae Haydon is. It was a sad issue. I don't have all the answers, and I'm unsure where to begin."

Callie breathed heavily, "How about starting at the beginning? I know it must have been important to François."

Valerie's blonde hair swung over her cheek. "Yes, it definitely was important to him. Mae is Lily Haydon's mother. Bryon Martos is the attorney for Dominic Jazzy, who owns Jazzy Cove Vineyard & Winery in Dundee. Mae Haydon and his wife, Bella Jazzy, are twin sisters... so that makes Lily Mr. Jazzy's niece by marriage." Valerie lowered her eyes, sipped more tea, and pushed a piece of fish around the lettuce with her fork before continuing.

"So, this wasn't François' case?" Callie was confused.

"No, it wasn't. After a meeting with Bryan, François found a file in his office that Bryan had inadvertently left behind. One day, when François left the office, he had his hands full—he was carrying his briefcase and two large files, determined to return the Haydon file to Bryan's office. Some papers slipped from his hands and slid to the floor in a big pile. He was upset when I bent down to help him pick them up. I noticed Dominic Jazzy's name. He was Bryan's client... I knew his friend, Denis Sorbets, worked there as their winemaker, but it was something else..."

"Oh? I know Denis. He's been at the house a few times."

"Yes, he'd visited our office too. I remember the look on François's face when he glanced at some notes in the margin. I knew he was upset, but he shook his head at me when I questioned him. He took the file home, but told me to keep it between us."

"What? François brought Bryan's work file home with him?" Callie was shocked. This was a man she thought always followed the rules. But the past few months had shown her that there was a lot about François that she didn't know.

"The next day, François was grumpy. He called me into his office and told me to close the door." Valerie looked at Callie bleakly. "He said to expect a showdown at the firm. Those were his words, 'a showdown'. When he told me the file's contents, I was stunned."

Callie sat up straighter, clinging to Valerie's words like ivy climbing a brick wall. She nodded for her to continue. "So, Bryan should have remembered the name when I asked him…"

"He knows both names." Valerie raised her eyebrows and held Callie's gaze. Her fingers began to fold and refold the note in her agitation. She blinked rapidly.

Callie had always trusted Bryan, but now she realized she no longer knew whom to trust, except for her close friends and Jules. Her deep brown eyes noticed Valerie glancing around the bar before leaning forward furtively.

Valerie lowered her voice and reluctantly continued. "Lily settled out of court. She was only twelve when he hurt..."

Callie's brain burned as she heard Val's words. "…When he hurt her?" The room began to spin around her as she waited for Val to continue.

Valerie's words suddenly caught in her throat.

Callie twisted around to see what had caught Valerie's attention at the nearby tables. When she brought her face back to her friend, she had slipped on her jacket and grabbed her purse.

"What happened? What did he do to the girl?"

"We have to go. Now."

She reached for Callie's coat and tossed it at her before blindly leading the way out of the restaurant, as if her feet had been set on fire. When they got on the sidewalk, Valerie turned and said, "I'm sorry, Cal. I have to go."

Callie stood in a blunted daze on the sidewalk, unsure of what had just happened.

CHAPTER 4

E arlier that morning, in his law office about three blocks from Jakes, Bryan Martos sat in his plump leather chair, lost in thought. His leather-tooled, glass-eyed racehorses filled the shelves of his wall-to-ceiling bookcase. Their life-like eyes followed him no matter where he sat in his office. They were all expensive, but his favorite was the replica of Lady Pepper, whose race brought him nearly $100,000 in winnings. He studied the small statues briefly before glancing at the FAX on his desk. His finger ran down the list of horses on the racing form running that day.

Bryan was a fifty-four-year-old bachelor who was methodical and focused. He had never been married and doubted he ever would be, even though he'd been in an intimate relationship with Bella Jazzy for five years. He'd passed the bar exam thirty years ago and was proud of his accomplishments. When his partner, François Beauvais, died three years earlier, Bryan had no intention of retaining his employees. Three disgruntled people left his firm. He had no wish to add another partner afterward. A private man with a few secrets he wanted kept that way, he hedged his bets and worked alone.

Since François's death, he never allowed his activities to jeopardize his firm's reputation. He was a gambler; watching the twitching race horses anxious to leave the gate, his chest tightened with excitement when he was at the raceway. He'd grown up around horses and wished he had a stable of his own. But race horses cost thousands, which he didn't possess.

He'd put himself through college cleaning tables in a local brew pub in Eugene. He lost sleep working at night and going to school during the day. He was an alumnus of the University of Oregon and liked to bet on the Oregon Ducks. He found humor in the fact that his life was made up of the whims of horses and ducks.

He'd learned at an early age the importance of money. His dad urged him to make horses his life's work, like he'd always done.

But Bryan knew, as a lawyer, he'd earn more money from crooks than grooming horses. Horses were in their blood, dad said. Bryan knew it was true; he'd only concentrated on betting on them, not grooming them.

He ran a finger across his eyebrow. Maybe his dad had been right. Because he'd gotten himself into a hell of a fix and wondered if he'd ever dig himself out of the self-made hole he now floundered in. He scratched his jaw, thinking about the money he'd lost and the people involved in his mess, and he let out a long, audible sigh.

At least he had Bella to warm his bed. She got his mind off his gambling issues and Charlie's nasty friends. He glanced at his wrist. Nearly noon. He grabbed his suit jacket and smiled. It didn't bode well to be late.

Bryan looked indulgently across the table at Bella, smiling as she lifted her lipstick tube to outline her lips. She met his smile with a come-hither look when she snapped it shut again. She lifted her head and swiped at the hank of blonde hair falling over one eye.

Bella pursed her lips when she saw the strange look cross Bryon's face. And then she craned her neck to see what had taken her lover's attention away from her. Two women had just walked out the doors, and Bryan was tracking them with his eyes. She didn't like the distraction and reached for his hand.

When Valerie Blume pushed open the glass doors that led out of Jake's Grill, Bryan's face turned solemn, and he pinched his lips together.

"Who are they, Bryan?" Bella Jazzy wiped her mouth and lifted a finger to her lips as she smoothed on a new layer of dusty pink lipstick. "You look like you just licked a piece of sour candy." She glanced out the window and saw a dark-haired woman with a swathe of silver bangs hug a taller blonde, before she turned toward Bryan again.

His eyes narrowed as the woman crossed the street. "Nobody you should be concerned about, Bella," he answered with deceptive calm.

"Well, you certainly seem to be. Who are they?"

He gave her a narrowed, glinting glance. "The short woman with the gray streak in her bangs is my deceased partner's widow. The tall blonde was his paralegal. The widow called me a few days ago asking about an old case. I played dumb. Now, she's undoubtedly quizzed Valerie about it. But she doesn't know anything." He hiccupped and checked his watch.

Bella studied the retreating women before they disappeared down the street, unsmiling. "Should I know her?"

Bryan's face closed. "I told you; she's my old law partner's widow. She wanted to know who Mae Haydon was." His face stilled.

Bella's puzzled face turned toward him. "Why does she want to know about Mae?" Some sixth sense awakened, and the nagging in her mind refused to be stilled. Despite being estranged from her twin sister, she was protective of her. A rock that felt as solid as a marble lodged in her throat. Each day, she woke up aching for the connection they'd shared and lost because of a child's lie. Surely, one day, Mae would miss her enough to see through the child, and their twin link would be restored. The widow asking about Mae now had her stumped.

"I don't know. Come on," Bryan said, "our room's waiting for us." He abruptly stood, expecting Bella to follow.

"Why would she want to know who my sister is? Is it something about that incident with Lily?" She let him lead her out of Jake's Grill, through the large, open breezeway to the elevator that would take them up to the third floor. Each week, they'd taken this same route.

"Of course not," he lied.

Bella's mind worked through Bryan's answers, and she didn't think his body language equated to his words. Something was amiss, and she didn't like it. Suddenly, her anger at Lily didn't seem so bad after all. Especially compared to the sadness that swept through her each day, because she missed her twin sister fiercely. She let Bryan guide her down the corridor toward their room and tried to shake off her melancholy.

Bryan's love patched the hole in her heart that had shadowed her since Mae was no longer in her life. She turned toward him, looked up and down the hallway, and then she squeezed his butt.

Whispering into his ear, trying to loosen his earlier mood, she kissed her earlobe.

He chuckled softly. "Let me get the key out first…"

She grinned up at him, her blue eyes demanding the solace she knew lay within the room. "Hurry then." Her voice was filled with impatience.

When he pulled her inside the room and spun her around to kiss her passionately, she knew she'd soon set aside thoughts of missing Mae. She was also sure the earlier conversation in the grill would be forgotten, at least for a while. But she couldn't shake the feeling that Bryan wasn't being completely honest with her. She let him have his way and tried to push Mae from both of their minds. Within minutes, he stopped thinking about the two women who seemed more important than he'd admitted.

CHAPTER 5

That Wednesday night in February, it was still too cool to sit outside for long, but Callie loved her outdoor room. She pulled her fluffy robe tightly around her and headed for the chaise lounge.

Still stunned by Valerie's abrupt departure from Jake's earlier, her mind reached for reasons why they'd nearly stumbled out the doors. She couldn't remember precisely what Valerie was saying when she'd seen someone or thought of something that froze her words in her throat. But, something in her urgently-whispered words triggered a muddled memory. This was about the file that François took home, not about Callie. It was about Bryan's file. Why had Bryan lied? If it was a big legal secret, why didn't he just say that? First, François, and then Bryan. What was so important about this woman and the money she received?

"Dammit."

She knew everyone had secrets. Everyone wore two faces. She was no different, but some secrets were better kept dark. Important secrets. She laughed uneasily. There were important secrets and not-so-important secrets; she doubted Mae Haydon was an important one. Not like the one she'd carried around like baggage nearly all her life. Now **that** was a secret.

She thought about the incident that had plagued her for nearly forty years. She wished she could face the memories, if not the man, head-on. Jules deserved a woman who didn't have that piece of baggage, one who didn't pretend those awful things happened to someone else... a woman who'd been too weak to fight back.

The sky was clear. Twinkling stars dangled above like pencil lights, and she realized why it was cold; the Big Dipper curved in her direction. Callie stared it down for the first time in years. She gazed upward at the cluster of stars and dared her throat not to clench in anger. She turned off her phone and sat in the dark; it was just her and the past. Callie blocked out all sounds to find the quiet of her mind.

Her memories whisked her back to the summer she'd turned thirteen. Her best friend, Diana, had invited her for a slumber party, and Callie had arrived with her backpack filled with all the stuff teen girls usually carried with them. The girls planned to watch movies, eat popcorn and pizza, and talk about boys. When she'd arrived, Diana's uncle answered the door. She'd met him before and didn't like all the black hair that covered his arms.

"Hi, Callinda. Diana went to the mall with her mother for some last-minute things. She was worried you'd arrive before they returned, so Helene asked me to wait for you. So, I guess it's just you and me for a while. She already ordered pizza," he said. "I'll get us some Pepsi while you put your bag in Diana's room."

He hadn't waited for Callie's reply.

When she had returned to the living room, her heart was hammering so loudly that she wasn't sure what to do. She didn't want to hurt his feelings, but the last thing she wanted was to share pizza with him. She kept glancing out the window, willing Diana and her mother's car to pull into the driveway.

"Hey, I'm on the patio. Come get some pizza and a Pepsi. I'm sure Diana and Helene will be back any minute."

She tried to hide her dismay, smoothed the pink sundress, and followed his voice. It was getting dark, and when she stepped onto the patio, the back light went out. She turned to go back into the house.

"It's okay, Callinda. I'll fix the light. Actually, the stars make it bright enough. Do you know where the Big Dipper is up there?" Jack Beaker pointed upward, and Callie's eyes followed his arm, still unnerved by the man and the darkness of the patio.

She chose her words carefully and watched the man warily. "I should go back inside, Jack…" The corner street light put the man in shadow on an already-dark patio. She felt a loud pounding in her ears, and she was set on flight mode.

"Nah, let's look for more stars. Here's your Pepsi. The pizza's hot. We can't let it get cold." His voice shifted. The man was standing too close to Callie, and she felt his breath on her face.

All of a sudden, she wanted to go home. Diana should never have left when she invited Callie over. When she set down her Pepsi bottle to re-enter the house, the man's arm yanked her roughly toward him. Her face pressed into his chest, and her heart raced like a sparrow in a spider's web.

"Hey," Callie cried. Before she could make another peep, he'd pulled her toward the massive, blue rhododendron bush at the side of Diana's house and clapped his hairy fist over her mouth. Her fear escalated into panic, and the night turned more menacing. She yanked herself backward, but his grasp was firm. He peered closely into her brown eyes, but she turned her head away as her small fists beat against him. The man was strong.

"Callinda…Callinda. You know you want this. I've heard you and Diana jabbering. You wondered what it was like to be with a man. And here I am." His laughter was mean, strange.

"Please…Jack...don't." She twisted against his hand, but it didn't budge from her face as fear rushed in and gripped her.

"You don't have to beg me, darlin'… I'm ready, and in a minute, you will be too." His grip tightened. The night darkened as calloused hands touched her where nobody had before. She saw the Big Dipper watching her from the sky, and numbness seeped in. That was the moment she started pretending. The heavy breathing, the quick removal of her panties, and the terrible pain that followed were happening to someone else. And then her world fell away.

The young Callie's face was wet with tears when he threw her aside and strode off into the darkness. She fell to her knees sobbing, as her fingers searched for her panties, but couldn't find them. She ran into the house for her backpack and didn't stop running until she got home. She never told anyone, not even her mother. And she wouldn't answer Diana's phone calls; she didn't speak to her again.

It had been a long time since thoughts about that night intruded into her life. She knew she should pack up her past and run toward the new one. She wiped her hands and thought about the Spanish language classes she would soon begin to turn Pablo Picasso's dream into reality. When she had found his old brandy bottles weeks earlier in France, she never imagined how they would impact her life. Was finding the Haydon women more important than the here and now?

Callie shook her fist at the Big Dipper, directing a withering stare at the stars that hung above her. When she returned to the house, she stood by the door and picked up the pile of rags she'd used to clean the glass and dust the baseboards.

She tossed the dirty towel into a pile with several others and reached for an orange. She smiled as she peeled it, thinking of her niece, Cendrine, whose baby would soon join the Beauvais family. "I wonder what they will call the child we've called Lulu for so long?" She slipped a wedge of orange into her mouth, attempting to shift her thoughts from the corners of her mind where she'd hidden her past to a new baby in the family.

~

On Thursday morning, she showered and got dressed for her appointment. Alexis arrived just minutes after Callie had started to pull herself together. The moisture in the air had curled her dark hair more than usual, and she stared at herself in the mirror. She looked tired, and her eyes drooped.

When the estate agent struggled through the door, both hands were full of papers, and a briefcase dangled from one arm. The woman had short gray hair that curled tightly to her head, and her bright blue shirt slipped off her shoulder due to the unbalanced load.

"Alexis, come in. Can I take some of that from you?" Callie questioned her organizational skills as she eyed the woman. But she soon quelled those thoughts when she saw the typed, evenly spaced list the woman placed in her hands.

"The sale's advertised in today's Oregonian; our flyers are being pinned on light poles and in store windows as we speak. We will have a woman sitting at a table around there," she pointed near the door. "And I'll be here to answer questions and push your items out the door." She grinned.

"Should I stay during the sale?"

"No, I would rather you didn't. Someone from my crew will monitor each room, and address any questions. Typically, it's much better if the owner doesn't see their furnishings and dishware walking out the door. It's much cleaner this way, don't you agree?"

Callie sighed. "You're right, of course."

She nodded. "You have seven days to finish up. My cleaner will come in on Thursday morning. If you can let her in and leave by

Friday morning, we can finalize everything by Sunday afternoon. I'll give you a call Sunday. That should work." The woman gathered her briefcase without waiting for Callie's response, and before Callie could count to ten, she was driving away.

Callie rented a storage unit for the boxes designated for France. After taping another box shut, she placed her hands on her hips and surveyed the nearly empty bedroom. Mentally, she was ready to leave. She thought it would be difficult, and on some days, it was. However, she felt relieved that it was almost over, at least in the Portland house. She still had to face the cottage and the lake shimmering behind it.

But first, Callie was determined to find Mae and Lily Haydon. She'd found Haydon's address online, surprised how easy it was to learn where they lived, but it unnerved her, too. Nothing was private anymore if one could tap a name into a computer and find anyone.

Her GPS directed her to the Laurelhurst District on the corner of 31st and Irving Street. When she saw the charming yellow house and the mature pink dogwood tree in the front yard, her breath caught. She imagined François's thoughts when he read the contents of that file. What could have prompted him to give her money? It was strange that he never brought it up. Not once.

Before she got out of her car, she stopped to dial Valerie.

"Hi, Callie. What…?"

"Val, did François confront Bryan about Lily's file?"

Silence. "Val?"

"François died five days after he found that file, Callie."

"Five. Days. After."

"Yes, that's why I was so upset. Bryan frightened me. That's why I didn't tell you anything about it before. If you hadn't found that note in that book…I'm sorry, Callie. I'm sure François would have made a stink once he rounded up all the facts, but he didn't have time to do that. I better get to work, Callie."

"Sure. Thanks, Valerie." Callie's mind was clouded. Valerie wasn't telling her everything; she was certain of it. But what? She glanced toward the front door of the Haydon house and noticed the curtains move. She couldn't put this off. Her life had just taken a sharp turn, and she didn't want to hit the brakes now. She took a qualifying breath and opened the car door.

A few minutes later, an elderly gentleman cautiously opened the front door of the house. His white hair stood at various angles, and a pair of rimless glasses perched on the bridge of his nose. His eyes were brown and friendly.

"Hello," she held the screen door open. "My name is Callie Beauvais. I'm looking for Mae Haydon. Is she home?"

The rheumy eyes examined Callie. "No. I haven't seen them since I bought this house two years ago. I don't know where they live." His voice was steady, his smile sincere, and then he closed the door.

Callie returned to her car, taking slow, thoughtful steps until she settled into the driver's seat once more. Then she slammed the door. She saw the octogenarian part the curtains as a final farewell.

"Well, that worked well."

She gazed at the tall trees lining the street. They reminded her of her childhood in Napa, among the grapevine community in California. She closed her eyes and rested her head against the side window. She imagined the houses, many resembling those along this street, and wondered what her life would have been like if they had never moved away. She longed to climb up into the tree like the one in this yard, the tree where she spent hours observing the people around her, wishing her father were part of their lives. She shook her head, marveling at the memories flooding her mind. Was it the trees? Looking for a mother and daughter? An old man who probably still watched her from inside, lonely and curious?

She glanced out the windshield again. The trees were tall and spindly. But she imagined the canopy they would create when leaves covered their limbs in spring. Trees had always been a haven, then grapevines, and now, it would be France. She blinked hard. She'd always needed a haven since that night long ago.

It was a nice neighborhood; a tricycle lay on its side next door. She felt the urge to set it upright, much like she wanted to straighten out her life. After gazing at the forlorn trike for a minute, she glanced at her clock. She had given herself two hours to connect with Lily. Now, how would she spend her time before meeting Olivia for lunch? The words bouncing and echoing in her head shifted from loud to deafening. She raised a hand to wave at the fluttering curtain of the yellow house and made her way toward the city.

CHAPTER 6

S he'd spent her extra time walking along the boardwalk beside the Willamette River. Joggers, mothers pushing strollers and people walking dogs avoided the bicyclists. For a cool February day, she found it pretty amazing to be in so much foot traffic. Glancing toward the bridges that spanned the river, she smiled at the beauty of Portland. On one side of the water, big city buildings stood tall beside her. On the other side was OMSI, a science and industry museum, Olivia's house, and probably Mae and Lily Haydon, too.

Oregon's largest city sits on the junction of the Columbia and Willamette rivers, in the shadow of snow-capped Mount Hood. It's known for its parks, bridges, and bicycle paths, as well as for its eco-friendliness and its microbreweries and coffeehouses. Iconic Washington Park encompasses sites from the formal Japanese Garden to the Oregon Zoo and its railway. The city hosts thriving art, theater, and music scenes. She knew she'd miss it, but each part of the planet held beauty, and she didn't belong here anymore. She belonged in France, but here, a bit of magic lingered.

Afterward, she felt the imposing presence of the buildings surrounding the restaurant as she walked along First Avenue. Callie approached the Veritable Quandary, sniffing the river and smelling fish, mud, and something she couldn't identify. The restaurant was a romantic spot with brick walls, a glassed-in dining room, and an outdoor patio near the Willamette River.

Once inside, the ladies ordered fried green tomatoes and grilled pork tenderloin skewers before discussing the mystery Callie had presented to Olivia.

"You mentioned something about Jules and François, and you wondered if it was *that* money. What were you talking about?"

"Jules needed financial backers when he started his computer business thirty years ago, when he was fresh out of university."

Olivia nodded.

"His sister Aurore and his best friend...François came to his rescue; they exchanged their money for shares in his new company. They promised they'd never sell their shares without giving him the first option to buy them out. François reneged on the bargain. Jules was so angry that he wanted to sue François for breach of contract, but he changed his mind. When he asked François why he sold the shares to an outsider, François told him he *needed the money*. Jules was angry at him for not publicly acknowledging Veronique as his daughter. So, he sold his shares to a stranger."

"What?!" Olivia's brows shot upward.

"Jules found out about the sale when the buyer asked the date of the next stock meeting. He was livid, of course. Aurore was so angry that --- as his lawyer--- she sent a forged letter to François threatening to sue. But Jules hadn't wanted to pursue it, and he'd told her so. He loved François like a brother. François signed a receipt for that letter the same day he died. The receipt was clearly stamped on the copy of that letter. When I read it, I was furious. I thought Jules might have inadvertently caused François's death. François was upset when he raced the boat across the lake in that wicked storm. Why? It's a question I've asked myself hundreds of times."

"How did you get your hands on the letter and dated receipt?"

Callie sighed. "Aurore was upset and wanted me gone while I was in Provence. You see, she'd already lost François to me years earlier, and she'd had François' daughter. She wanted to hurt *him* then and hurt *me* now. Veronique and I were getting too close for her comfort, and she wanted me gone. Period. She thought after I'd read that letter, I'd leave France, I guess."

"And the letter?"

"Yes, the letter. She'd stuffed it into the window frame at the cottage, and Jules found it. When he gave it to me, he didn't have a clue what it was, and when I read it...Well, I went berserk. It was touch and go for me and Jules last month because it took us days to iron out the details and talk about it."

Olivia ran her tongue across her lips. "I see."

"**This** money must be **the** money from that sale. I've finally gotten past my anger at François over Veronique. Now, another one of his secrets crosses my path. Now, I wonder... is this personal or business? There's no entry in his checkbook. He gave up one daughter because he didn't trust me enough to tell me. Could this be another personal liaison he hid from me? Maybe another child? This girl, Lily? My god, when will the secrets stop?"

Olivia didn't have an answer for her.

"At this point, I'm intent on talking to Lily Haydon."

"It seems very important to you." Olivia tapped her white-tipped nail on the table. "Are you telling me everything? You look so agitated, and I feel like I've missed a page of the story." Her blue eyes stared into Callie's face.

The waiter interrupted their conversation when he delivered their lunch, and the women ate in silence until Callie looked up and said, seriously, "I need to find the Haydons. When I went to their last address this morning, an old man answered the door—the new owner."

Olivia thought a moment, her forehead creased. She snapped her fingers. "If Lily was twelve... three years ago...doing the math, she's now in high school. After my divorce, I wanted the children to stay in the same school district. I didn't want any more turmoil for them, and they had lots of friends there. So, if Mae Haydon lived on 31st Avenue between Sandy and Glisan Streets, what high school is nearby? If you can figure that out, you may be able to narrow it down."

Callie's eyes rounded. "Good thought. I'll look up schools. Soon. I'm tired of packing, but I should get back. I only have a few days before the estate people set up. Then, I can start looking for Mae again."

"Are they going to put the lake house things into the sale too?" Olivia pulled another breadstick from the nearby container and dipped it in butter.

"No, two sales. One here and one at the lake. The logistics didn't make sense. So, if she worked in Portland, I could still go to the lake so I could sleep at the cottage after the first sale." She grinned suddenly. "Besides, when Jules flies over, he'll expect a place to lay his head..." Callie's eyes turned warm at the thought.

Olivia laughed. "Are you sure you want him to wait? That man is ready to jump on a plane right now. He can either help you find the woman and her daughter...help you with what's going on.... Or maybe he can talk you out of it." Her eyes locked on her friend.

Callie's face closed up. "No! Nobody is going to talk me out of it. Let's just say it's at the top of my list before I move to France. I won't leave until I talk to Lily." Callie dropped her hands into her lap, suddenly wishing she were already gone. She loved her friend, but she couldn't explain her obsession with Lily Haydon to her or to herself. But then, again, maybe nobody could. She had so many different people inside her, it wasn't surprising. She stared across at Olivia, unblinking.

Olivia's face changed from laughter to shock in a heartbeat. She studied Callie shrewdly a moment longer before finishing her tomato.

CHAPTER 7

Broad shouldered, Dominic Jazzy was tall and smart. He had a head of prematurely silver hair that curled around his ears, a handsome man who knew it too. Although he was a few pounds overweight, a product of too much fine wine and dining with very little exercise, he eased himself onto the stool in the Jazzy Cove tasting room. He sighed, as the stool creaked beneath him, loosened his tie and wedged his heel onto the foot rest.

He took a long swallow of the Pinot Noir. Savoring the dark red wine on his tongue, he knew it was one of their best. An arrogant smile chased across his lips as he contemplated the J scrawled across the label. Maybe it was time to add a Reserve to their offerings. He made a mental note to talk to Denis. His winemaker would make it happen, even though his pickers were due, and life would be busy.

He was confident, just as his father had been and his grandfather before him. The vineyard had been in his family for three generations, and he took pride in their achievements and, of course, the grapes they grew and the wine they produced. He tapped his thin cigar on the edge of the small ashtray on the bar, aware of how much his wife, Bella, disliked the offensive smell. But he loved it, and no woman would stop him from smoking in his own place. His eyes darkened as he thought about her.

She had been so amiable when he first met her at this bar over ten years ago, smiling, eager to please, and quick to bed. He ground the cigar stub into the ashtray in frustration. Now, the woman was so focused on her status, his money, and everyone who could make a difference in her lifestyle that she had no time for him. But did he care? She was an ornament and likely realized it early on, so could he fault her disinterest now? No. And he was glad because it left Dom Jazzy the freedom to pursue his own interests. He had kept his eye on one. He smiled in recollection.

She had dark curls that cascaded to her waist and a smile that brightened her freckled face. When he had gazed into the girl's almost transparent, blue eyes, he fell deep into her youthful soul. As she passed by the vineyard after school, he timed his stroll to the mailbox to match the arrival of her school bus. In the afternoons, she rode her bicycle through the far end of the vineyard, taking a shortcut to her house. A few weeks earlier, she'd been afraid he'd yell at her, tell her to stay out of the vineyard, but of course he did no such thing.

In fact, he had encouraged her to ride through his vineyard whenever she liked. She always had something funny to say and laughed at his responses. Yes, he definitely had his eye on her. He stubbed out his cigar and briefly thought of the Pinot Noir as he headed for the house, still thinking about the girl's long curls and happy laughter. He ignored the rest of the memory… when she'd stopped laughing as he reached his hands out to touch her face.

He'd had another dream last night, and he hadn't been able to shake it all day. They had been coming more frequently lately, the burning vineyard and his grandfather's mean face glaring at him. He felt anxious about going to bed tonight because he had woken up in a sweat the night before. Bella had shaken him awake. He hated showing signs of weakness, and that's how it felt. Weakness.

Old Amenzo Jabez Jazzy had always terrified Dominic with his angry voice. Dom couldn't recall ever seeing the old man smile. When someone failed to obey him, he'd strike the poor hapless soul with a thin strap. These were stories his father, Thomas Jazzy, had shared with Dom. Between the tales and the fearsome appearance of an old man with white hair sticking out in every direction, Dom wanted nothing to do with him. But Amenzo Jazzy had other plans.

The old immigrant had sacrificed meals, left Italy for America, and endured a cold winter on a drafty ship to find the real deal. Dom grunted. He'd heard the old man say that often, the real deal. He hated the saying. His father had loved old Amenzo. Dom hadn't. He was careful not to show it, of course. He didn't want that strap used on him. But he was observant, cautious, and patiently learned to care for the vines and make wine.

But he'd wanted to paint. He loved watercolors, and the idea of wandering all over Europe to be a copyist in the beautiful museums of Italy, France, or Spain had intrigued him. He'd been confident that one day he would leave copying behind and paint as Dom Jazzy.

But old Amenzo had other ideas.

It was 1907 when the Italian immigrant arrived from Italy with a grimy, cloth-wrapped bundle. It was tied up like a Christmas goose, dirty and worn. When he finally stepped off the old clunker he'd sailed into San Francisco on, he wrapped his arms around it as if it were gold. He found himself among a few hundred Italians and Germans, all hoping to find a prosperous life in America. On the ship, he'd made friends with another Italian whose brother lived in Oregon. Amenzo heard that Oregon had fertile grape-growing soil, so he traveled north and never looked back. He took loving care of that plump bundle and didn't let anyone near it. The old man had a plan, and he wouldn't let anyone stand in his way. He glared at those who came too close to his rootstocks. When he reached Oregon City, the men separated by the river. Amenzo headed toward the coast.

He arrived in Dundee and joined the other 124 residents in the area at that time. He met William Reid, a Scot who established the Oregonian Railway into the Willamette Valley. A deal was made when the men realized they could assist each other.

Amenzo Jazzy planted his carefully tended Pinot Noir grapevines and signed a contract with the railroad man to transport his grapes and wine to market. That relationship forged a connection between wine and history.

Dom stared at the ceiling in the dark, wide awake. Bella snoozed softly beside him. He exhaled, harboring vague thoughts of swallowing a sleeping pill. The old man's grumbling voice echoed in his mind as he squeezed his eyes shut, willing himself to sleep.

He thought of an easel, a paintbrush, and a view of the valley. He had eventually traded his painter's dream for Pinot Noir grapes. Was he sorry? Not really. His eyes blinked rapidly, and the girl's face drifted through his mind. He couldn't remember when he first admitted that something was wrong with him. Some days, he worried about it, but most days, he didn't.

A fire broke out in the vineyard the next morning, and Dom jumped out of bed so quickly that he hit his head on the dresser. He couldn't put on his pants fast enough or breathe clearly. The smoke drifted into the house, thick and suffocating. Bella wasn't in bed, which surprised him; she never got up early. He stumbled as he twisted around the corner, ran toward the door, and screamed for her. When she didn't answer, he hurried across the back patio and changed direction toward the burning vines while lifting his cell phone to his ear. Every time he tried to dial 911, the phone died. He stopped to dial more carefully, wondering why there was no one in the field. Where was everyone?

He dialed again, pounding in the numbers. The phone had no service this time. His eyes squinted through the smoke. He saw a figure running toward him. The man was carrying a large pole of some kind. Dom pulled out a handkerchief to press to his nose. Was it Denis? The pickers? When the white-haired apparition descended upon him, he was struck dumb. "Grandpa?" It couldn't be.

"You're burning down my vines!" the old man screamed. His mouth was working, and spit was flying. I should have known better than to leave my vines in Thomas's care. You were a dud from the day you were born. You cried all the time, and your mother didn't even want you. That's why she left. Now, my good Thomas is gone, and here you are, making a mockery of my vines. You tried to burn them down so you could go paint like a girl." The man's breath panted through the smoke as he ranted.

Dom felt like he was a child again and hunkered down near the closest vine stalk like he had years ago. "No, I didn't do it." He cowered, shaking and sweating. At least he hoped it was sweat he felt running down his legs. His arms felt heavy as he raised them above his head. He knew what was coming, and he wasn't wrong.

The first time the pole hit his shoulder, Dom grunted and tried to push back deeper into the vines. The second time the old man slashed downward, he hit Dom's left ear. Blood pounded in his head, and his ear rang like a bell. "Stop! I didn't burn anything. I tried to call the fire trucks, but my phone won't work!" Dom held his cell phone up to the man.

The next moment, his spine tingled with fear when he saw the old man's eyes turn from anger to something worse. "What's that? Another idiot idea?" Skeletal fingers reached for the cell phone and curled around Dom's wrist instead.

Dom broke free and stepped back after he managed to get his legs moving. He attempted to run. When old Amenzo Jazzy grabbed the collar of his shirt and tried to spin him around, Dom's arm reacted, and he slammed it against his grandfather's skull.

In the next moment, Dom heard someone crying. He struggled to breathe through the smoke and glanced behind him.

"Dominic! Wake up! You nearly took my head off. Stop screaming!" Bella cowered against the headboard.

Dominic saw the fear in her eyes. He shook his head violently.

Bella's eyes widened, and her face appeared angrier than concerned. "What the hell?" Her blue eyes impaled him.

Dom sat down on the bed and cradled his head in his hands. His heartbeat raced so fast that he pressed his fist against his chest, urging it to slow down. The dream was so real, he smelled the smoke.

Bella wasn't surprised. It wasn't the first time Dom had flailed and yelled in his dreams. The first time it happened was just after their wedding, and she had been stunned awake, unable to move quickly enough. His arm had slammed into her hip, nearly causing her to faint. He had apologized, but it happened again a few weeks later. That time, she had heard him muttering loudly, arguing with someone, and she slipped out of bed. When his arm crashed down onto the bed, it landed near her pillow. She shivered, thinking about how close she had come to getting her head bashed in.

The next morning, she realized she had made a mistake by questioning him about the dreams. She'd asked him how long they'd been occurring, and he'd acted as if they were unimportant, a gnat in the grand scheme of things. When she suggested seeing a mental health therapist, he'd hit the roof. In fact, he hadn't spoken to her for several days afterward. She'd never brought it up again with him.

She no longer slept soundly. When he made noises in his sleep, she would get out of his way. She struggled with the fear that surrounded her, often wondering if he had a significant mental issue. Maybe he was hiding something from her. After a few years, she no longer cared and could usually stay clear of him. She never understood what triggered the violent dreams. Once, in an attempt to avoid them, she had made another suggestion that angered her husband.

"Maybe I should sleep in the guest room. Years ago, all married couples had private bedrooms. That way, I wouldn't have to walk on eggshells while we're sleeping. You scare me sometimes, Dom." She thought it was a perfect solution.

Dom hadn't. He didn't need to say a word to convey that; his body language had said enough. She never brought it up again. When she talked to Mae about it one day while they worked in the tasting room, she told Bella she had felt her fear but hadn't understood it.

"Just like when we were kids. You cry, and I feel the tears." Mae wiped all the wine glasses dry and set them carefully on the shelves behind the bar. When she turned around, Bella was staring at her.

"What?" Mae reached toward her.

"Mae, I think something is wrong with him." Bella squared her shoulders. "I want to sleep in separate bedrooms." She glanced around. "We rarely have sex anymore anyway. I'm not sure why he wants me in bed with him." As those words left her mouth, she regretted saying them. Her twin sister's eyes reflected her feelings.

"Bella," she whispered as she squeezed her twin sister's shoulder, "are you okay?" Mae briefly sensed her sister's weariness before Bella straightened up and gazed into the distance.

"I'm fine. There's just a lot going on around here. I shouldn't have said anything. I love it here. I love Dom and everything connected to the winery…the vineyard, and the Dundee community. It's such a sweet feeling to walk down the street and see people look at me like I'm important. It's not like when we were kids, when we were just ordinary. And poor." Bella sniffed, twisted a diamond earring in her earlobe, and then brought her eyes back to her sister's questioning face. "Forget what I said, okay?"

Mae lifted the pale hair off her sister's forehead and stared into her eyes. "We're a team, honey. You can say anything you want to me, remember? Now, let's get busy. The tasting will begin shortly. I put Lily in the office, where she's folding napkins and practicing her math. Get ready to roll." Mae had winked at her. God, she missed Mae.

CHAPTER 8

A cross town, Callie shivered and wrapped her arms around her knees as she gazed outside the picture window at the street she knew so well. Hamilton, a curving street lined with majestic firs and graceful pines, had once been her entire world. Her hands circled the hot cup of tea as she pulled her feet beneath her.

A sense of foreboding unnerved her. She saw the best in others, despite her past being cloaked in dark memories. She would stop people with a hand if anyone jumped into a conversation without first saying hello, believing that good things happened to decent people. But ever since François left her a widow, she had felt the terrible sensation that nothing would be the same. Then Nate opened the hidden door in her heart. It was Jules who later showed her she could walk through it.

After dinner, Callie balanced her glass of wine on a small plate filled with crisp crackers and cheddar cheese before making her way outside through the back door. Standing at the corner of her wooden deck beside the row of rose bushes, she shivered slightly, hugging her thick sweater tightly around her.

The garden looked much like it had when François worked the soil, though her gardener had now removed the daily growth of weeds. No half-smoked pipe lay on the stone pillar. No book casually rested on the table beside his Adirondack chair. Three years had passed, yet Callie could still remember the scent of her husband's cherry pipe tobacco. She'd always thought it was the most comforting smell in the world. Deceiving, more like, because it made her feel safe, sheltered, and loved.

She cradled the stem of the wine glass in her hand as her gaze scanned the room. She could still hear the echo of her husband's laughter and imagine the slight smile he could coax from her, even when she was in one of her gloomy moods. She could feel his arms around her, protective, as if he would never let anything bad happen to her. And she had believed that, too, in her naiveté. She believed it until the night the boat accident tore him from her world.

It turned out that her husband was flesh and blood, just like everyone else. The solid ground she had thought her life was built on had been washed away like a sandcastle in the surf—first, François, then Mom, the following year.

As she sipped her chilled white wine, she remembered her husband's ashes given to her in a neat box. The image floated to her mind: the feel of the box in her hands, the ache in her heart. She shook her head to cast the image aside until just its shadow remained, knowing she would soon leave this house filled with memories. She sat in his chair and held the glass to her chest as she reminisced.

Not since the last time her husband stood in this garden had she felt completely secure. Since then, her life had teetered on shifting sand; all Callie could do was hang on and maintain her balance. Before Jules began to fill the space in her heart that François had left behind, Nate had nudged it open.

But now, Jules had become her sun, moon, breath, and heartbeat. She had lost so much to the tides of life that day at Devil's Lake. Would she be able to extinguish the anger simmering inside her toward François so that she and Jules could enjoy a future together? As condensation dripped from her glass, she lifted it to her lips and suppressed the ever-present anger over the secrets that kept exploding around her. "I am so ready to get past this headache…." She mumbled the words in the quiet garden. She closed her eyes and leaned back.

They popped open again to gaze at the plaque on the stone column beside her. The light streaming in from her living room windows caressed the silver-hued stones that had been mortared together so long ago. Looking beyond her memories, she thought of the hidey hole François had installed to hold his tobacco pouch and tamping tool. She smiled sadly. Setting down her wine glass, she leaned over to swing the hinged steel plaque aside, revealing the arched door behind it. She pushed her hand into the small space. When her fingers delved into the dark hole to pull out the packet of old tobacco, she felt a metal key instead.

Frowning, she quickly held it in her hand and stared at it in confusion. She had never seen it before. It resembled their safe deposit box key, but why would François put it in his little stash compartment on the back deck? "Oh, god, not another puzzle." She pursed her lips and lifted her wine glass with a trembling hand.

Until François died, she had led a relatively normal life, but wedged between searching for a missing nephew in Provence and discovering those old Spanish bottles of brandy just a couple of weeks earlier, she was now burdened with more questions than answers. Again. With the sun beginning to set and her shoulders tense, Callie gripped the key and headed back into the house.

She pressed her back against the wall as she reached the kitchen door. She stared at the key and walked over to the counter to place it there, pressing her fingers into each tine. She heard the screams in her head before a scream erupted from her throat, and she kicked the side table across the room, breaking its leg.

"What were you doing, François!? Why can't you stay dead? I already went through this before, the not knowing why, the anger, the grief!" She spun her hand around and knocked the half-filled box of dishes off the countertop, sending everything crashing to the floor. She snapped her mouth shut. When she saw what she'd done, she began to shake and bent down to inspect each piece of broken glass and china.

"Well, that's just less I have to pack," she grumbled.

Grabbing her broom and dustpan, she thrust the broom at the mess before sitting down to burst into tears. Her anger had settled back in to stay.

~

The next morning, Bryan Martos couldn't stop thinking about Callie Beauvais. He jabbed the end of his pencil into the large calendar tablet next to his phone, tap, tap, tap, before throwing it across the room. What was the woman up to? Turning to look outside his office window, which faced Mount Hood in the far eastern sky, he flexed his fingers and pressed the palms of his hands flat against the desktop.

His secretary brought a stack of papers and placed them on the corner of his desk. "These are the Smithson papers to sign." She left as quickly as she'd arrived. He could hear her stiletto heels tapping a rhythm on the tiled floor outside his office, and then they faded away. He knew she'd reached the carpeted area near the library.

Pulling the racing form from beneath the file where he had stashed it a moment ago, he glanced at the clock. He needed to call his bookie before noon or risk losing the chance to bet on the next race.

His father had raised him in the racing stables where he'd been a groom and caretaker. He taught his young son to love and respect horses. He said they were not pets, but animals trained to win money. He could love them if he wanted to, but he always remembered why they were there: to make money. His father taught him what to watch for when the horses ran. He knew which horse won the most often. He observed their jockeys and how they rode in the rain, sun, and cold. He monitored how fast they rode on each set course and distance.

Bryan smiled sadly. He missed his dad. The man had been dead for nearly twenty years. He'd also wanted his son to follow in his footsteps and become a racehorse groom. But Bryan wanted to be rich, and his dad never was. In fact, they'd often wondered where their next meal was coming from. He'd never starved; his dad made sure of that. But Bryan knew money would not line his pockets caring for horses, and his father finally agreed.

He'd become friends with Charlie, a man who hung around the stables and showed him how to slip into the bleachers to watch the races. His young fingers had itched to mark the sheets, be one of the bidders, and be part of the excitement.

From the time he was ten years old, Charlie showed him how to observe and place his bets. He'd slip Charlie the hard-earned tips he'd earned from working for other grooms. His dad didn't like Charlie, but Bryan liked it when Charlie handed him winnings. Bryan managed to hide their friendship.

Now his father was gone, and his son had taken up gambling. Bryan knew how to bet on the horses. Sometimes he lost, but more often he won. There was just that one occasion when he lost big. He had to pay off his bookie. Then the next time, he did it again. The firm had plenty of money, and Bryan always reimbursed the firm's account the next time he won. It seemed like a perfect solution. But François didn't see it that way.

François Beauvais. He had liked the Frenchman. The men worked well together. Bryan protected clients like Dominic Jazzy, while François defended vineyard owners facing issues with vinicultural laws. It was a perfect partnership.

Until Lily.

Bryan felt a pang of guilt, but only for a heartbeat.

He looked at the racing form in his hand once more and reached for the phone. His heart raced against his ribs, and his breath came in short gasps. The next race was crucial, and he didn't want to miss the opportunity to place his number in the winner's circle.

He wouldn't worry about Callinda Beauvais right now. He had always been able to manipulate, maneuver, or control everyone in his life. François had been a surprise he hadn't counted on, but his little wife? Bryan grimly conceded he would have to keep an eye on her. He had heard about her battle the previous year when she took on a high-end doctor and an Oregon senator for Larkspur Insurance. She had won. He chuckled. But they were wimps, and he wasn't.

While Olivia prepared dinner that night, Bram Carle shook his head as his wife recounted her conversation with Callie. He gently caressed her arm when she placed a plate of spaghetti in front of him.

"I can't understand why finding this girl is so important to her, Bram, but she's not budging. She wants to talk with Mae and Lily Haydon, and that's that." She sat across from him, lifting her napkin without eating.

"If there is a signed settlement agreement, there's not much they can do because if they open the case, they'd have to return all the settlement money. There's probably a clause that would penalize them a set dollar amount for each person they talk to about the event. Sometimes that's as high as $100,000 per person. Who knows if a court case would help them? Unfortunately, oftentimes the victim is painted as the one at fault."

"But a child?" Olivia's face reddened. "$100,000 per person? That seems so extravagant."

"Well, the penalty must be high enough to incentivize the victim to pay attention. So, if she tells one person about it to help with another case, maybe that other person would waive the amount and pay for the information…to settle the penalty themselves." He twirled strands of spaghetti around his fork and carefully brought them to his mouth. "What was the charge Lily made against the vintner? You haven't told me that."

Olivia sipped a glass of Chianti and dipped some bread into the small oil plate beside her. "Callie didn't say. I don't think she knows. There's more to the story that Callie isn't telling me. And I know she won't leave for France until every loose end is tied up here first."

Bram lifted his wine, finished it, and set it beside his empty dinner plate. "I think she's anxious to learn Spanish to start her trustee duties for Picasso's dream." He laughed indulgently, "And there is that new baby ready to push its way into the world any day and…"

"Yes, I know a lot is waiting for her in France, Bram, but you didn't see her face when she talked about this Lily thing. There is something I just can't put my finger on…." She got up to clear the table and stared at her reflection in the window above her kitchen sink. Her short blonde hair hugged her head like a cap, and she gazed into the darkness at nothing. "I'm worried. Something is going on.

Bram's face met hers in the reflection before he kissed her neck and handed her a towel to dry her hands. She grinned, and they left the dishes for.

Bella Jazzy's short blonde hair fell across one blue eye. She reflected on her conversation with Bryan and the questions from the Beauvais widow as she watched her husband pour his second glass of wine later that evening. How could she bring it up? She tapped a red-tipped nail against her perfectly aligned teeth. How could she initiate the discussion without revealing that she'd been with Bryan? She observed Dom lift the glass to his lips and thought about how handsome he was. His premature silver hair gave him the look of a movie star. She felt it was a shame that his looks were the only nice thing about him.

"So, Bella, what did you do in town today?" Dom swirled the wine in his glass and gazed at it before lifting his eyes to her.

"Nordstrom's had a sale, so I spent the morning there. Then, I had lunch with an old friend...you remember Kit, the woman who used to run the little dress shop in the small Dundee strip mall?"

He wasn't listening to her. "Bryan was going to call me today, but I guess he got busy." His eyes lingered on the dark red Pinot Noir, and his finger caressed the glass.

Her eyes turned warm. "Oh, I forgot to tell you Bryan called."

"When? Did he leave a message? He's working on something for me." Dom sat up straight, anxious.

She had no idea what he was talking about, but knew it was the perfect opening for her. "Yes. He said to tell you that François Beauvais's widow was asking questions about Mae."

Dominic's face swiveled around toward her, definitely listening now. "Why?" He had to concentrate on carefully placing his glass instead of throwing it across the room. He stared at his wife.

She shrugged. "I don't know, but I think it bothered him. What would she want to talk to Mae about?" Bella saw her husband's face cloud up and his fingers tighten on the stem of his wine glass.

"I don't know. Why don't you call your sister and ask her?" He reached for the wine bottle and angled his glass again. "All I need now is Lily to bring up old history while..."

"Lily? ...While what?" She noted his set face, clamped mouth, and fixed eyes. When he didn't answer, she said, "Mae hasn't talked to me since Lily told that story about you...And it's been three years. I miss Mae. I liked it when she worked in the gift shop and the tasting room. And I miss Lily too, but...that was so awful." When she reached for the wine bottle near Dom, she didn't see the look on his face. She'd gotten the message to him, and that's all she cared about. Bella pressed her lips together to stifle a smile.

A muscle twitched angrily at Dom's jaw. She didn't even notice he had left when he reached for his cell phone and exited the room to take a private call. He elbowed the office door shut and dialed Bryan's number. No answer. He didn't leave a message, tossed his phone onto the chair, and gulped down the remaining wine in his glass.

~

At ten o'clock the next morning, Dominic Jazzy stormed into the Martos Law Firm without an appointment, demanding to talk with Bryan. His mouth was tight and grim. With a harsh voice, he demanded, "I want to see Bryan now."

Jeannie Greene's hair was the color of a rusty pipe. Startled, she looked at the man, and her face clouded. "Please have a seat, Mr. Jazzy, and I'll see if he's available."

When she left her desk, Dom fumed and remained standing.

"Mr. Martos?" She knocked on his partially open door. Her apologetic voice instantly captured his attention. A hand pushed her hair back from her face as she tucked the rusty curls behind one ear.

Bryan looked up from the papers on his desk, unhappy about the interruption, and let out a sigh of resignation.

She lowered her voice, deliberately creating an air of mystery. "Mr. Jazzy is here, and he looks furious." Jeannie appeared ready to flee when she noticed the expression that crossed her employer's face.

Bryan's stomach tightened. Just what he needed: to babysit Dom Jazzy. His face tightened for a moment as he readjusted his mental state and retrieved the thick file from the corner of his desk.

He turned to Jeannie. "Show him in."

His eyes turned black, and he schooled his expression to hide his distaste. When he had accepted Jazzy's retainer fee, he had no idea how offensive the man could be. But without the retainer, Bryan Martos couldn't keep his bookie satisfied. He smiled as Dominic walked into his office. He stood up, shook the man's hand before closing his office door, and sat down behind his desk again.

"What the hell does that Beauvais woman want with Mae Haydon?" His voice was tense with frustration. He leaned forward and pressed his knuckles against the top of Bryan's desk, his blue eyes challenging his attorney.

Bryan met the stare without flinching. He wasn't pleased to learn that Bella had shared their conversation about Callie with Dom. Dammit, he shouldn't have said a word to her. Why hadn't she warned him?

"With this new abuse accusation building momentum, the last thing we need is someone stirring the pot with Mae. The case with Lily can't come up, especially now… during your negotiations with Heidi Mason's parents."

Bryan's stomach tightened another notch. "Sit down, Dom. I went through the good widow's house and tore it apart. I wasn't sure if François had saved anything that might incriminate you about Lily. There was nothing there. The man's been dead so long now; I'm sure everything died with him."

Dominic swung his head up. "Why would your old partner know anything about the case? He wasn't involved in it at all, was he? What did you expect to find there? And why is she asking about Mae if there wasn't anything there? Where did she hear Mae's name?" His brow furrowed as he tried to calculate the answers while looking directly across the desk at his attorney.

Bryan heaved a sigh. "François saw the file before he died."

Dominic Jazzy jumped up and pointed his finger at Bryan. "Well, the file better be dead and buried. Why in the hell didn't you tell me this before?" His eyes flashed with smoldering anger.

"Because it was on a need-to-know basis and didn't make a difference. The suit never went to court, and Lily's deposition was buried. Trust me. There is only one copy, and it's in my locked file. This new case should be settled this week or next." He shook his head to erase the image of the girl's parents seated across the table from him at their attorney's office. He was unsure if they would settle at all. They wanted Dominic Jazzy's head. He felt relieved when Dom turned and left the way he'd come.

"I wish I'd never met the man at all," he mumbled.

He saw the reflection in the glass of his office door as Jeannie knocked and entered, her footsteps muffled by the thick carpet. "What is it now?"

"Your mail." She flinched at the tone of his voice as she set the stack of envelopes on the corner of his desk. Then she moved away, her jaw tightening.

"Good," he growled. "Leave it and get out."

Two hours later, Valerie Blume and two attorneys from her law firm left the courtroom, busily discussing the scene they had just left behind. Their case looked promising, and their voices reflected this through their laughter and conversation. As Valerie threaded her way through the crowd with them, she felt a tap on her shoulder and turned around with a smile.

When she saw who stood beside her, the smile died on her lips.

"Nice to see you again, Valerie," Bryan Martos said, but his eyes indicated that was a lie as he gestured for her to step aside. Nodding to her coworkers, she signaled that she'd be just a moment.

She had no choice but to make light of her caution and follow him. Her blonde hair slipped across her shoulders as she clutched the files to her chest, as if they could serve as a barrier between her and the malevolence she saw in his eyes.

"What in the hell do you think you're doing, Valerie? I saw you talking with Callinda Beauvais the other day at Jake's. I know what she's after because she called me, too." His eyes darkened as he gazed at her speculatively.

Valerie didn't answer but looked towards her friends, who waited by the large glass doors of the courthouse, chatting.

"Remember --- what happened in the Beauvais Martos Law Firm *stays* there. If I learn you've broken client/attorney privileges, I'll come after you with both feet, and you won't even know what hit you. Do I make myself clear?" He pasted a fake smile on his face and glanced toward the men waiting for her.

She stammered a few words before feeling his large hand shove her aside as he pushed the door open and stepped outside. She saw him glance both ways along the busy street and pull his coat closed before disappearing. She wasn't sure her legs would carry her out the door. Trying not to panic, she avoided the curious gazes of the men as they walked back to the office.

Her thoughts were dull and disquieting. But she was afraid.

CHAPTER 9

Callie glanced at her watch, surprised to see it was only noon. She jotted down the school's phone numbers, logged off her iPad, and lifted her phone. After calling three high schools, Callie finally hit pay dirt when a young girl recognized Lily's name.

Callie's mood shifted from disappointment to delight.

"Yes, I know Lily Haydon. We've been friends since fourth grade. We lived a few blocks from Laurelhurst School before my parents bought a house in the Alameda District. We were neighbors."

"Oh, that's good news! Do you know where she moved after her mom sold their house?" She'd finally be able to connect with the girl. As the thought raced through her head, she heard a loud commotion and an angry retort on the other end of the phone.

"Hand me the phone, Julie." Callie jumped when she heard the irritable voice and rolled her eyes.

"Who's calling, please?" The woman's voice felt like a splash of cold water after the student's friendliness. After Callie explained, without revealing too much information, the woman replied, "Hmmm. I'm sorry, but we do not give out personal information about our students. I heard Julie tell you that Lily Haydon attends Grant, and that's all we can tell you." With that, she hung up.

Callie bit her lip, wishing she had asked the girl for her last name. She could have found her after school. Taking a deep breath, she closed her eyes. Why was it so important to her? Shouldn't she pack, sell everything, and move to France as quickly as Jules could get her there?

When the phone rang in her hand, she smiled when she saw Jules' face light up the screen to announce his call.

"*Halo?*"

Her voice became warm. "Hello, Jules." Callie's mood suddenly brightened, and within minutes, she was able to push the gloom away. When they hung up, euphoria filled the spaces where worry had receded.

That night, Callie browsed Facebook. Indeed, most teenagers have a Facebook page. When she logged on to Facebook and typed Lily Haydon into the search box, she was stunned to find six girls with that name. But then she smiled; only one of them lived in Portland, Oregon. She sent the girl an instant message, introducing herself and sharing her number, expressing her desire to meet. Knowing her message would go into the other folder, she also realized it might be a while before she heard back, if at all.

She was wrong.

Lily Haydon saw the message from Callie Beauvais, and her stomach cramped. "Mom? Come see this," the girl called from her bedroom after checking Facebook before bed. Her thick blonde hair slid over her face as she peered at her laptop screen. Her knuckles gripped the sides, and a wave of anxiety churned in her belly.

Her mother padded into her room in fuzzy green slippers, carrying a cup of hot tea. She looked over her daughter's shoulder. "What is it?" She read the message. When she sipped her tea, she yelped as it burned her tongue.

"It's from François Beauvais's wife. She left her phone number, Mom. I don't want to talk about it again. It was all so horrible. Should I talk to her since François helped us so much?"

Mae Haydon sat on the edge of her daughter's bed before answering. Finally, she whispered, "Honey, if you don't want to talk with her, you don't have to."

She turned into her mother's arms. Their matching blonde heads huddled together as Lily whispered, "Will you call her and tell her I can't talk about it, Mom?" Her heartbeat surged, and a strange numbness began to slip through her body as she remembered her uncle's face burrowing where it didn't belong. When her mother gave her a final squeeze and left her room, Lily pushed the laptop onto her bedside table and closed the lid.

She stretched her legs as far as they could reach when she lay on her bed, until her bare toes touched the footboard. Reaching her small hands toward her face, she pushed her cheeks outward, moved her hands toward her ears, and ran her fingers through her pale, shoulder-length hair. Then, she traced her neck, her chest, and danced down her body, willing the numbness to go away. It always did, but it was never fast enough.

Lily didn't want to talk about that night. She was surprised to receive the note from Mrs. Beauvais and couldn't imagine the reason for the unexpected message. She had been sad and cried with her mother when they read the newspaper about François Beauvais's death. He had been their knight in shining armor, and she would never forget him. She loved his French accent when he spoke with them, much like how his eyes seemed to cry without tears when he looked at her. He hadn't asked her to tell him about that night; he already knew everything. He had read the words another man made her repeat. She hated it all. And now Mrs. Beauvais wanted to reopen it. Why?

Jolted out of innocence, she had gathered a boatload of shame, and the thought of discussing any part of it shook her. She burrowed down in her bed, swung her legs under the blankets, and fluffed her pillow. Her fingers rose to her mouth as she thought about her uncle, and she bit off the nails that dared to grow. Her fingernails were already a wreck. She wore only jeans that were too big, loose sweatshirts, and clunky shoes. Her uncle had said she was pretty. Lily vowed never to be pretty again.

She felt the tears coming, choking her throat and rushing through her body. When she could no longer hold them in, she buried her face in the pillow so her mother wouldn't hear her cries. Her mother had cried enough for both of them. Lily wondered if she would ever stop.

The next day, at a law firm near Jamison Square in the Pearl District, Valerie Blume couldn't focus on the files piled on her desk. Her thoughts kept drifting back to her conversation with Callie. Her hands trembled as she recalled her fear when Callie inquired about the incident between François and Bryan. She knew she ought to have told her friend everything.

She pounded the file in front of her with her hand and flipped the blonde hair off her shoulder. She had already lost a lot of sleep over it. She hadn't told her friend what she knew. Val hadn't lied to Callie, but she hadn't been entirely forthcoming. She told herself it wasn't important, yet admitted she was afraid to bring it up again. The papers were safe for now, but she wondered if she should give everything to Callie and not worry about it any longer. But would that put Callie in jeopardy? Would François want her to do that? She placed her head in her hands, clearly undecided and concerned about Bryan's threat. Valerie remembered that she also hadn't told Callie why Lily wanted Dominic Jazzy in jail in the first place.

Callie's fingers hovered over her phone. It was late in France, but she made the call anyway. She'd missed her niece and nephew and hadn't connected with them since her arrival. Her mind kept drifting back to Provence and the new baby. She didn't want to miss the baby's birth, but she might have to. She growled a bit, recalling her arrival in France after Thanksgiving. At that time, she felt guilty for missing her best friend's wedding while trying to find Cendrine's husband. But Olivia and Bram had brought their wedding all the way to France. This time, she knew Cendrine could hardly make it to the delivery room in Oregon. She snickered at the thought as the phone began ringing on the other side of the ocean.

"Callie, *halo!*" Cendrine's voice always made Callie smile.

"How's my favorite niece and Lulu tonight?"

"Lulu is still waiting to tell us if she is a girl or a boy," Cendrine answered with a warm chuckle. "Olivier tells me I cannot call his boy Lulu. But of course, I wouldn't do that. Veronique ate dinner with us tonight, and we think the boy will be named Michel Jacques after our grandfather. Do you like the idea?"

"I love that, *ma petite.* But if it's a girl?"

"Chloe, I think."

Callie smiled. "Of course, you should name the child for your mother. How are you feeling? I'm so happy that you and Veronique are connecting. I can hardly wait to be part of the big family there." Callie hated being so far away now that her pregnancy was nearly full term. She had gone through too much stress after her husband disappeared a few weeks earlier, and the women shared a special closeness. It felt like the baby would be her grandchild instead of a great-niece.

"I am fine. I miss you. Jules misses you very much, but I know you must end things in Oregon. The baby is being naughty. I am ready, but the baby is not. Maybe she waits for her auntie to be nearby first?" Cendrine teased.

"Well, I'd better hurry up then, *ma petite*."

"It is late, and I will call again soon. Kiss the children for me?"

"*Oui, bon nuit*, Callie."

"Good night to you, too."

When Callie hung up, she had a smile on her face.

And then she remembered the key.

She lifted the phone again; this time, she clicked on FaceTime. When Jules raised his phone, a pang of guilt struck her when she saw his sleepy, scowling face. Then, his expression softened like a gentle river upon seeing Callie's face fill the screen. He sat up and gazed intently at her.

"I'm your alarm clock this morning." Her voice held a tingling hint of laughter, and her lips curved into a smile.

Jules ran a hand through his tousled hair. "You are sassy this morning, *ma belle*." He grinned back at her as he stood up and tried to keep the phone steady when the clock's alarm buzzed beside him. "I must lie you down a moment," he said as he reached across the bed.

"That sounds like a promise," she responded.

He chuckled, a low rumble in his throat. When he picked up his phone again, his eyes twinkled. "Yes, absolutely sassy," he repeated. "What are you hiding? Out with it, as Americans say." His eyebrows rose.

She closed her eyes and felt her lashes brush against her cheek. When she looked up again, she repositioned herself against her headboard and took a deep breath. "Tonight, another hundred questions popped out of a little box."

Jules looked at her in confusion. "A little box?"

She shook her head back and forth, bit her lip, and thought for a moment before she began. "I found a key tonight. Something that François hid away in a small box; he saved it for his pipe and tobacco. I sat outside, staring at the stars, and remembered his little stash place. I was surprised when I pushed my hand inside to clean out the old tobacco. The only thing in the box was a tiny key I have never seen before, Jules." Her eyes lifted with a tiredness that overwhelmed her, then they snapped angrily. "Another secret our friend held to himself. Now, I must find where the key fits. And I have a terrible feeling that it will reveal more secrets and raise more questions wherever it goes. Maybe I should write a book, expose François, a man whose very existence is proving elusive because I don't recognize him anymore."

Jules sighed and sympathized with Callie when he saw the anger splashed across her face. "My darling, it could be the key to nothing important. I think you are in a vulnerable place right now. You are saying goodbye, and you are still upset he is no longer there to answer questions about Veronique. I think this key is something he should have told you about if it was important. But Callie, you must have secrets inside of you that you don't share with everyone, am I right?" His voice was soft, filled with love.

Callie's face changed swiftly from anger to something else. She cleared her throat and gathered her wits. "You're right. I may be looking for problems where they don't exist. I knew there was a good reason to call you. Maybe I should do it every time my head gets crazy, but then again, I'd call you a few times daily." She laughed uneasily, thinking of the dark secrets inside her heart—secrets she planned to keep to herself.

"Sassy or not, if you called me that often, you'd never finish your packing, and I don't want to wait much longer before you're here with me." He touched his fingers to his lips and lifted them toward her face on the phone. "I should get ready for work now, *ma chère*."

Callie puckered her lips into a kiss and pressed the red button. His face disappeared instantly, leaving her to reflect on his words. He was usually right; it probably wasn't important. But she had an unsettling feeling that he might just be guessing this time.

CHAPTER 10

Morning didn't come a minute too soon. Her bed sheets were a tangled mess from all her fretting, trying to decipher why François had hidden the key. And where did it belong? Where did the key fit? She'd pulled out her safe deposit key from her key ring last night and compared both keys. It was a sister to hers, but with different teeth and numbers. Were they both from Chase Bank? Or were safe deposit keys universal in size and shape? Those were just a few questions that leapt through her mind all night.

She pulled herself out of her mussed bed and padded through the house. It echoed around her now that she had emptied the rooms. While the coffee brewed, she glanced at her watch. She'd give herself another hour before calling Bram. He'd know the Oregon law regarding a surviving spouse accessing a safe deposit box.

The key still rested beside her cell phone. She turned it over a few times, wondering why François kept it in his hidey hole. It had been outside all this time, and if she hadn't been reminiscing last night, she might never have looked in the box. She would have sold the house, moved across an ocean, and a stranger would have discovered it and thrown it away.

She poured her coffee into a saved mug, vowing to stash it in her bag for the trip to the cottage. She couldn't keep every sentimental dish, cup, vase, and picture frame, but she also wasn't going to walk away from everything that meant so much to her. She prided herself on having saved only twenty boxes. She made a mental note to move them into the storage unit before Alexis brought her team in to tag everything.

She leaned back and blew softly across the brew before trying to drink it. Callie rechecked her watch. Exactly nine minutes had passed since the last time she had peeked at it. She set the mug down and picked up the key again, holding it in her hand to stare at it. "François, I wonder if I knew you at all."

Olivia answered the phone on the first ring. "Callie? What on earth has you up this early?" Her voice sounded worried.

"Good morning. Did I catch Bram, or did he already leave?"

"No, he's right here, chewing on a bagel. Hold on." Olivia and Bram exchanged glances as she passed him the phone.

He wiped his mouth and dropped the bagel on the plate. "Hi."

"Hi, Bram. Last night, I found a safe deposit key in Francois's hidey hole on the patio. I've never seen it before. Will the bank let me open the box? I don't know if it's our bank, but I wondered if Oregon law will allow me access to it since my name won't be on the card."

"Huh. Good question. I believe any bank will allow you to open a safe deposit box if you can prove you're the sole beneficiary. Take François's Will and his certified death certificate. That's all you should need. Let me know if I can help, but I'm sure that will work."

"Good. It was creepy to find it last night. What are the odds of my finding something so small outside in a tiny spot like that? I wonder what I'll find in the box... obviously, something else he's hidden from me." Her words sounded strained and angry.

Bram raised his eyebrows and looked at Olivia, who stood beside him, trying to make sense of the one-sided conversation. "Oh, another thing. When you find the bank for the key, you won't be able to open it without a bank officer beside you. Additionally, the bank will need to make copies of everything inside the box before allowing you to take the contents. Oregon law is pretty clear."

"Nice to know. Thanks, Bram. Hug Olivia for me, and I hope both of you have a good day. After I find the bank, I'm afraid of what I'll find inside that box."

"It sounds rather like an adventure, but I'm not sure if it's a good or bad one. Why else would François hide it?"

"My sentiments exactly. Bye." She hung up and finished her first cup of coffee. While waiting for the banks to open, she filled a bowl with cereal, sliced a banana, and grabbed the carton of milk from the fridge. She glanced toward the back window and the hidey hole that seemed to mock her.

Two hours later, Callie felt exasperated. She had called the bank, but they wouldn't provide her with any information over the phone. A personal visit was necessary, and now she wondered how many banks she would have to visit with the stupid key to find the right keyhole. She poured herself more coffee.

She approached the Chase Bank manager and explained her predicament. The woman retrieved the safe deposit index cards and flipped through them. Callie idly wondered why it wasn't on the computer.

"Why does the bank still use index cards in this day and age?"

The woman shrugged. "The records are digitized, but we still hold the signature cards for proof." The woman's fingers paused as she lifted a card. She extended her hand to receive Callie's key and compared the numbers. "Yes, this is our key. Mr. Beauvais signed the card a little over three years ago, and it looks like he only came in once. Do you want to open it now?" The woman's eyes were kind.

"Yes, I need to see what's inside."

"Do you have a copy of the Will proving you're his sole beneficiary and a certified copy of his death certificate?"

Callie retrieved both documents and handed them across the counter. "I'd also like to get into my other safe deposit box and empty it. I'm closing it today because I'm moving out of the country."

"I'll be sorry to see you go, Mrs. Beauvais." The woman lifted the hinged countertop and led her into the private area of the bank. Rows of large and small safe deposit boxes lined the wall on three sides of the small space. "I must go in with you and make copies of everything. You understand? Oregon rules."

Callie shook her head, anticipating it after her conversation with Bram.

Nervously, she moistened her dry lips. She inserted the key next to the bank's key, and the woman placed the box on the small counter beside the steel door. She waited for the woman to copy all the contents, and her shoulders sagged when she was left alone.

She fished out a thick packet of papers, one business card, and a folded, wrinkled piece of paper. Callie thumbed through the documents, recognizing legal forms, unsure of what she held in her hands. She pushed everything into her briefcase. She'd look at the papers later. At least it wasn't full of hundred-dollar bills or gold bullion. She chuckled a second before pressing a hand on her chest to calm the beating of her heart.

Then, she turned to her personal box and removed one hundred silver coins, her life insurance policy, several stock certificates, and four small silver bricks that François had purchased before their marriage. She picked up a soft drawstring bag that contained her small, pink, pearl-handled gun. Next were two boxes of bullets and a pocket knife etched with scrimshaw. Her fingers danced in the box. Empty.

Her oversized briefcase felt full and heavy as she lugged it to the car, her pulse racing and adrenaline surging through her body. All she needed was for someone to knock her on the head and steal her bag. She wasn't usually so fanciful or cynical, but these days felt anything but normal. Inhaling deeply, she focused her mind on arriving home without a mishap.

As she pulled away from the bank, she wasn't as anxious to look at the paperwork as she had been earlier that morning. She was afraid she might find something else to throw her off kilter.

As she drove toward the 405, she remembered the business card she had tossed into the bag with the folded piece of paper. Her curiosity got the better of her, and she couldn't help herself. The big stuff could wait, but she wanted to take a look at the note and card. She changed lanes suddenly, waved a hand in her rear-view mirror at the honking stranger, and pulled into a parking space a block from Starbucks near Portland State University. Angling inside her briefcase, she found both small pieces and pulled them into her lap.

CHAPTER 11

The business card was a surprise. Denis Sorbets, Jazzy Cove Winery. She turned it over and read the note: Ask Denis about Lily. Seeing François's handwriting made it hard for her to swallow. When she unfolded and read the words on the crumpled paper, she froze, and her throat tightened. Swallowing hard, her numbed fingers turned the car back toward the Willamette River.

Within minutes, she was parked at 2nd and Madison. She glanced at the briefcase sitting on her passenger seat. Thinking it over, she glanced around, noting there were few pedestrians, and opened the trunk. Lugging it with both hands, she plopped it inside the deep well and gripped the note. Of all the places where I shouldn't get robbed, it's in front of the police station.

The marble façade of the Portland Police Station had undergone a significant makeover in the past few years. Her eyes were drawn across the street, momentarily, where green grass lay beneath a canopy of tall, budding Douglas firs. She barely took it in because the frightening note burned a hole in her pocket.

After going through security, she walked up to the front desk and said, "I need to talk with someone about a possible murder."

The large woman behind the desk raised an eyebrow before she approached a man wearing jeans and a dark sweater nearby. Detective Ross Goldberg was in charge of homicide. When he swung around to shake her hand, tears glistened in Callie's eyes. "I think my husband was murdered." Callie burst out, clearly agitated.

"I think we need to find a place for you to sit down." Ross Goldberg led her through the busy area to a side conference room. He pointed to a chair beside a desk, asked a young man with a crew cut to bring in coffee, and returned to the room, shutting the opaque glass door behind him. "Mrs....?" His light hair was threaded with golden highlights and matched his shaggy brows that rose above kind eyes.

Callie took a breath. "Beauvais. Callinda Beauvais."

Ross Goldberg's eyebrows lifted. "Now, please start from the beginning." He pulled a pad of paper toward him, picked up a pencil, and waited.

Callie said, "My husband's name was François Beauvais. When he died on Devil's Lake near Lincoln City three years ago, his death was declared an accident. Today, I found something telling me it might not have been accidental at all," she said brokenly.

He leaned toward her. "What makes you think so, Mrs. Beauvais?" He pushed the glasses up on his nose, and his green eyes looked deeply into hers, clearly interested.

She handed him the paper she had pulled from the safe deposit box. "I found this today. Someone was threatening my husband. This note was in a safe deposit box my husband rented just a few days before his death. I didn't know it existed until I found the key last night. I'm selling my house and leaving the country, so when I found this…I knew…there was more to the story." She knew she was babbling, but couldn't stop.

The detective's eyebrows rose an iota before his green eyes returned to her face. "It's definitely threatening. But since you touched it, your husband touched it, and who knows who else touched it, the fingerprints have been blurred. I think the author of this note watches too many movies." He read the words glued onto the paper in pieces from a magazine.

Callie shivered.

Detective Goldberg turned to his computer and pulled up the medical examiner's report on François Beauvais. The man's cause of death was deemed an accident. He looked at Callie sympathetically and thought for a minute before he said, "Mrs. Beauvais, let me look into this. What's your phone number?"

She nodded and wrote down her number before he showed her out the door. Callie imagined he would drop that note into a slush pile to get lost. It was a cold lead. Did he take it seriously? She sure as hell did.

The traffic moved like molasses along the Sunset Highway toward the Sylvan Exit. Her mind was in overdrive, filled with chaotic thoughts. She felt the papers in her trunk tapping a rhythm along her spine. Maybe the detective believed her. Perhaps he'd find something about… She could give Goldberg the benefit of the doubt, but…

In the meantime, she would talk to Denis Sorbets. François had obviously spoken with his friend about Lily, and Callie had the creeping realization that there was a connection. The men had been friends in France since Denis had worked at Beauvais Vineyard right after university. When they each learned that the other lived in Oregon, they were delighted.

The day they got together was enjoyable for everyone. They drove to the Dundee West End Harvest Gathering, sampled wine, listened to music, and engaged in French conversation. But if he talked to Denis about Lily, why hadn't Denis mentioned it to Callie afterward?

After the memorial service, she shared a glass of wine in the city with Denis while she and Olivia were at Jake's. She remembered that Denis had been very sad about losing his friend. They shared memories of his apprenticeship in Provence and of François. But nothing else.

Despite the bulging briefcase calling to her from the trunk, she wanted to drive past her Sylvan exit and head toward Dundee instead. She knew her anger was making her act irrationally, but she didn't give a toot. If Denis had information that could help her, she'd find out. Once again, it brought her right back to Lily.

She had been disappointed when Mae Haydon told her that Lily didn't want to speak with her, but she hadn't given up. Maybe if Denis could shed some light on the mystery, she'd have another reason to call Mae. If she could get past the mother, she might reach the girl.

Callie pounded the steering wheel, exited the highway, and made a complete U-turn. Heading home, she braked at the stoplight on Walker Road and let her mind mull it over. She had to think about meeting Denis after she'd checked everything in the trunk. Callie couldn't remember being unsure about laying everything out, making decisions, and finding answers. She was a list maker, a doer. This time, she felt like she was running in pause mode. The man behind her honked his horn. It reminded her of one of François' sayings, "They go on green here in Oregon…" As she wound across Walker Road and northeast toward home, it eased her heart.

Within minutes, Callie was pulling everything out of her large bag. Papers were piled into three stacks. She had stashed the coins, stocks, and silver bricks inside a small portable safe along with the insurance policy. When she reached for the papers on the table, she paused. Hot tea would help her procrastinate, so she moved toward the stove.

"Nothing is as it appears," she whispered. Jules told her it was probably unimportant, and she took his words to heart. Maybe the key had been left there by mistake, slipped out of his tobacco pouch. Perhaps it was just a fluke; his business safety deposit box was his to fill. It had nothing to do with her. She lifted the steaming kettle and poured hot water over the Constant Comment teabag. But he'd hidden that threatening note. That did have something to do with her. Time to dig. Her eyes returned to the papers. She placed her cup beside the pile.

She plopped herself down. The first stack of papers was clipped together and organized by date. François had circled names and dates, then drawn red lines to one name on the sheet: Dominic Jazzy. How were all these names related to this vineyard owner? She peered closer but couldn't find a common denominator. What h

Callie sipped her tea, pulled a banana from the fruit bowl, idly peeled it, and let her eyes roam over the next page. More circles and another intersecting red line. Gazing out her window, she tried to recall if she had ever seen François make these notations. She didn't think so. Giving up on the first stack, she reached for the second.

Callie recognized these as depositions and noticed Dominic Jazzy's name was listed on each. "Why was François interested in this man?" There were two sets, and both depositions were from residents of Dundee, where the vineyard produced Pinot Noir. She didn't read the depositions beyond the first pages; each discussed the vineyard.

The last packet contained some papers, a contract of sorts. Callie thumbed through them and raised her eyebrows. It was an employment contract between Denis Sorbets and Dominic Jazzy. She read every word, and there was nothing unusual there. At the bottom, she saw François' handwritten words, 'non-compete, how long?' Callie finished her banana and washed it down with the rest of her tea.

She started laughing as she slipped all the papers back into a small box. This didn't make sense; maybe that's why François hadn't shared it with her. It wasn't important. She had worked herself into a tizzy over a silly key that led her to nothing except a note that scared the crap out of her and Denis Sorbet's business card about Lily.

She wished she had kept the note now, but couldn't say why. Someone had painstakingly cut those damning words from magazines and pasted them into that note, someone who wanted to frighten François into silence.

All of a sudden, her spine tingled.

She remembered being in Provence to scatter François's ashes; his *Maman* had asked her to wait until the beginning of December. His mother didn't want her son's ashes spread so close to his November 19th birthday. She and *Papa* had wanted his memorial to stand on its own. How had she forgotten that when she met with the detective this morning?

Whoever sent that frightening note meant it. François hadn't lived to blow out another birthday candle. She pressed her fist to her mouth to stifle the sob threatening to escape.

"Who wanted François dead? Someone who had a lot to hide. François must have gotten too close to someone's secret. How could he investigate something so sinister without sharing it with me? The man must have been careless, and François noticed. But murder?"

Callie got up, turned off the lights, and lay on her bed in the dark. Her heart thumped so loudly that she could hear it in her ears. When she moved a hand over her stomach, she felt her heartbeat throbbing in her belly. Thump. Thump. Thump. Her mind tried to deny it, but she couldn't ignore it. She knew her heart was pounding in fear... it was tattooing out a message. Someone may have killed her husband.

She would call the detective tomorrow to tell him about the birthday François never saw and the candles he didn't blow out on his cake. She would make him listen. It was too real now. "And nothing will stop me from finding his murderer." Her voice echoed through the silent, half-empty house.

~

Mae Haydon felt conflicted; she had been experiencing a wrenching feeling for a few years. Her heart had been shattered since her twin sister turned her back on Lily, forcing her to make a choice.

She had been connected to her twin since birth. They finished each other's sentences; one would respond to the other before a word was spoken between them. They were mirror images, yet Bella had erased their connection as if she'd wiped an eraser over their lives. She missed her sister more than she had ever missed anything or anyone in her life. Losing her husband early in their marriage and raising Lily without him had been difficult. Losing her twin sister had been catastrophic. She pushed her short blonde hair behind an ear, the identical shade on her sister's head.

They grew up in the small town of Ashland, Oregon, near the California border. Mae was the introvert, and Bella was the extrovert. They had always been soulmates, never needing to speak while still communicating volumes with their eyes. The connection had been uncanny. Their friends teased them, trying to figure out how they could be so close yet so different.

Mae's large blue eyes filled with tears. She lifted her cup to her lips to sip her lukewarm mint tea, wondering if Bella still drank cinnamon tea, one of the few things they had differed on. Mae had always been more reflective about her inner world; she thought everything through before making decisions, a process that had always worked for her. Bella was impulsive and sometimes made poor choices. Mae drew energy from others, especially Bella, who had always brightened up a room just by walking through the door.

Bella was the shining part of Mae's glow. She had always protected her, and they would laugh because Bella was born ten minutes before Mae, just after midnight. That strange twist made their birthdays one day apart. Bella was the eldest and treated Mae as her younger sister. Always. The twins were named Zella Mae and Bella Raye.

Mae finished her cold tea and wiped her eyes. God, how she hated the name Zella. Once, when Bella had called her Zella out of anger, Mae had smacked her in a rare, uncharacteristic blast of fury. Bella never did that again.

When Bella dragged her along on double dates during high school, Mae went, albeit reluctantly. She didn't venture out much and generally preferred a quiet evening with a book to the chaos of Bella's parties.

But with Bella's persistence, Mae had emerged from her shell and met her husband, Mack. He had been a dream and a good man. When they fell in love and got married, Mae was sure her heart couldn't expand any further. Then Lily was born, and she realized she had been mistaken. The sweet little girl had grown into a lovely young woman. Over the years, Mack had missed his daughter's laughter, her tears, lost teeth, sore throats, bicycle falls, and so much more. That was long ago, before the horrors of Afghanistan shattered Mae's world and made her a single mother.

Mae took a deep breath and thought of her daughter, who was sleeping two rooms away from where she sat. The girl was the sweetest breath of fresh air in a sometimes-frightening world. She was born with the best of herself and her twin. She wasn't sure where Mack's DNA fit in, since Lily resembled her and Bella so much. Blonde, blue-eyed, with freckles. She had a dewy complexion that her mother and aunt shared. People often thought Lily was Bella's daughter, more outgoing, more like her auntie.

Until her bastard husband changed everything in their lives.

Mae hiccupped and felt the minty tea surge back up into her throat. The clock struck midnight. Mae didn't move. Her body experienced the twinless grief exploding through her chest, as it always did when she thought of Bella. Her hands trembled as she took her cup into the kitchen, wondering for the thousandth time what her other half was doing at that moment.

Was she laughing? Could she really live her life without Mae being part of her day? Was Mae the only one grieving? She shook her head in despair. As much as she missed her beloved twin, Lily's well-being was the most important thing in her life. Her daughter had to come first.

Mae tried to keep her mind from drifting back to the day Bella expressed her worries about her husband, Dom. Her twin's face kept interrupting her thoughts. She had felt fear that day, not specifically directed at Dom, but particularly concerning him. Her concern for Bella over the past few years had grown to the point of shattered pieces of love. She would always love her. Why was life so hard? Why did people have to choose between their loved ones at all? As the pain on Lily's face emerged in Mae's mind like a ripple over a clear lake, her disjointed thoughts began to wobble and shake.

When the tears stopped flowing, her thoughts turned to Callie Beauvais. The woman seemed determined to talk with Lily. Why? What did she believe she could accomplish that Lily's mother could not? Mae glanced toward the hall, aware her daughter was sleeping fitfully, still haunted by nightmares of Dom Jazzy. Her mind wrestled with the persistent worry that never left her.

Rethinking the idea of Lily having another channel to vent, maybe she should consider what their conversation might hold. She had been insistent, and something touched Mae when she heard a special timbre in the woman's voice over the phone.

She would sleep on it and talk with Lily in the morning. When she slid into bed, she tried to push aside the emptiness of missing Bella and her ache for Lily.

And she slept.

CHAPTER 12

For the first time in days, the drizzle stopped and the sun peeked through Callie's car windows. The white, puffy clouds moved as if a giant wind chased them across the sky. She glanced at the trees as she drove away from downtown Portland and frowned; their branches stood still. She wondered how the wind could be so wild up among the clouds, but here, there was no wind at all.

Valerie had reluctantly agreed to speak with her again. Callie was confused and perplexed by her strange behavior; she sounded frightened. She drove toward O'Connor's Bar and Café, located next to Annie Bloom Books. Over the years, she and Valerie had met some of the Larkspur ladies there intermittently. Callie hadn't been there in a long time.

When she walked inside, Valerie was already waiting at the door. The memorable bat clock still hung upside down over the bar. It had stopped working one day, so someone thumped it over and set it on its top, and it has run ever since. Callie's forehead creased when she saw the cloak-and-dagger way Val situated herself in the café.

"Valerie, you're scaring me." She twisted the colored scarf around her neck and pinched the ends as she followed the waitress.

Val tossed her blonde hair, which bounced against her shoulders. Soft black jeans were tucked into her black boots, causing her hips to sway like the smooth gait of a horse. "That's because there's a reason to be scared," Valerie answered cryptically.

Callie's eyes widened as she followed her friend to a back table. She noticed that Valerie had chosen the chair facing the front door. Again, Callie's antennae rose, but she didn't say a word. She wanted to avoid scaring her friend away again. She needed the information Valerie had kept to herself.

Plates of stuffed cabbage rolls, croissants, and glasses of white wine were placed in front of them, but Callie remained silent. By then, her belly trembled as her impatience grew with each minute the big clock ticked.

I need to tell you something else about that note you found, Callie. I couldn't tell you at Jake's because Bryan was there, and I was afraid...

"Bryan was at Jake's?"

Valerie stared at her.

"I'm listening." Callie curbed her impatience. She couldn't mess it up now after finally getting Valerie to open up, so she stuffed food into her mouth.

"François learned that Dominic Jazzy had been accused of sexually molesting his niece. Lily told her mother, but the case never found its way to court. Jazzy had Bryan Martos shush it up. Mae Haydon refused to put her daughter on public display in a courtroom, so it was easy for Bryan to settle out of court. But Lily didn't want the money. She wanted her uncle sent to jail. Jazzy is a pillar of the Dundee community. He has a lot of money, backs many local businesses, and his wife volunteers for numerous organizations. Lily was only twelve and a half years old when it happened." Valerie's breath hitched when she saw Callie's face go white.

Callie's stomach dropped. She stared blankly for several seconds before placing her fork on the table. Then, she reached a hand to her throat as it threatened to smother her. A roar in her ears sounded like a freight train on full throttle, and she didn't know how to stop it.

Valerie's brows flickered a little. "Callie?"

Callie frowned into her glass. It felt as if a steel rod held her upright, and her head ballooned, threatening to explode. She had kept that door shut in her mind for countless years, and now one conversation from her friend had wrenched it open so violently that she almost heard the door slam against the wall. Callie turned her gaze back to Valerie. She reminded herself to breathe in the good and exhale the bad. She refused to let the vileness in, a feeling of filth she had kept locked away since she was thirteen. She looked at Valerie steadily, "Go on, Val."

Valerie's eyes narrowed for a moment as she reached out to Callie and tapped her fingers. "Are you okay, Callie? You look pasty white."

"Yes, please go on. I want to hear it all." Callie's nails dug into the palm of her hand to stifle the loud roaring in her ears.

François said the paperwork implied that Jazzy settled $300,000 on the girl, which obviously...to François and me, trumpeted the man's guilt." Her green eyes flashed angrily.

Callie forced her voice back under control. "$300,000? The note mentions more than one check

"Yes, that's the kicker, Cal. François discovered that Dominic Jazzy settled that amount with Lily, but Bryan Martos handed Mae Haydon a company check for only $50,000. François wanted to find out where the other $250,000 went, and that's when...." Valerie held herself in check before divulging anything further. When she finished her wine, she raised her arm to call the waiter.

Callie sat back in her chair as her body trembled and chills ran up her spine. "Well, I know what François did. He replaced that missing money out of his own funds. He cashed in some shares in his friend's computer firm. I hadn't known about that until recently." She gripped the edge of the table, thinking about that poor young girl. She was sure she was going to vomit.

When the waiter arrived, Valerie held up two fingers. "Two more Chardonnays, please." Valerie's eyes flit around the room in agitation.

With a glass of wine in her hand, Callie battled the encroaching darkness and sweltering heat that threatened to overwhelm her. Taking deep breaths, she gazed into the glass.

"Callie, for god's sake, are you okay?"

Callie nodded mutely before lifting her wine. "Where are all those papers now, Valerie? Proof that Bryan kept Lily's money?"

Valerie's mouth slammed shut. She lifted her glass and glanced around the room. "I...I have no idea. When François died, I left the firm. The last thing I wanted was to stay and work with Bryan Martos. I think he was eager for me to leave too. He was nasty to me after the memorial. Maybe he thought I would take clients away from the firm." She snorted. "As if I could...His eyes were mean and...well, I won't go into that. He frightened me a little. Does this help you understand the note and the people involved?" She wound a hand through her thick, pale hair.

Callie leaned back in her chair and gulped some of her wine, still fighting off the emptiness that gnawed at the edges of her mind. "I want to speak with Lily. I found her on Facebook, but her mother called to say no. But now, I absolutely must talk with the girl!"

Valerie gasped. "Whoa, Callie. Client/attorney privilege has already been breached with our conversation. Mae Haydon won't be happy I've told you all this." Valerie nervously tucked her pale hair behind one ear and glanced around furtively again

Callie stared at Valerie. "Her note showed that she was happy François stepped in when Bryan…Wait. Did François find that missing $250,000? And how did François explain the second check to her? All of this seems unclear to me."

Valerie pushed her plate away. "He told her there was a financial glitch, and the second check finalized the settlement. He lied to her. What else could he say? One other thing I just remembered. François told me that Bella Jazzy and Mae Haydon had a terrible fight because she wouldn't believe her niece's story. Mrs. Jazzy said Lily was lying. Her husband was mentoring the young girl to be a winemaker one day, but he must have done much more than that…" Valerie shook her head sadly. "François was going to talk with Denis, but I don't know if he got to it."

The words hit Callie hard. Maybe someone stopped him before he could speak with Denis. Her own secrets weren't going anywhere, but wouldn't she be tearing herself apart if she talked to Lily? François helped that girl, which was a bittersweet thing for him to do…and he hadn't even known about Callie's gloomy history. He did it because it was the right thing to do. The right thing to do.

I must talk with her. Did Bryan know that François was aware of the money? François confronted him, right?"

Valerie bit her lip. "I don't know. Maybe. I hope I'm wrong, but…well, money can make a person do bad things, you know?"

Callie thought about the shares François had sold out from under Jules, his best friend. She hated that he did it. However, hearing this information about Lily certainly influenced her thoughts on the matter. One action seemed to cancel out the other, but she still didn't know what to make of it. That was a lot of money to give to a child from his cash, especially when his partner had probably embezzled the original money.

Her mind spiraled as she contemplated the enormity of François's actions. How could Bryan Martos have gotten away with such a monstrous breach of ethics and all that money? Wouldn't François have tried to shake it loose or force Bryan to return it? Was the reputation of his firm at risk? Money. It was morphing into something bizarre in her thoughts, and she didn't like where her mind was heading.

~

Callie hadn't told Denis why she wanted to see him, but his response to her call indicated that he was curious. François respected him as a friend and winemaker. Now, Callie needed to rely on those qualities herself.

Callie tried to focus on the traffic, but distracting thought bubbles kept appearing. She gripped the steering wheel and tapped her fingers to the jazz piano tune on the radio as she drove through Tigard on Highway 99 toward Yamhill County's wine country. She had visited many of the now 300 wineries scattered throughout the Willamette Valley, most of them in Yamhill County, but she'd never been to Jazzy Cove.

She drove for miles, trying to understand what she had learned that morning...François' death, once thought to be accidental, was now shrouded in mystery. She hoped Denis Sorbets had answers.

As she drove along Yamhill County's main artery, she reflected on the titans of wine tourism: Newberg, its satellite Dundee, and McMinnville farther north. While McMinnville typically shone brightest in terms of size and the variety of dining and shopping options, Newberg and Dundee boasted the majority of wineries and tasting rooms. As the wife of an avid wine lover, she was surprised they had never attended any of the events that she knew Dominic and Bella Jazzy offered to their wine club members. She wondered idly if François was avoiding the winery or its owner.

She knew Jazzy Cove was close to the small town of Dundee and not far from Argyle Winery. She had seen the signs several times, but now, feeling anxious to speak with Denis, she wasn't sure she would find the place without help. Her GPS guided her as she hurried her way west.

The mountain views were breathtaking and seemed to stretch on for miles. She had always loved the drive; the same road led her to her cottage at Devil's Lake. The Argyle Winery had consistently been one of their stops on the way to the beach. Miles of vineyards and sprawling homes adorned the hills around her. The sunshine lifted her spirits. Just one mile to go. Denis asked her to meet him near the western corner of the vineyard, where he lived in a small house, a fringe benefit for their winemaker.

Fifty minutes, 19 stoplights, and 30 miles after Callie left her house, she finally found the signs for Jazzy Cove Winery. Following the GPS voice, she turned right off Highway 99. Stone and wood buildings dotted the yard as Callie passed the Jazzy Cove Vineyard sign hanging from a stone column near the old highway. She drove slowly toward the outbuildings and beautiful wine tasting rooms attached to a large barn-like structure. She knew that was where it all happened and felt like she was home again. The vineyard was quiet, except for the group of cars in the parking lot she passed, tourists eager to taste Jazzy Cove wines. She noticed workers to her right, some picking grapes and others hauling boxes to a vast metal container on wheels. Once more, it felt like home.

The tidy white house came into view, and she stopped on the loose gravel driveway. The vineyard extended behind the house and spread for miles toward lavender-tinted mountains. The small house featured a charming porch, with inviting lawn furniture spilling onto a front stone patio.

Denis opened the door with a friendly nod. Short sandy hair fell over his forehead, and he wore a crisp white shirt, corduroy pants, and boots. The fact that she took time to appraise the man indicated how apprehensive she was. He beckoned her inside with a broad smile on his work-worn face and hugged her warmly.

"*Entrez*. Come in," he invited. He reached to slip off her jacket and pointed toward his kitchen. She preferred sitting in kitchens rather than the living room, where finding a place to set down a cup or glass could be a challenge during conversations. Her mother always conducted her business around a kitchen table, and it was one of Callie's quirks that she consistently followed.

He studied her while they sat at his round kitchen table, each with a cup of coffee before them. His black-framed glasses made his brown eyes appear larger than usual, and although he needed a shave, his smile remained warm.

She glanced out the window to take in the miles of grapevines. Callie missed Beauvais Vineyard. She dragged her gaze back to Denis. "François and I went to several vineyards around this area, but never found time to come here. Strange, isn't it, since you worked at this one? It is beautiful here in the valley with those purple mountains in the distance."

He nodded proudly, "I have been happy here because it reminds me of the Loire region of France and just a bit of Provence too," he responded with a wistfulness in his voice."

Callie drew a deep breath and tilted her head to one side. "I'm sure you wonder why I called out of the blue, Denis."

His mouth quirked with humor. "*Oui.*"

"I need your help." She lifted her chin to meet his gaze evenly.

"Me?" His dark eyebrows rose. "Now I'm really interested."

I'm trying to uncover the truth about François's death. I'm not convinced it was an accident. Guess I'd better start at the beginning.

"Oh?" He looked confused. Lifting his cup, he froze mid-air with a look of alarm as she explained the events leading up to her arrival. "So, that's why Mae and Lily stopped coming around. Nobody would answer my questions. When I called Mae after she stormed out of here one day with Lily in tears, she wouldn't talk to me. I left several messages, but she never returned them. I loved having them around, especially Lily. I could never understand it." His voice trembled—that poor girl.

"So, you didn't speak with François about it?" She pulled his dog-eared business card from her purse and turned it over for him to read.

He read the words out loud, "Ask Denis about Lily." He frowned. "François called me. We planned to meet in Portland for lunch several times, but we got busy and... He sounded cautious and serious, so I wondered what it was about. By the time we finally made time for each other, he died." He reached for her hand. "I'm sorry, Callie. That sounded harsh. I don't know why he wanted to speak with me." He pointed to the card, "But it was obviously about Lily. Why he kept it inside a safe deposit box with legal papers, I don't know." His eyes filled with tears.

She paused to settle her mind, and her jaw clenched.

Denis turned to her. "I'm shocked to hear Lily accused Dom. The other papers in the box...did you look at them yet?"

"Yes. I was upset and thought I'd learn why he kept everything hidden. First, I went to the police station." Her voice began to break, and her words wobbled.

"The police?"

"Yes, I found a note threatening François. So, I knew he was in danger. That's one of the main reasons I came here to see you. Since he got involved with Lily's claim, I thought it was part of the threat." She looked directly at Denis. "Do you think Dom Jazzy could kill someone? The man obviously didn't want anyone to know about Lily's claim."

"Oh my god, I wouldn't think so. He's a moody guy and I doubt he's ever been held accountable for his actions... He thinks he can do anything to anyone, and his money buys him out of it. I've seen this happen in the business a few times, but it's never been anything like this...although..."

"Although what?" She leaned forward, her coffee forgotten.

He glanced out the window to ensure no one was near the house. "A few weeks ago, when I was walking through the vineyard checking on the vines, I heard a commotion that sounded like a squeal, followed by someone crying. When I ran in that direction, I was nearly crushed against the grapevines as a teenage girl came tearing down one of the rows. I reached out to help her, but when she twirled around with such fear on her face, I instinctively dropped my hands. She was sobbing. She said, 'Please, please don't touch me.' She ran all the way down the row of vines and never stopped to catch her breath.

"Do you know who frightened her? Did you see anyone afterward?" Her brown eyes were round with apprehension, and she tried not to jump to conclusions. But what if?

"No…not then. But I was surprised to see Dom snipping vines in an area I'd just finished. I wondered what he was doing in the vineyard. It was unlike him. He usually stays close to the cave and rarely comes out into the vines unless the pickers are here and he wants to monitor their pace." He scratched his dark head and rubbed his neck.

Callie felt as if her chest might shatter, and tears threatened to fall. She lowered her head to battle the dark memories, but quickly looked up when Denis slammed his hand against the table.

"Lily is a good girl. How could this have happened, and I not heard about any of it? My god in heaven, just the thought of what she…She wouldn't make up something like this. I know it, so it must be true…," he finished in a whisper, his eyes turning glassy with tears.

Callie looked him in the eye. "If Dom Jazzy victimized that child and there's a possibility he may have hurt the girl you saw in the vineyard that day…maybe he tried to stop François from shining a light in that direction to find out the truth."

Denis didn't blink, but shook his head in disgust and despair. "What should I do now? I can't continue working for a man who…" He gulped and rolled his eyes toward the ceiling.

Callie stood up and pulled on her jacket. "Well, that's one problem I'm glad I don't have to consider. I have enough problems of my own. I found Lily on Facebook, but she refused to speak with me. Her mother sold the house they lived in at the time of her attack. I know she lives near Grant High School, but that's all. Do you have any idea where they moved?"

Denis shook his head.

"I'm selling both houses, and an estate agent is handling everything I'm not taking to France, so I have a lot to do." As she leaned down to hug the man in the chair, she noticed a look of deep sorrow etched across his face.

He looked up in surprise. "France? You're moving back…?"

She nodded and turned a watery smile toward him. "As soon as I find the person who wrote that threatening note. As soon as I find out who killed François." She eased away from him.

Denis Sorbets hadn't moved from his chair. His elbows were pressed against the table, and he supported his head with both hands.

When she opened the door, he said, "Callie?"

She turned while gripping the doorknob with her fingers.

"I'm giving a vineyard tour to a group of agricultural students from OSU this morning. Then, I will conduct a personal tasting discovery afterward. Would you like to join me? I know you have the vines in your blood after living with François." His eyes seemed to plead with her, as if he wasn't quite ready for her to leave.

Her lips parted in surprise; her hand unclenched from the doorknob. "Yes, I would like that, but I'm unsure how to keep my mind off Lily right now. I used to walk through the vineyard with your old teacher, Andre. Some of our best conversations took place among those grapes. I can still feel the Mediterranean dirt under my feet. It would be nice to stop thinking about…Yes, please. Lead the way, *mon ami.*"

The sun shone on them as they walked along a narrow wooden boardwalk near his house. It led to the tasting room, the wine cave, and the outer buildings. Callie noticed it was well-maintained, even though it was likely built years earlier. She followed him and saw that he pulled his beret low over his right eyebrow like Andre back in Pertuis. His boots made a thumping noise compared to her casual shoes. Since the earlier rain, she didn't have to worry about dust, but she grimaced, thinking about trudging between the rows in such unsuitable shoes.

Shrugging, she decided it would be worthwhile to redirect her thoughts. She wouldn't think about the papers in her trunk, the horrible note someone made to threaten François, or the little girl running through the vineyard in tears. For now, she would follow this Frenchman, immerse herself in grapevines, and taste the wine. She pulled the cuff of her jacket back from her wrist. It was nearly noon, and wine time in France. She inhaled the fresh air that the rain created. Her face relaxed as she glanced at the many shades of green leaves just beginning to shoot out of the canes.

She heard the group of students before seeing them. They stood in clusters, pointing at the bare vines and chatting with two women in coveralls. When the tallest woman noticed Denis, she smiled expectantly and raised her hand in greeting.

"*Bonjour*, Kit."

Callie glanced at him quickly when his voice changed. She suppressed a smile when she noticed his face light up. The woman was clearly more than a tour guide to the winemaker.

With an adventurous toss of her head, the woman spoke to the shorter woman, who raised her hands for silence. "I'd like to introduce our winemaker, Denis Sorbets. He will be in charge of the first phase of the vines tour. Please hold all your questions until the last; he will happily answer them when we enter his domain in the cave or the tasting room."

She turned toward Denis with an amused look in her eyes.

Callie glanced at him discreetly and saw the color in his face deepen as he turned toward the group. When he had their attention, he pointed to the end of the first bank of vines and motioned for them to follow. Kit joined Callie. They watched him lead everyone down the row with long, purposeful strides.

"I'm Kit." She studied Callie intently and reached for her hand.

Callie grinned. "I'm Callie Beauvais. Denis was a good friend of my late husband's. He knows I love everything about vineyards because my husband's family produces wine in Provence. Denis was an apprentice with Andre, their winemaker."

Callie noticed the other woman's shoulders relax. The beginning of a smile lifted the corners of her mouth. "He has spoken of Andre and the Beauvais wines. He tells me they also produce pink sparkling wines?"

"My niece, Cendrine, is in charge of the sparkling wines, and yes," Callie kissed her fingers and made a smooching sound. "The best."

Kit's eyes crinkled into another smile.

Denis stopped suddenly and bent toward a row of brown, dormant grapevines. "Today, please notice the mulching berms and protection methods we use here at Jazzy Cove. There are several protection methods for overwintering grapes. Choosing a variety that is hardy to your area is one of the most important things you can do to ensure their survival. In cold climates, grapevines are generally covered with about eight inches of mounded soil, like this." He pointed to the long furrow parallel to the vines.

"Frigid regions should also add some insulating mulch, such as straw or shredded cornstalks, which are more water-resistant."

A man with brown hair that curled to his shoulder raised his hand. Denis stopped and nodded toward him. "You mean along every row?"

Denis smiled indulgently. "Yes, if it is very cold. I will happily answer all questions when we finish the pruning, *oui?*"

The man's face showed an apology.

Callie had heard it all before, but hearing it again with a French accent reminded her of François. Now feeling a bit melancholy, she turned to study the students' faces and tried to visualize Denis listening to Andre say these words. Her mind returned to Pertuis, the older man, and all the memories waiting for her. She had to shake her head to bring her thoughts back to Jazzy Cove, where she listened to Denis teach these young people.

Since mounded soil above ground can still get quite cold, some grape gardeners prefer using other methods, like deep ditch cultivation, where ditches are approximately 4 feet deep and 3 to 4 feet wide. The vines are planted within the ditch, and soil is added as they grow. Although this method takes significantly more time to completely fill the ditch, it provides adequate winter protection. It never gets that cold here in this valley.

The students whispered to each other and shared laughter.

"Another method, which can be used in less cooler regions, involves using shallow trenches, like these." He pointed his finger toward the dirt at their feet. "Dormant grapevines are carefully removed from their support structures and lightly wrapped in old blankets or burlap. They are then placed into a slightly sloped trench lined with sand. Another protective covering is placed on top, along with a layer of black plastic or insulating fabric. This can be anchored into place with soil or rocks. Once spring arrives and buds swell, the vines can be uncovered and reattached to their support structure.

Callie's eyes glazed over. When Kit saw her face, she pulled her aside. "I know you've been through this already, Callie, and he will show the students how to prune back the vines. Shall we go to the tasting room?"

I'd like that. May I walk through the vines after the tasting lecture? Sometimes wandering through the vineyard in the fresh air helps me think.

Kit nodded and led Callie back the way they'd come.

As they walked into the tasting room, she heard the woman behind the bar discussing the wines they would offer the students. A younger woman with wispy black hair listened closely and stared at the labels of each bottle. The taller woman had short, blonde hair, and large, gold hoops hung from her pierced ears. Her face was calm and beautiful. When she noticed Kit bringing Callie toward the bar, her expression shifted to confusion.

"Is the tour over already? I thought we had another twenty minutes to put things in order, prepare the crackers and pitchers of water for the tasting room." The woman's face reflected a mix of surprise and stress.

Kit laughed. "No, Denis is pruning the vines now, and then he'll lead everyone to the cave. Bella Jazzy, meet Callie Beauvais, a friend of Denis'. She's lived around vineyards for years. When I saw her face, I thought a little glass of wine would help clear her head."

Callie gazed at Dominic Jazzy's wife.

Bella quirked one blonde eyebrow and lifted a bottle of Pinot Noir. "Are you from this area, Callie? Your name sounds familiar to me." She poured two fingers of red wine into the stemmed glass.

"Not really. I grew up in Napa Valley, and before my husband died, he inducted me into the grapevines and winery community both here and in Provence. His family has a vineyard producing reds and pink sparkling wine there. Denis and my husband were good friends." Callie lifted the glass with a grateful nod of her dark head.

"Ah, Denis told us he learned a lot from a man named Andre in Provence. Is this the same family?" Bella leaned her elbows on the counter for a moment before filling several pitchers with cold water.

"Yes, Beauvais Vineyard," Callie answered proudly. In Napa Valley, she had enjoyed working at a winery, but later her love for everything about vineyards grew. She recognized the expression on Bella's face.

She tilted the glass of wine over the bright white surface of the bar to examine the color. Then she swirled the wine in the glass, making several revolutions to release the aromas of the bouquet. She heard Bella and Kit chuckle as she held her nose above the glass to inhale.

"She knows what she's doing, right, Kit?" Bella's face lit up.

Callie turned to look at the woman. She sipped the wine, letting air enter her mouth. A grin spread across her face when the air mixed with the wine, releasing an explosion of extra flavors. Rolling the red wine around in her mouth before swallowing, she closed her eyes.

Both women chuckled as they watched her.

"Maybe we should hire you to stand behind this counter," Bella said teasingly. She glanced at the large, antique wooden clock on the wall opposite the bar and counted. "Five minutes and the rush will be on."

Kit slid behind the bar, poured Callie a few inches of wine, and winked at her before lifting the remaining glasses toward the plate of small crackers. And not a minute too soon, as the doors opened and the laughing students entered the tasting room.

Callie met Denis Sorbet's eyes, and their earlier conversation returned to her mind. She sipped the wine and chose to listen, idly wondering how often Bella Jazzy went through the spiel. She also contemplated whether the great Dom Jazzy ever participated in the tastings. Her mouth turned down in a frown as she thought about the man she'd never met and hoped she never would.

Her phone rang, displaying Valerie's face on the screen. Each time she thought of her friend, her stomach tightened in knots. Whenever they spoke, another nugget of information knocked her sideways. Tapping the phone, she left the group and whispered, "Hello?"

"Hey, Callie. I remembered something else Bryan told me when I left the firm that last day. He warned me to take care of myself. He might have sensed that I questioned François' death because something didn't feel right to me…

"Why didn't you mention this to me before now?"

CHAPTER 13

Valerie sniffled loudly, as if crying, and Callie gripped her phone tightly, focused on her answer.

"I don't know. I could do nothing and didn't want to be next, just in case it was true. It was hard to believe anyone could hurt him, and it shocked me to think that someone might have killed him. I'm not saying it was Bryan. Hell, no. But I wonder if Bryan knows who might have?"

When Callie started to respond, the phone was dead. She turned toward the young crowd standing at the bar and watched Bella and her assistant pour, speak, and tag each glass. As she watched the familiar scene, her chest rose and fell like a steam engine.

She would have slugged Valerie if she were in the same room with her. Feeding Callie information in little pieces that could have been important was getting on her nerves. Why couldn't she spit it all out at once? Was Valerie telling her everything now? Or was she still lagging behind with facts? Callie closed her eyes and took a huge breath while she pulled her thoughts back to the present.

Her stomach gurgled. When she opened her eyes again, she glanced at the gift shop one step down from the tasting room. Knowing she couldn't return to the conversation near the bar, she browsed the shelves. A small green frog caught her eye, making her laugh. There were three shiny frogs, each in a different position: one lounged on its back, another sat cross-legged, and the last one sprawled on its belly, all relaxed and holding miniature glasses of red wine. She chuckled and picked up the squatting frog. She knew it was perfect for Cendrine, and she felt better as she returned to the bar with her find.

Ten minutes later, Callie looked down at her shoes, hesitated for a moment, and made a quick decision. Walking through the rows of vines with wild abandon prevailed over keeping her shoes clean. Some rows had leaves, while most did not. This was the time of year when canes were pruned to prepare for a good harvest of grapes. She traced her fingers along several canes as she wandered through the field, reflecting on her conversations with Denis and Valerie.

Most of the old wood had already been removed. Her gaze shifted to the next field. Green leaves signaled that it was more developed, and she moved toward the grapevines. Her thoughts bounced between Provence, François, and a sobbing girl running through the vineyard.

Across the way, Dom Jazzy walked into the tasting room and waved to Denis and the students who were gathered at the bar. Denis clenched his jaw and rested his foot on the footrest near the floor. He lifted his glass in a stiff greeting and then turned his back on him.

"There are five things I always say when people taste our wines," Denis said, raising his glass to match theirs in a toast.

"First, avoid the price trap. High-quality wine doesn't always come with a hefty price tag. Second, listen to your taste buds. Simply drink what you enjoy. Third, think small. Whenever possible, seek out wines from small, family-owned vineyards like ours. Fourth, drink it right. There are no strict rules, but a few tips can enhance your enjoyment. Cold? Lightly chilled? Room temperature? And fifth, be an explorer. Sometimes, the most exciting wines can be found off the beaten path. I've roamed the world's vineyards and believe that small is the best approach. So, drink up and enjoy Jazzy Cove Pinot Noir. It's one of the best." His smile lingered long after the students sipped their wine because he believed every word.

Dom's eyes deepened with condescending thoughts as he studied Denis's body language. When he reached the others, his wife pushed a glass of Pinot Noir toward him, assuming that was why he'd arrived after the tour. He didn't often join groups because he had too many irons in the fire, but when he did, he enjoyed it like an adventurous child. His gruff grandfather might have beaten it into him, but the old man had also instilled a love for the vines in his grandson.

Without a word, he lifted it to his lips, savored it, and watched the group of students. He listened to Denis answer various questions, but heard Bella and Kit whispering about something else. He leaned in.

"What was that?" His silver hair gleamed beneath the lights as he scanned the students. He half-listened to Denis while leaning toward the women.

Denis brought a friend to listen to the tour. When we offered her some Pinot, she went through all the steps a wine connoisseur would take, well beyond wine tasting 101. Bella chuckled.

Dom took another sip and raised his eyebrows. "Who

Kit answered before Bella could open her mouth to respond. "Her name is Callie Beauvais. Her husband's family vineyard is where Denis apprenticed. He and Denis were good friends."

His smile faded.

Dominic Jazzy choked back his wine and reached for a napkin. His eyes shot toward Kit. "She was **here**?"

Kit and Bella gave him a strange look.

"Here, in my tasting room… What was she doing here?" His voice turned cool, and the line of his mouth tightened slightly.

Kit turned his face toward him in surprise.

Bella said, "She was visiting Denis. What is the matter with you?" His face was ashen. When she continued to question him, he raised his hand to silence her. He glanced around the room before leaning in and lowering his voice. "She left?"

Bella nodded.

His lips formed an even deeper frown. As he narrowed his eyes in contemplation, the women exchanged a glance. Dom's eyes appeared hooded like a hawk, prompting them to step back from him.

Kit was the first to speak up, muttering hastily, "She left a few minutes ago. She wanted to walk through the vineyard because it reminded her of Provence...said the fresh air would clear her head."

Dom's face broke into a forbidding smile. He handed the glass back to his wife with formality, as if presenting her with a nosegay. When he left the room, the women noticed him heading toward the vineyard like a man on a mission. He craned his neck to look over the top of his vines and began to jog slowly.

"What the hell was **that** all about?" Bella asked aloud.

Kit refilled the pitchers and the cracker dish. "I wondered the same thing."

Callie wandered through the grapevines like she'd seen Andre do a hundred times. She heard his voice, "As the grapevine grows, it is trained onto wire, removing all shoots between the wires and cutting back the shoots along the lower one to two buds. Mature vines will have four to six canes with five to ten buds on each and four to six renewal spurs with two buds each." Callie laughed softly at the voice in her mind. She missed the old guy.

She raised her eyebrows as she meandered down the next bank of rows. These vines were thicker and more advanced than the ones she'd just walked through. Jazzy Cove was well tended, and she made a note to talk with Andre and tell him his teachings had made a dent in Denis's head.

Abruptly, a noise interrupted her thoughts. The grapevines were five and a half feet tall. She was five feet two. Even stretching up on her toes didn't reward her with a view. Her insatiable curiosity urged her forward. As she hurried from the center of the row to the berm, her shoes slid in the mud, and she went down.

"Damn," she muttered. She pushed herself up again and saw that mud had soaked her black pants and the cuffs of her jacket sleeves. She pulled her fingers away from the mess. Another noise diverted her attention from the muck, and she stood up. She tilted her head forward and then twisted around to look behind her.

The man was large. Blocking the end of the row of grapevines, he stood with his hands on his hips, staring at her. Then, the tall figure approached her. She couldn't make out his features, but her heart quailed at the body language that urged her to get moving.

Turning away from him, she speed-walked toward the opposite end of the row. She nearly fainted when she glanced behind her and saw the man break into a jog. She pushed herself, slipping and sliding in the muddy soil toward the end post. One last look behind her, and she sprinted toward the outer buildings on her right.

When the man yelled, she didn't slow down until she felt his hand on her shoulder. Her body stiffened in shock. Knowing she wouldn't get away, she turned abruptly, causing the man to fall over her.

His hands gripped her shoulders, his face inches from hers, and his lips twisted in annoyance. He stood with his back to the sun, obscuring the features of his face. "What do you think you're doing, trespassing here alone? Why didn't you stop when I called you?" His voice was harsh, but he was slightly out of breath from the exertion.

Callie's words caught in her throat, "You scared me. What did you expect me to do when I saw a big man running toward me like a charging bull?" She spat the words out.

"I can walk every inch of this vineyard," he drawled. The sun slipped behind a cloud, exposing his silver hair.

"Mr. Jazzy," she acknowledged with distaste.

He noticed her tone of voice, and his eyes narrowed. "And, you are?" He played dumb, stared at her beneath hooded lids, and enjoyed the look of uneasiness on her face.

She saw him fist and unfist his hands as if he wanted to hit her. A cloud of fear enveloped her chest, but she tried to relax. The unwarranted anger that thrummed from him nearly knocked her down. "I'll leave now. I won't be trespassing again." When she moved away, her foot slid. She grunted as she started to slip and reached for the end post, but instead fell into the rose bush planted to ward off insects. She felt the thorns tear into her soft flesh.

Dom Jazzy watched her slide to the ground. A warning cloud settled on his features as the sun shone again, darkening his face.

Callie stupidly expected the man to catch her fall. When she stared up at him angrily, she froze. She wasn't a fifty-year-old woman lost in the maze of Jazzy Cove Vineyard anymore; she was thirteen, scared out of her mind. It wasn't Dom Jazzy standing above her; it was Jack Beaker, her childhood abuser. She raised a hand to ward him off and pushed her feet in the mud, trying to slink away from him. Finally finding a grip, she pulled herself up with the aid of the post and ran toward the buildings.

Dom Jazzy ran too. When he caught her, he firmly gripped her elbow and twisted her around to face him. His fingers clamped over her trembling chin. "Hope you enjoyed the wine, Mrs. Beauvais."

He smiled when her eyes snapped with anger as she jerked from his clutches and fled.

His laughter followed her as she trudged through the mud toward her car. He'd known who she was during the entire encounter, and his slyness angered her, bumping his evil up another notch.

All the way home, Callie fought against the images of a young girl running through the vines, crying and helpless. She imagined a wicked Dom Jazzy stooping over the vines, snippers in hand. She was glad he hadn't held those snippers when he found her nonchalantly walking through his vineyard. She feared he might have used them on her.

Denis's words echoed in her mind and lingered there. Her heartbeat finally slowed. She swore she might never drink Pinot Noir again. Well, maybe. Taking ragged breaths, she glanced at her speedometer and lifted her foot quickly. All she needed was a speeding ticket to add to the stress building like tiny rocks falling off a mountainside.

Now dried mud flicked off her cuffs as she squeezed the wheel. She hadn't brushed off her pants before jumping into her car, jostling the key, and tearing away from the winery. She didn't care what Denis might think if he had seen her speeding away. She just wanted to get as far away from Dominic Jazzy as possible.

As cars vied for calculated positions along the highway, traffic hummed its afternoon song. It was nearly five when she got home after crawling through late afternoon traffic through Tigard up Highway 217 to reach her side of town. She wished she could call Jules, but it wouldn't be fair to wake him up at two in the morning to whine and cry on his shoulder when he was an ocean away.

By 8:00 that evening, Callie had rifled through the thicket of papers from the bank again. It still didn't make sense to her, but a few key pieces looked important. She changed her mind and woke him up. Hearing his sleepy voice reminded her of sharing his bed and burrowing into his arms. Wishing she were beside him, she whined a little, unsure where to start.

"Jules."

"*Bonjour, ma chère.* What is wrong?"

You're right. I need you here, but not until this house is cleared out and we can go to the cottage.

He heard the tears in her voice as she told him everything that happened that day. Then he cursed the distance between them. "I can come to you quick

Callie smiled, thinking her love for him would carry her away. The anticipation of being in his arms was intensely delicious.

"You still hope to find the girl, even though this man practically accosted you?"

"Absolutely."

"Did you look on Facebook? When Veronique was Lily's age, she was on Facebook all the time. Maybe you can find her there?" His voice rose, filled with hope.

I did. I sent her a private message, but her mother called me. Lily doesn't want to discuss it with me. Our great minds work together."

"Because we work together better as a team, my darling."

"I love you, Jules."

"And I love you. I will be there soon."

"When I go to the cottage, make a plane reservation, *oui*?"

"*Oui*," he answered, but she knew he wasn't happy to wait.

~

Each room stood emptier than Callie had imagined. Her framed artwork was propped up in rows of four. She counted twelve and shook her head, feeling as if she were turning the heavy page of a giant book. The effort felt mind-numbing. She spotted throw pillows, two ottomans, three floor lamps, and a three-foot-tall metal angel painted to match her throw cover. A laugh escaped her as she walked past five small tables and the antique wooden smoke stand lined with copper. Where did all this stuff come from? Had she tried to gather two or three of everything? Once the laughter started, she hugged her belly and bent at the waist. She realized how good it felt to clean house.

The end of her life with François was truly over. She had experienced an emotional time in the last few days and sat with a half-empty coffee cup on her lap when the phone rang.

"Hello?"

"Mrs. Beauvais? This is Mae Haydon."

"Oh!" Callie sat down on the dining room chair with a thud.

"Lily changed her mind. If you still want to talk with her, can you come to lunch tomorrow? She goes to school for half a day. She isn't sick; she needs time to..."

"Yes, of course! What time? I'd love to talk with her, Mae." Callie's mood lightened and darkened simultaneously.

"I'm not sure if anything you have to say will lift my girl, but I think she could use another ear. I hope you are as sincere as you sound, because if you upset her, you'll be out on your butt. We liked your husband, respected him, and we owe you the courtesy of a visit. Please go slowly, Mrs. Beauvais. My daughter is strong but still a child, and I hope she can become a functioning adult one day. Many days, I walk on eggshells around her. I'm always afraid I'll say the wrong word or discuss something that brings all the bad memories to mind for her. You will take care, won't you?"

"I understand how she must feel more than you could possibly know. And yes, you can depend on my carefulness. There are a few things I need to clarify. I didn't know my husband stepped in to help you and Lily until two weeks ago. Please forgive my saying so, but I also know a little about what happened to Lily. No child should go through such a thing."

Mae sniffed. "No," she whispered.

"Thank you for letting me in." After she scribbled down the address, she danced at the sink and refilled her coffee cup.

She turned away from her half-finished, very late lunch and watched a robin dive for a wiggling worm. When it jumped into her jade pot, laughter erupted again. She was feeling tipsy.

~

The house was nearly ready, and she was in a good place with Jules. Now, if she could convince Lily it wasn't her fault, she might believe it herself. She focused on her, and refused to take depression into their house --- one thing at a time.

Suddenly, the day was brighter, the flowers were thinking about budding, and maybe Callie would make a difference after all. If François hadn't started the ball rolling, it would have fallen to the wayside along with Lily.

"François, I'm still so angry I could spit, but you've made me pay attention again."

CHAPTER 14

Callie met Mae and Lily Haydon the following afternoon. Her GPS led her up Sandy Boulevard to 48th. When she pulled up to the brick house, a blonde teenager was climbing the front steps.

Turning toward Callie, she smiled tentatively. "Mrs. Beauvais?" The girl's blue eyes were interested, but hesitant.

"Yes, and you must be Lily." She saw a girl on the brink of womanhood with pale, golden hair parted in the middle. It gently swooped toward her slender neck around a heart-shaped face. Her lips lifted in a smile that reached her eyes, eyes older than they should be.

Lily nodded and opened the door. When they stepped inside, Callie saw Mae beside the window, her fingers still on the curtains where she had watched them walk toward the house. Her arms were crossed tightly over her breasts, and her blonde hair slid across one eye. It was cut short, just barely covering her earlobes, which held large gold hoop earrings. Light hair swung freely when she moved her head, and her expressive blue-green eyes watched Callie below carefully arched pale brows. If Callie hadn't known she was looking at Mae, she would have bet it was Bella. The resemblance between the twin sisters was uncanny, although Mae appeared softer or quieter. She couldn't quite put her finger on it.

Mae was hesitant at first but led Callie into the brightly lit living room and gestured toward a loveseat pushed against the wall. The sun's rays poured through the glass, giving the room a sense of openness and cheer. A bowl of chocolate-covered raisins filled a dish by her elbow.

Mae twisted her hands. "Why don't you change clothes, honey?" she suggested to Lily, who shrugged and left the room.

While Lily changed clothes, she turned to Callie. "She's quiet and doesn't talk to strangers. She doesn't talk much at all except here with me and to one of her friends. She's changed so much since... She doesn't act like a typical teenager, not after..."

Callie reached outward, clasping Mae's beckoning hand as a flicker of sympathy crossed her face. "I know Lily's nearly sixteen now and should be laughing, talking on the phone, and sharing notes about boyfriends with her school chums. By the sound of your description, Lily doesn't fit the usual age group, and I know why. I've been there too, Mae."

Mae's shocked face paled. "Do you drink tea, Mrs. Beauvais?"

Callie nodded, fighting to keep her eyes from brimming over. "Please call me Callie." She had battled her own demons for years. Deep down, she understood that's why she wanted to talk with Lily. Maybe if she helped her, the silence she'd kept corralled inside her head would disappear. The images no longer crashed around like marbles as they did when she was Lily's age. She had managed to lead a normal life by pretending none of it had happened. She formed satisfying relationships and learned about the love between a man and a woman, despite the terror of her youth.

During the next two hours, Callie learned that Mae Haydon had worked at the Jazzy Cove tasting room since Lily was little and that her twin sister, Bella Jazzy, had always been very close to her. Bella had been thrilled to discover Lily wanted to be a winemaker, and she'd asked Denis Sorbets to mentor her. He had already been Jazzy Cove's winemaker for five years. Bella was confident he'd be the perfect tutor when her niece turned twelve.

"When Lily and Denis talked winemaking, my girl was lost in the clouds," Mae said with a smile. "Lily knows more wine and vineyard lingo than I ever knew, and I'd worked in the tasting room for a few years too. Jazzy Cove's specialty is Pinot Noir. It's the perfect weather for the grape, and the Pacific Northwest is one of the most prolific Pinot Noir regions. Jazzy Cove's Pinot is very good, and Lily was proud to be part of it all.

Lily quietly listened to the women's conversation as she sat in the rocking chair, gently tapping her foot to move the chair back and forth. "I miss Denis, Mom," she whispered.

Callie glanced at Mae, who shook her head before continuing.

Denis was always good to Lily, patient and kind. When Dom wanted to take over Lily's tutoring just before her thirteenth birthday, everything changed." Mae grimaced, and her voice turned thick.

"Mom, do we have to talk about that part?" Lily gripped the arms of the wooden rocking chair, rocking so fast that she was a blur.

Mae looked at her daughter and stifled a sob with her fist.

Callie reached for Lily's fingers, now clutching the edges of the oak armrest like a lifeline. She moved closer. "Lily, my husband was very concerned about what happened to you. That was why he made sure you received the missing money, but he wanted to do more, I think."

"…Missing money?" Mae asked, catching her slip.

"Well, not missing, just incorrectly distributed…" Callie refocused herself

Lily squeezed Callie's fingers in response. "Uncle Dom said I lied. He said I was a stupid kid who wanted attention by making up stories. Aunt Bella believed him. She called me a liar." Tears welled in her eyes.

Anger flashed across Mae's pale face as she played with one of her earring hoops.

"When I told Mom, she believed me. I never wanted to go back there. When Mom said we needed to stop him from hurting anyone else, I wanted to do that, so that's why we called Mr. Rubin. He was my friend's father's lawyer...but it didn't help," she whispered.

When darkness enveloped Callie's vision, she controlled her breathing.

"I didn't want Lily to sit in a courtroom and listen to my brother-in-law's attorney paint her as a teen slut. I knew he would do that because of the questions he asked me about Lily. I couldn't do it. It wasn't fair." She pulled a box of Kleenex toward her and blew into the tissue twice.

Denis didn't want Uncle Dom to train me. He wanted to teach me himself, but Uncle Dom yelled at him when he asked if I could stay in the cave with him. Uncle Dom told him to make wine...that's what he did best. He also claimed he could make wine with his eyes closed and that he should be teaching me, not Denis. I remember the look on Denis's face, his eyes were angry, but sad too. He knew I wanted everything to stay like it was. Maybe somehow, I gave Uncle Dom the idea that I would…"

Mae rubbed her daughter's shoulder. "No, that's not true!"

In her mind's eye, Callie saw herself as a scrawny thirteen-year-old sitting in the living room, waiting for her friend to return. Her dark, curly hair was French braided to her head. She wore her new sundress and a soft brown cardigan, her bare legs swinging back and forth. Across from her, Jack Beaker's face leaped from her memory. He had stared at her and invited her onto the porch. Callie didn't want to go, but she followed him… Callie felt the past and present collide around her, and the world seemed to go dark.

They stared at her. "Are you all right, Callie?" Mae sounded disturbed.

Jerked back to the present, she glanced at Mae and Lily, forcing herself to smile before looking away. "Forgive me, I guess I...." When Callie saw Lily's face up close, she began talking to the girl, almost forgetting that her mother sat less than two feet away from her.

She gathered her wits. "Lily, you are not alone. When I was thirteen, I learned that terrible things can happen to good girls. There was nothing either of us could have done to stop this from happening. I've never told anyone what happened to me. You and I both know how difficult it is to discuss it. I used to blame myself because I didn't scream, yell, or fight. But when you're thirteen, crying seems like your only option because you're scared. I sure was. I tried fighting, but a child's strength is nothing compared to a man with a mind filled with nasty thoughts."

Lily's eyes watched her. "I couldn't push him away," she whispered. The girl's blunt-nailed fingers dug into the rocker arms.

Callie's eyes lit up with understanding. "My mother would have been horrified. I was too scared to tell her. I didn't want to tell anyone. When it happened to me, I guess I thought if I didn't talk about it…just pretended it didn't happen, then the images would go away. It wouldn't be real. Eventually, my emotions and fear belonged to someone else. In fact, they disappeared deep inside my brain so well that the images didn't completely surface again until I learned why my husband helped you. When I found out, I knew I had to talk with you. I wanted to tell you it's not your fault. You are a beautiful girl, no matter what happened to you." The heaviness in Callie's chest nearly knocked her down.

Lily raised a hand to her lips to stop them from trembling and shrank into the chair. Callie noticed that the girl's fingernails were bitten down to the quick; she wondered why they weren't bleeding.

Her body was shaking, but she held firm to Lily's hand as the girl stared at her. Tears rolled out of her eyes and down both cheeks.

"I can't talk about it. Callie, please don't ask me to do that?"

Callie and Mae exchanged a look.

"Give her time, Callie. Maybe one day…but not today." Mae's look was like a mother lion who brooked no argument.

"You don't have to, sweetheart. But sometimes saying the words makes the bad things go away." Callie reached over to hug the girl before heading out of the house, her mind racing all the way to the car. Could she possibly finish what François started?

She slid into her car seat. Memories of her childhood forced their way in against her will and flashed through her mind. She shook her head violently, eyes squeezed shut, her hands covering both ears. Throughout her life, her mother had implored Callie to be good, not strong. But she knew her mother would have believed she'd never invent such a story. The images and, words were welded inside her, belonging to another child, not Callie. Didn't they? Callie laid her head on the steering wheel. "Lily told her mother. Why couldn't I? Lily had more guts than I did, that's why! And her mother did something about it, but then money got in the way and shut her up. Dammit!"

Her mind was overflowing with words, images, and memories. She could usually push it all aside, focusing on other thoughts, but not today. The memory of Lily was difficult to bear. The memory of Mae was heartbreaking.

And since learning of Lily's abuse, Callie's hurts screamed to get out again. She did her best to push such dark thoughts aside, but this time they refused to leave. They'd swamped her since her conversation with Valerie. Nobody knew how vulnerable her heart was, since she'd never shared the nightmare, not even with François, and never with her mother. Millie Augustine would have murdered if she'd known what the man had done to her teenage daughter.

Callie had tried to tell her mother, but her tongue always stuck to the roof of her mouth. Millie Augustine would have done something about it—Callie was sure of that. However, she admitted she hadn't wanted her mother to bear the sadness, pain, and anger. Eventually, Callie had pushed it into a teeny, tiny box and watched the images from time to time as they happened to another girl, never to herself. That had kept her sane, helped her love, and… pretend. But this time, the images couldn't be stopped.

She had known this might happen when she spoke with Lily. However, before speaking with Valerie, she hadn't known why François was so obsessed with helping the girl. She should have understood it was pretty damned important. Nothing could have sent François into that spiral if the case had been trivial. But a child being molested? Of course, he would lift every rock and mountain to help a young girl. She might still have reservations about some of the thorny secrets he had kept from her and question whether she truly knew the man she had married. But she never doubted his ethics and morals, nor his rancor toward Dominic Jazzy now that she knew the truth.

When Callie arrived home, she called Valerie. They talked for over an hour. Afterward, Callie felt thoughtful. Her friend still sounded evasive and cautious, yet also vulnerable. Was she still holding something back? Her voice nearly broke a few times during their conversation, but Callie didn't want to press her. Surely, her friend wasn't so afraid of sharing information with Callie that she'd conceal anything of real value. Would she?

A dark SUV had followed Callie from the Haydon house. The car switched lanes to keep her in sight and rolled to a stop in her cul-de-sac. Its owner stared through the tinted windshield and thumped the wheel with a menacing look on his face. Growling under his breath, he said, "That nosy woman has to be stopped." He waited until she'd closed the drapes before pulling away from the curb an hour later.

CHAPTER 15

The following morning, Callie had her answer. Powell's Book Store started as one large building with used books filling 75% of its shelves and the other 25% with new. Author reading events took place in one corner, and later, a tiny coffee shop opened on the main floor in the back. Over the years, it had expanded into several buildings, a parking lot, and a large café that rivaled its neighbors along West Burnside Street.

Callie entered the main building and inhaled the beloved scent of books. She had always cherished the place. The main arterial street bustled with activity, and parking was limited. The underground lots attracted throngs of people to the bookstore, and she followed the crowd into the depths of the garage.

Valerie's phone call on Saturday morning both dismayed and surprised her. Of course, she would meet her at the café, as soon as she could get there. It took her fifteen minutes. She hadn't wasted time on cosmetics. Instead, she'd slipped shaking fingers through her hair and jumped in the car.

She didn't notice the dark SUV parked on her cul-de-sac, nor did she see it pull into traffic behind her. All she could think about was the fear she'd heard in Valerie's voice. She ran two stop signs when the intersections were clear and took the shortest route over the hill and down Jefferson Street. The back way was second nature to her, and she knew it as well as her own name. That morning, in her rush to meet her friend, she was glad it was Saturday because the traffic was unusually light.

After she'd pulled into the underground garage, the SUV rolled slowly by the entrance and parked at the corner. The man followed Callie into the building and eased his way down the aisles of new books. When he followed her into the bookstore's café and then saw Valerie Blume waving from a window seat, he returned to his car. He smirked as he sat behind the wheel, watching the women through the glass.

The table in the far corner was covered with magazines. Callie pushed them aside after she sat down. The aroma of the hot croissant nearby made her stomach growl. She had left the house without eating anything or drinking a cup of coffee. When she saw Valerie holding a cup and munching on a breakfast roll, Callie figured a few more minutes wouldn't hurt. The information Valerie hinted at surely wasn't going anywhere.

Minutes later, Callie watched Valerie struggle, so she told her about her visit with Lily and Mae. Lost in the memories that surfaced for a moment, she crushed them back where they belonged. Then she was jerked back to the present when Valerie clutched her hand.

Valerie whispered, "That's not all François found, Callie. Mae Haydon's attorney disappeared as soon as Jazzy settled with Lily. I called his law firm so François could meet with him, and I was told he left the firm. Poof, disappeared. Then, François gave the second check to Mae for Lily. She was a pretty little thing, and I felt sorry for her. There was a photograph in the file, though I never saw her. François told me she had the biggest blue eyes he'd ever seen and was afraid of her own shadow. Jazzy did that to her, and he got away with it. François couldn't do much because it was settled out of court, but he wanted to make a difference for that girl."

"I know that already, Val. So, what else are you talking about?"

François wanted to review the financial records for the firm and Bryan's personal accounts.

Callie's face scrunched up as she leaned back to stare at Valerie. "He didn't trust Bryan? Did you get the records?" She tore off a piece of croissant and popped it into her mouth. Her mind was now racing in new directions.

"Yes, I copied the records. I gave it all to François. He told me he wanted to talk with his friend who worked at Jazzy Cove. Maybe he thought the man knew something that could help him. Since François was a viticulture attorney, not a criminal attorney, he knew he had to be careful. This was his partner's client, and he shouldn't know about Lily's case because Bryan hadn't discussed it with him. There was a copy of the child's deposition in that file... it was so horrible; I couldn't finish reading it. Afterward, I think François only showed it to me so I'd be angry enough to get Bryan's personal bank information for him."

"Why didn't you tell me this before? I knew you were hiding something, Val." Callie's voice trembled, and the bread lodged in her throat. She reached for her coffee to wash it down and coughed into her napkin.

"You asked me about the note and Lily…I didn't think it was important…oh, hell. Yes, I did, but I was still a little scared because Bryan was acting strange and François had already died."

"So, what made you tell me about it now? Your guilty conscience?" Callie tried to stop her crude retort, but couldn't help herself. Everything was getting muddy in her head, and she couldn't think straight.

Valerie glared at her and took a deep breath. When she glanced out the café window, her eyes filled with tears. She half-covered her face when she turned toward Callie again. "I think I'm being followed. It happened a few nights ago when I left the office; I was sure footsteps were closing in on me after I got off MAX. I ran like a scared child into my building and climbed the stairs three at a time to hide in my condo. Then, it happened again yesterday during lunch. I have a terrible feeling it's about all this stuff creeping up again. I can't shake it. Sometimes I think I'm imagining it, but dammit! I don't think so." Valerie's hair fell across her eyes, and she placed her elbows on the table to rub her face dry.

Callie was speechless, helpless.

"I should have brought everything to give to you. When François died, I took them from his office and hid them at my mom's house in Salem. I'll get them soon… if you want them? Maybe you can do something, but I feel danger in the air. Maybe we should burn them and forget it?"

When Callie saw the expression on her face and heard the alarm in her friend's voice, she covered her mouth with both hands. Exhaling loudly, she shook her head vigorously. "Oh god."

Valerie gathered their empty cups for the trash and started to get up. Callie touched her fingers as they clutched the napkins and stared into her face. "Let me think about this, huh? I have so many balls in the air, I'm not sure which one to catch first. Be careful, and if you see someone following you, call the police, will you?"

Valerie nodded tensely and looked around the café with unease. Callie pulled her into the book aisles and whispered to Valerie, "We need a break. It's Saturday, and my last Saturday Market. Let's ride MAX to Front Avenue. I'm sick of all this subterfuge, and if we stay together, maybe we can even find something to smile about. The papers are worrying me, and so is everything else."

Valerie shook her head as if to disagree with the plan, but then thought better of it. "Okay, let's do it. Leave your car in the garage and let's walk. The rain stopped, and we can blend in with the crowds. You know what it's like in the Pearl District and the riverfront on Saturdays when it's chilly. At least the sun is trying to come out."

"You want to walk fourteen blocks?"

Valerie smiled weakly.

The women headed east.

The man watched the women exit Powell's and banged his fist against the steering wheel. His car slid past them slowly before he gunned the engine and sped up Burnside. His gut clenched. He knew his secrets were battling their way out, but he was just as determined to shove them back in again. And those women weren't going to get in his way. He watched them in his rearview mirror. Although they were already out of range, his mind was already calculating how to silence them, so he slowed down and tracked them toward the Burnside Bridge.

~

"I know I'm wasting time, but we both need a diversion." Callie's calves were burning. She hadn't walked this far for a while, and her body noticed. Bright red lanterns hung above the arched entrance to Chinatown.

Saturday Market was everything Callie remembered: the largest continuously operated outdoor market in the United States. She had visited many times on Saturdays or Sundays from March through

Christmas Eve at Tom McCall Waterfront Park. It stretched from beneath the Burnside Bridge to an adjacent plaza at Skidmore Fountain. Since 1976, it had become an iconic economic engine for the historic Old Town Chinatown neighborhood. Everything was handmade.

When the women arrived at Skidmore Fountain, Callie sat on the stone bench. "I'm out of shape. And we have to walk all the way back to Powell's afterward. What were we thinking?"

Valerie laughed. "We can stroll, come on."

Callie followed her with a roll of her eyes. "I'm taking too much back to France with me. If I want to buy anything, slap me."

Valerie chuckled as they linked arms and walked toward the first vendor stalls. "There's a wooden earring holder that mounts on the wall; I want to buy for my mother. Hang on."

The man trailed behind them at a slower pace. It took him nearly thirty minutes to find them after he finally slipped into a parking spot. The place was so crowded that he could barely move. He hated it—the busyness, the parking, and the noise. Muttering to himself, he followed Callie's red jacket.

He kept pondering ideas. Since sweet Valerie must have confided in the good widow, he now had to take care of both of them. And he couldn't delay it any longer. God only knew who else they might share their information with. If only he could be sure there was nothing to connect him to…

"Watch out, sir. MAX is coming, and when those doors open, the crowd will knock you down if you stay here."

"Thanks," he said gruffly and followed the red coat. He was sure the leaky spout had been dammed up when François died.

When a woman with three children bumped into him, he hissed at them. She glared at him and huffed away, pulling the kids out of his path. He narrowed his eyes after them as a thought burrowed into his mind. The woman has to go back for the car. Why am I here in this madhouse when I can just wait and take care of the problem then?

A sly smile chased across his face, and he reversed his steps.

By the time Callie and Valerie returned to the fountain, they both collapsed onto the bench again, huffing, puffing, groaning, and whining.

"I told you to slap me if I bought anything!"

"Ha ha. I heard the tone in your voice when you said, 'Lulu would love this.' When you held that crocheted baby sleeper in your hands, I knew I couldn't have slapped you hard enough to keep your wallet shut."

Callie snickered. "And the green earrings? And the plaid scarf? And the earring holder for my wall?"

Valerie eased a shoe off one foot. "Too bad they didn't have those little crocheted slippers. I could use them about now."

Callie mumbled her agreement and glanced at her watch. "Do you feel like walking to Huber's for a glass of wine and a sandwich? I am not walking back to Powell's. We can call a cab."

Valerie's breath caught. "You had me at 'wine.' Let's go."

Back at Powell's Book Store, the man was so agitated he was practically steaming as the day turned to dusk, and the women still hadn't returned. He'd nearly sprained his wrist twisting it to check his watch every few minutes. His big plan to resolve two major problems was slowly disintegrating.

When he glanced up to see the rain beginning to splash across his windshield, he cursed and started the car. "Next time, I won't be so patient. Next time, I'll get her at her place." His thick knuckles gripped the wheel, and his tires squealed as he pulled away from Powell's.

CHAPTER 16

Callie picked up the phone on the first ring. "Brunch tomorrow? 10:30?"

Yes, I'll be there, and I've wanted to talk with you and Bram about something. I'll bring your favorite stuff.

Livvy chuckled.

Callie welcomed the invitation to brunch with her friends. She'd been stewing over several scenarios, least of all Valerie's fear that she was being followed. Was she opening a hornet's nest? Is that what François did? She kept remembering Valerie's face. The woman had always been very independent and in control, but today, she'd seen a woman afraid. The financial records might be vital, but could Callie put Valerie and herself in danger by pulling them out into the open? She was glad they'd spent the day together, even though she now had blisters on both big toes and one heel. She started the hot water running in the tub, looking forward to a long soak.

She'd stared at the assortment of boxes filled with clothing she'd prepared to donate to Goodwill and bedding she'd piled up to give Olivia, yet she couldn't see any of it. The weight of stress that had burdened her since Valerie informed her about Lily's sexual abuse, along with everything else, was overwhelming. Maybe Jules was right. She bleakly wondered if she should leave it, but could she do that? Could she forget those glazed blue eyes? Could she live with herself without solving the remaining puzzle?

A distraction pulled Callie back to the present when she glanced out the front bay window. Didn't she see that car there yesterday? She leaned forward and pulled the curtain back for a better look. When she opened her front door, the SUV drove away. Shrugging and biting her lip, she shut the door again. When she couldn't quiet her mind, she knew a sleeping pill would follow her bath.

~

She stopped by the little bakery in Hillsdale on Sunday morning and purchased giant cinnamon-nut rolls drenched in caramel—Bram's favorites. When she grabbed a bag of Irish Cream coffee beans for Olivia and a latte for the road, she realized how eager she was to spend time with her friends. She'd miss them. But they'd always have a free bed and breakfast in France.

When Callie pulled into their driveway in southeast Portland and sprinted up the redwood steps, she smiled. The house on the Willamette River always filled her heart with peace. It was a far cry from the year before when she had raced up these same steps to rescue Olivia from Hunter Roget. Her mind spun back for a few minutes, but she abruptly halted when Olivia's angry face met hers.

"This is the day you invited me, right?" Callie laughed.

Olivia pulled her inside and guided her to the kitchen table, where Bram had poured her a cup of steaming coffee. The Oregonian was spread out haphazardly in front of him, and his eyes warned Olivia to

Callie handed the bakery bag and coffee beans to Olivia. When she sat down, she stared at Bram and Olivia in confusion. "What happened?" She asked, knowing she would not like the answer.

Bram pushed the paper toward her and tapped the headline.

Prominent Vineyard Owner Questioned
By Richard Ellis

Police have confirmed that a silver-haired man raped a thirteen-year-old girl while she rode her bicycle home from Evergreen Middle School two weeks ago. She'd often taken a shortcut from the school across Jazzy Cove Vineyard. This time, an older man reportedly grabbed her in the vines.

The girl, who has not been named due to her age, feared reprisals from her attacker, but told her school counselor. Oregon law states the counselor has a responsibility to report abuse to the police. The girl's parents plan to press charges naming the winery, which will be filed by Anderson, Santiago, and Romulo in Circuit Court. The sun was bright, and she admitted she couldn't see the man well but remembered silver hair.

The lawsuit does not identify a single person. It says the vineyard is responsible for the blatant disregard for its visitors' safety on its premises. The matter is currently under investigation.

Dominic Jazzy adamantly refuted her story and demanded that this journalist keep this reported accusation from the paper. The school counselor, Mrs. Pierce, described the vicious attack, and the girl's parents pulled her from school as the counselor suggested. At present, it is my understanding that Mr. Jazzy offered to pay for a psychological evaluation for the girl.'

If someone had dropped a pin on the floor, it would have echoed through the kitchen while Callie read the article. The darkness swelled in her head and nearly knocked her off the chair, but she shut her mind against it. When Olivia pushed a cinnamon roll toward her, Bram shot her a look.

When the roaring in her ears ceased, she inched her fingers toward the plate and broke off a piece, letting the caramel drip through her fingertips. Without saying a word, she pushed it into her mouth, reassuring herself that she wouldn't have to speak because she couldn't. Instead, she chewed

Two cases involving the same man is not coincidental. Bram wiped the caramel from his lips, waiting for Callie to respond.

She flinched, and her eyes turned stormy.

No. And I think he's guilty as hell. He just can't hurt any more young girls..." She bit down on another chunk and raised her eyes to her friends. Her eyes were sad and angry as she tried to slow her racing heart. The adrenaline rush was almost more than she could endure, but they didn't know her story, and she wouldn't tell them. She slammed that little door again and raised her cup for more coffee.

Just minutes after taking away the offending newspaper, the three enjoyed golden hash browns, crispy bacon, and omelets. Then, everyone pretended it was just an ordinary Sunday brunch among friends.

In Dundee, Bella Jazzy's white knuckles gripped the Oregonian, and her eyes flew wide. Across the table, Dom was meticulously spreading strawberry jam on toast. His fork idled on his plate. She methodically folded the fifth page with shaking fingers so the bottom column was in clear view. Without a word, she pushed it toward the man she married ten years earlier, while seething inside.

Dom Jazzy raised his eyebrows and took a sip of his coffee as he picked up the paper. When he read the headline, coffee spewed across the table, splattering the front of his wife's dressing gown. Large brown stains grew in a wide circle and burned her chest, but her eyes didn't leave her husband's face. She waited.

After he read the piece, he stabbed the paper with his index finger and raised his eyes toward her. "It's not true, of course. You know it isn't. Some journalist wants to make a name for himself. This guy, Ellis, is known for sensationalism. He's also a bleeding liberal." He wiped his chin and refilled his cup, but his hands shook slightly, and his wife noticed.

"You bastard."

Dom raised his eyes in shock. "I **told** you it isn't true."

"Just like it wasn't true that you hurt Lily?"

His eyes widened in surprise. "Of course I didn't hurt Lily. She lied about that, and this girl did too. I don't know who hurt her in my vineyard, but I'll sure as hell find out." His last words carried such vehemence that they gave Bella Jazzy a twinge of uncertainty.

He stalked off to his office, and she slowly pushed everything into the sink. She also reached for the newspaper and tore it to shreds. What would her friends think if this were true? She'd just volunteered for the fashion show brunch at the new boutique in New Town Center, and she didn't want anyone whispering about this damaging article. She thought of Lily again. Maybe there was something she could do.

Five minutes later, she was talking to her sister.

"Mae. I know we haven't spoken for years… since Lily said…" She struggled to find the right words but straightened her shoulders and lifted the still-wet gown from her breasts. "I suppose you've seen the morning's newspaper?"

Mae Haydon's eyes narrowed. "Yes, Bella. Lily and I both read it."

Bella forged ahead. "Dom said it isn't true, and things are probably going to get pretty sticky around here. Please ask Lily not to bring up what happened...what she said happened when... It will make this new girl's claim worse for everyone," she finished awkwardly.

"For everyone!?" Mae yelled into the phone. "If Dom didn't hurt my Lily, why did he pay her $50,000 to shut her up and then pay the other..."

Bella Jazzy had slammed down the phone before Mae could tell her about the rest of the money François paid Lily. She stomped into her bedroom, ripped off her offending gown, and grabbed a pair of designer jeans from her closet. Pulling a sweater from the drawer near her closet, she thumped down on the bed and pushed each leg into the pants, nearly ripping apart the seams. Glancing into the mirror, she saw her pale hair sticking out from her head like Medusa, and she ran her hands down each side, pressing hard against her skull to push away her twin sister's words.

"$50,000? My god, Lily didn't lie."

felt the knowledge slam into her chest like a large stone. The past three years had been sad, and she had stuffed her grief inside like a piece of paper. She had become so good at stifling her feelings that she had almost forgotten what her sweet sister's voice sounded like. What had she done? She had taken sides with her husband because she refused to believe her niece's words. She had assumed Mae was overthinking it like she always did. Her throat became so thick that she had trouble swallowing. Her sweet Mae, always the logical one, the big-hearted, clear-thinking twin. And Bella had tossed her away like debris.

She replayed their conversation in her mind. She thought about the money Dom had paid Lily to silence her, and disgust clawed at her chest. For all these years, she had pushed her twin sister to the back of the closet, and when she finally found the guts to connect, she had minimized the entire issue. I still couldn't believe Lily; I didn't want to believe that anyone I trusted could hurt someone I loved so much. All Bella had wanted was to silence Lily. Was she any better than Dom? Could she even look in the mirror again, knowing the nasty person she'd become?

Bella's blue eyes clouded, and the hole in her chest bloomed large and dark. As terrible as the situation had become, something greater was happening here. She couldn't quite let go of everything she had worked toward. He wasn't the man she believed he was. She hadn't truly loved him for a long time. She slumped her shoulders, pushed her short, pale hair out of her face, and stared at her perfectly manicured fingernails.

She needed to outline the plan brewing in her mind. She had to make a last-ditch effort to slow down the momentum and fix things. Squeezing her eyes shut to block out the pain of hearing Mae's voice and to push away the twist of guilty conscience, she headed toward the kitchen. A cup of hot cinnamon tea was what she needed to clear her head. And then she had to make another bad choice.

Meanwhile, in Dom's office, he paced like a caged lion while Bryan Martos's voice attempted to calm him down over the phone.

"I don't know where the leak came from, Dom. Not from my office. Only my secretary and receptionist are here, and neither know about this new accusation. It's media hype, that's all."

Dom yelled into the phone, gripping the receiver like a hammer he wanted to pound into the wall. "That's all?! It lists my name and my vineyard for god's sake. Media hype, my ass."

Dom couldn't hear Bryan's response because Bella was banging on his office door. When she flung it open, he waved her out, but she stood with her feet braced and her hands on her hips. She wasn't going anywhere.

"Hang up the phone…now!" She spat the words out angrily.

Dom Jazzy was so surprised that he sputtered. "Bryan…I'll call you back." He turned toward her in anger. When she jerked toward him and tapped her finger into his chest, he was so surprised that he sat down in his chair and stared at her. His brows drew downward in a frown.

"You paid Lily $50,000 when you said she made the whole thing up? Why pay to shut her up if you hadn't hurt her?" She paced the the same path he had nearly worn in the rug moments before.

He stared at her. $50,000? He had settled for $300,000. "Where did you hear this?" His fingers twisted around the paperweight on his desk as if to throw it at her…

Her face was red. "I called Mae to ask if she repeated Lily's story. She said you paid Lily hush money. I nearly fainted when she told me the amount. I want answers."

But Dom's mind focused on the dollar amount.

He spun her around to face him, and looked deep into her eyes. "Bella. Pull yourself together. Believe me. Lily lied, but she was so upset, I wanted to make things easier..."

Before he could finish his lie, she fled. The sound of pounding heels on the floorboards left no doubt about what she believed.

Dominic Jazzy ran his thick hands through his silver hair and walked slowly back to his desk. He could hear his heartbeat as his anger intensified. "Damn Bryan Martos to hell."

He dialed the attorney's number. When he answered, Dom hissed into the phone. "Meet me at the Bistro in Dundee within the hour." He slammed the phone down and wondered what his grandfather would say if he read Jazzy Cove Vineyard in the same article with the word, rape. The old man would have probably used that pole on his head instead of the shoulders he usually aimed for.

~

Callie and Olivia stood before the large glass window and watched the river glide by. Large rhododendrons lined the riverbank behind their house, and ivy clung to an arbor built before Olivia purchased the home. Its charm ignited the romance in her blood; she hadn't allowed anyone to chop it down. Now, it sprawled over the arched frame in disarray, with coils of streaming vine slipping in and out of the trellis.

Callie stared at the discombobulated brown vine and shivered. "I think Dominic Jazzy may have killed François. Maybe he thought François was going to throw him in jail for hurting Lily."

"If he did, the man may come after you next if you keep asking questions. Please go to the police. Better yet, ask Jules to join you."

"Not yet. He wants to come over, but I need to do this alone. I know I'm being a little pig-headed, but...."

Olivia chuckled. "A little?"

Callie poked her in the arm. "There's something else I'm worried about. François' former paralegal...she's the friend who told me about this mess with Lily. She stashed some financial papers at her mother's house, and she's getting them for me. She said she was afraid when she left the firm after François died."

When Olivia's face paled, Callie continued. "She thinks someone has been following her and she's scared." Although Callie's nightmares had gradually faded, it took only Valerie's statements and Lily's incident to flick the switch on. After reading this morning's article about another young victim, Callie knew she would now face more sleepless nights. She also knew it was time to break the pattern.

She sat down and pulled her knees up, her bare feet resting on the coffee table. She struggled to grip the napkin between her fingers while balancing her cup of coffee with both hands. She lost the battle, set the cup down on the table, but held the napkin tightly.

"There's something else going on inside that head of yours. What is it?" When Olivia's blonde cap of hair swished over her eyes, she pushed away the strands distractedly.

Callie twisted the napkin between her fingers and kept her mouth from trembling. "Yes, there is something, but I'm not ready to tell you, Olivia. It's a part of my life that I've stashed away for years, and it isn't ready to see the light of day."

Her friend's eyebrows rose in astonishment. She reached over to still Callie's jittery fingers, gently removing the frayed napkin from her hand. "Okay," she said slowly, "but I'm here when you want to talk about it."

Callie blinked hard. "Let's have a glass of something wicked."

Olivia agreed without hesitation. "It's cocktail hour somewhere. I'll ask Bram to make us something strong." She left Callie, removed their cups, and slipped into the kitchen.

The Hot Buttered Rum was stout, and they sipped it slowly, as the conversation turned to Bram and Olivia's recent wedding in Provence. They relaxed again when they talked about the Spanish brandy and the project Callie set for herself in Spain as trustee for the money from the sale of Picasso's bottles.

"Life in the fast lane." Callie raised her mug. "Too bad I'm not gathering as many answers as there are questions."

Olivia tapped her mug with her own, unable to stop the reluctant smile that crossed her face. "My god, Callie. Does trouble follow you, or do you follow trouble?"

CHAPTER 17

When Bryan Martos walked into Dundee's Bistro that afternoon, he was already fuming at his client's demands. It was Sunday, and he'd planned to spend the day at his cottage. Instead, here he was trying to calm down a man who thought the world owed him everything. He smoothed down his hair that stood on end from the windy breeze and grimaced when he saw Dom Jazzy's flushed face.

As Bryon approached, he tapped his fingers rapidly on the table. At least it was away from the other patrons, so Dom could tear Bryon apart because of the Oregonian's article. As if he could prevent it. He sighed and pulled out the chair to join his most lucrative client. If he didn't need the man's money to satisfy his gambling habit, he wouldn't be here at all. But there's the rub.

Dom waved the waitress away when she approached the table. "Give us a few minutes," he mumbled, and she disappeared. His voice was hard when he turned toward Bryan. "How in the hell could you allow that to happen? I pay you to look out for my best interests."

"No, you pay me to get you out of trouble. And I do it. I don't have clout with the Oregonian or Richard Ellis if he's on the scent of a story, Dom." He reached for a breadstick in the basket near his hand.

"It's not about the article," Dom growled.

Bryan's head jerked toward him. "Well, why the hell did you bring me all the way here to Dundee then?"

"It's about the money, you ass."

Bryan's gaze held Dom's. He bit the inside of his lip, and his jaw thrust forward. "What money?"

"Lily's settlement. I gave you $300,000. You gave her $50,000. Where's the rest of it?" His eyes were sharp and assessing.

The color left Bryan Martos' face, and the bread he'd just bitten into turned to ash. He knew there was no way around it this time. Caught out, he swallowed and washed the dregs down with the water that waited for him. He closed his eyes a moment before he answered. "I bet on the horses with it. There's no easy way to tell you. I use your money to gamble with. You have your weakness and I have mine." His eyes bore into Dom's, challenging him to look away.

Dom was nonplussed.

"François Beauvais found the discrepancy and came up with the missing money to pay Lily the other $250,000. I don't know how he found out about it, but when he put two and two together, he wasn't happy with the results in our firm's bank account."

"So...that means his wife has something. That's why she's talking to Mae and Lily. Is there anything else 'out there' that could hurt me?" His eyes bulged, and Bryan could feel the heat emanating from the man's body.

"Everything is under control now."

"Really? And that's why the Oregonian has just plastered my name and Jazzy Cove across the newspaper, practically branding me a pedophile? That's your definition of 'under control'? His voice was filled with such animosity that Bryan pushed his chair backward a few inches.

"I'd imagined we could come to an agreement with the Mason girl's attorney and settle like Lily did. How could I know this would go south?"

Dom Jazzy pressed his fingers across his eyes. "Bella was so angry after reading the paper that she nearly killed me. I couldn't blame her. But when she heard about the money...Well, if she'd had a gun, she would have used it."

Bryan shook his head and bit his bottom lip, bemused and irritated, as he considered what Dom had just said.

"Wait a minute," Dom's mind clicked something into place. "If François Beauvais hadn't noticed that missing money, he wouldn't have started looking under rocks. Lily would have had her money. And this wouldn't have come out in the open. So, this is all on your head." He stared at his lawyer. "And now your partner is dead. Was that all he found under those rocks?"

The men stared at each other without blinking.

~

Later that Sunday afternoon, a guttural voice growled into the phone, "You just don't pay attention, do you, Valerie?" The voice sounded raspy and old, as if it had come to her from Middle-Earth.

She heard heavy breathing, and her palms turned sweaty. "Who is this?!" Dropping the file she had held in her fist, she sat down with a thud. Her desk was cluttered with folders. On Sundays, she usually ignored the phone when she was deeply engrossed in researching a case. This time, she picked it up without thinking.

The man laughed. "You know who this is, Valerie. And if you think for one minute that you're safe after talking with Callinda Beauvais, you have a screw loose. But not for long. I told you to watch your back after François died, but you didn't take me seriously. Now I'll do the watching."

Valerie squeezed the receiver. "What do you want from me? What could I possibly tell Callie that would hurt you? Why are you doing this?" Her frantic questions fell into space as he abruptly cut off the call. Still, she screamed queries. Dead silence answered. She dropped the phone, her body shaking, and she couldn't think straight. She had to do something, but what? Call the police, a voice in her head commanded, but what could she tell them?

Most Sundays, she worked with a skeleton crew at the law office, and today she shared the space with two other paralegals. She stared at them blindly before snatching up her files, banking them, and returning them to her desk.

"I'm leaving," she yelled as she passed the conference room. Hearing their muffled responses, she slipped through the heavy glass doors and punched the elevator button.

Within minutes, she spoke with her mother in Salem, forty miles south of Portland. Half an hour later, she was driving on I-5. Her eyes continually darted to her rear-view mirror. She wasn't sure whether she was more afraid for herself or Callie. But one thing she knew for certain was that the papers that had lain dormant for three years needed to be brought out.

Her mother was worried about her; she had hoped her daughter would stay and visit for a while, but Valerie was on a mission. She pulled out the old briefcase filled with bank papers and other items that François had asked her to find, and hugged her mother goodbye. She watched her daughter toss the bag into her car.

"Another thirty minutes can't hurt, Val. I will brew a pot of tea." She'd held onto her daughter's hand, hurt glittering in her eyes.

Valerie stepped out of the car, hugged her mother, and whispered, "Mom, this is important. I promise to spend next Sunday with you, okay? Tonight, I have to get back to Portland. This is something I should have done a long time ago. Okay?"

A smile found its way through her mother's mask of uncertainty. "I love you. Drive carefully. See you next Sunday, then. I'll make us cinnamon rolls." Her face creased in a loving smile.

Valerie squeezed her mother again and kissed her forehead.

The lights of Portland twinkled against the dark sky as Valerie returned and took the 14th Street exit. She stared out the window as sleet dashed against the glass. Pedestrians hurried along the sidewalks, their umbrellas buffeted by the wind that whipped through the city streets. She couldn't help but throw a surreptitious glance over her shoulder. Convinced she saw Bryan Martos everywhere, she found that the crowd would shift. Was her mind playing tricks on her?

She realized she was being followed when she drove into her underground garage in the Pearl District. With trembling hands, she clutched her cell phone and dialed Callie. It went straight to voicemail.

"It's Valerie. I think I'm in trouble. I'm in my parking garage, and there's a black SUV driving slowly toward me. It's the same one that followed me from my office yesterday. Now it's here again. The windows are dark, so I can't see inside. Oh my god, I know I should call 911, but they'd never help me in time. I want to tell you…I have information that might help you find out what happened. He's threatened me, so be careful. I know he's feeling cornered."

Valerie saw the car in her rear-view mirror, and her breath caught in her throat. "He drove past me. I caught the license numbers only as JM something and an 8. I couldn't get the last two numbers. Maybe I'm just nervous, and scaring myself. I'll call you again as soon as I can." When she hung up, she was shaking.

Valerie hurried toward the elevator. The silence of the parking garage felt eerie. Sounds echoed with every footstep, amplifying the stillness. She glanced over her shoulder, and the ghostly quiet unsettled her. Her heart nearly stopped when a black-gloved hand prevented the elevator doors from closing just after she jumped inside.

~

"*Halo*, Bram. Nice to hear from you. How are you and your new bride?" Jules had just been thinking about Bram and Olivia, knowing he'd see them again soon.

He heard Bram sigh on the other end of the line.

"Bram?"

"You didn't answer the email I sent last night, so I decided to call. Olivia is worried about Callie, and to be honest, so am I."

Jules put down his coffee, and his face stilled. "Why? I haven't looked at my email yet this morning. What's happened?" Adrenaline surged as he tapped his computer awake.

"Callie told us you wanted to fly over here. We know she wants to finish up the packing first, but you shouldn't wait. Something is happening here that I'm uneasy about, and Livvy agrees with me. Callie's onto something that could be dangerous."

His heartbeat quickened. "I'm leaving within the week. I decided to surprise her because she sounded sad in our last phone calls." Callie had been worrying him for a few days, and this made it more real. His imagination had run wild, but he'd been mistakenly lulled into complacency during their last conversation.

"Jules, we think she has demons to face, like all of us. She will surely tell you in her own time. This girl, Lily, has dredged up some old memories for her. Olivia thinks Callie may feel that if she helps the girl, it will also heal her own wounds. She doesn't know what it's about and doesn't know how to help. She needs you, my friend."

"I will be with her very soon, then."

"Good." Bram's audible relief crossed the miles to France.

Jules couldn't stop thinking about their conversation. He couldn't figure out what Bram meant. He hadn't noticed anything that could be defined as demons when it came to Callie. He idly pinched his earlobe. She had a sassiness he hadn't realized was missing from his life. Having worked among his computers for so long, he'd almost lost his way, and his zest for life had become fragmented. Since his niece was now an adult, raised without knowing that François Beauvais was her father, Jules had stepped in to take over.

His eyes turned warm. Callie had taken them all a hundred steps further. She had learned about her husband's illegitimate daughter, swallowed her pride, and loved the girl François left behind. Then, she introduced her to the Beauvais family, who opened their arms to her. Veronique now had an interior design shop, grandparents, a stepmother, and new cousins.

If Callie had demons, she had hidden them well. He had known her for only three months, but during that time, they had shared so much that his mind felt unsettled. He loved her. He wanted to marry her. And if she had problems to work through, he would help her.

He pulled up his airline itinerary on the computer to print it. Holding the paper in his hand, he took a deep breath and returned to work. Between him and Claude, they would get everything taken care of. Then he would fly to America and surprise the woman senseless. Jules had never been happier in his life.

He was a soft-spoken Frenchman who owned one of Provence's most successful computer businesses. He had silver eyes, dark hair with a hint of gray, and a broad forehead. At just over fifty, he took pride in his athletic frame, although he knew that drinking too much wine would go straight to his belly. He was a trusting individual, and his generosity was well-known throughout Provence; he donated laptop computers to schools, and his employees trained the students to use them effectively. He was a good guy who had finally found focus beyond computers.

His sister, Aurore, and best friend, François, had believed in him. With their help, he'd lived a pretty good life, had the usual ups and downs, a short, failed marriage, and good friends. When François betrayed him by selling his shares without first offering them to Jules, he was hurt. But, regardless of his betrayal, he had moved forward.

He'd found love with his best friend's widow and would not let that happiness slip through his fingers. With Callie and the connections she'd linked between his niece, Veronique, and the Beauvais family, he was determined to bring her back to France and marry her. If Bram Carle was worried, Jules knew there was a damn good reason.

CHAPTER 18

When Callie heard Valerie's breathless voicemail message Sunday night, she called her as soon as she walked in the door. She pressed her hand against her chest, fearing the worst. She nearly cried when Valerie answered the phone.

"I'm sorry I upset you. I was so scared that when a neighbor held the elevator door open, I nearly fainted. I was starting to unravel. He could see I was upset, so he gave me a Ruby beer from his McMenamin's stash. I nearly lost it when I saw his hand stop those elevator doors."

Callie unclasped her hand and took a deep breath. "Well, drink the beer slowly and count to a hundred."

Valerie chuckled again and hung up.

The voicemail had unnerved her. After their conversation, Callie poured a glass of Merlot and dialed Mae Haydon's number. She had thought about the damn article all the way home and worried about Lily's mental health after reading it. She was sure Mae must have seen it.

When Mae answered, Callie jumped in with both feet. "You read the Oregonian today? I was so upset that I couldn't see straight, and I could only think about Lily."

Mae's voice broke. "She's so upset; she wants to skip school tomorrow. She's locked herself in her room and won't talk about it. The article brought everything back again. I think the timing is perfect if you want to talk to her. Come by tomorrow for lunch if you can fit it in?" The woman's voice was strident and hopeful.

Callie quickly agreed. "I have a coffee date with a friend in the morning, so lunchtime will be perfect. Thanks, Mae." When she hung up, her face was thoughtful, and her deep sigh echoed in the room.

~

On Monday morning, Valerie glanced at the clock above her stove and poured out the cold coffee remaining in her mug. She had plenty of time before meeting Callie, so she decided to walk to work instead of taking the light rail. The night before, she had stared at the stack of papers and two thin files she had brought from her mother's house. Then, she stuffed them into a large, heavy-duty envelope to give everything to Callie at the downtown Starbucks later that morning.

yan's the voice eerily echoed in her mind, and she urged herself not to panic again. She had saved the bank statements and other papers that François had accumulated, hiding everything for three years. Having second thoughts, Valerie hesitated. She withdrew her finger from the envelope. Should she unearth it now? Could she allow herself the pleasure of discovering if someone killed François? Was she strong enough to endure Bryan's tremendously manipulative presence? She wasn't sure. When she handed the envelope to Callie, would her fears vanish or multiply?

The next instant, she saw François' kind face in her mind's eye. He had been a charming, lovely man. She even had a little crush on him when she started working for him, but upon meeting Callie, she laughed at her fantasies. The couple adored each other. Valerie knew she had no choice. If Callie could find anything in this pile of papers to resolve the question of François's death, she would applaud the results—no more hiding. No more ignoring her gut feelings. She knew what she had to do. Callie needed to know the truth.

Call it instinct, but she decided she needed a backup plan. She knew she should have told Callie everything at Jake's that first day. Surely, Bryan wouldn't find out about it... But maybe he was watching her building now. Her heartbeat quickened. She'd wanted to help François because it was the right thing to do. But the nightmare was becoming more extreme than she had expected.

Making a quick decision, she chose to mail the envelope before heading to Starbucks. It was better than handing it to her in a public place. Within minutes, she hurried along Burnside Street near Powell's Books. Shielding her umbrella against the light drizzle, she pushed through the crowds leaving the bookstore.

She crossed the street when the light turned green and rushed toward the corner. Careful to hold the bulky envelope inside her coat, hardly allowing it to breathe beneath her stiff elbow, she slowed and slipped into the Blanchard Building. She knew there was a small postal window in the lobby. Lowering her umbrella, she took a deep breath and dashed inside to scribble Callie's name across the packet. Eager to dispose of it, she sent it in care of Olivia at Larkspur Insurance. She had no idea whether the mail would reach her at the house since she was leaving town.

When the postal employee stamped it and dropped it into the bin, she sighed with relief. Valerie walked back outside, pushed through the revolving door, and paused for a moment. She inhaled the misty air with a satisfied smile, letting her shoulders relax.

As the SUV barreled through a wispy coil of steam rising from the wet pavement, she was too focused on opening her umbrella to notice the whoosh of tires so close. The crosswalk glistened with rain when its heavy bumper crashed into her unsuspecting body. A white pain tore through her as bones crunched inward, and she was thrown into the intersection like a rag doll. She was dead before the screeching tires sped away again.

Callie looked at her watch again. Valerie was twenty minutes late, and her latte was nearly finished. Craning her neck to glance up Broadway Street, she watched the crowd moving in her direction. Her mind returned to the voicemail message Valerie had left the day before. Uneasiness clawed at her stomach as she redialed her friend's cell number. She had already left a couple of messages without receiving a response.

Searching through her purse, she found Valerie's card and called her office. Maybe she had misunderstood the time or place? When she talked to the receptionist, she discovered that Valerie had an early meeting. She wouldn't be in the office until eleven.

Callie's mind felt scattered. The rain poured harder outside the café's circular glass windows. She was tired of the rain. Pulling out her iPad, she started typing. She checked her email and responded to Jules. Yes, she loved him too. She messaged Cendrine, "don't have that baby until I get there." She smiled when she replied to the email from her stepdaughter. Yes, use red and yellow for the flamenco wall in the shop. She snapped her iPad cover shut and looked up—still no Valerie.

When Valerie was thirty minutes late, Callie ordered another latte and a breakfast sandwich before sinking into her chair to reflect on the previous day's events. While waiting for the barista to froth the milk, she checked her cell phone to ensure it was working. It was, and there were no messages. Her thoughts about Valerie distracted her from focusing on the bigger picture. It was so uncharacteristic of her, especially since she had told Callie the papers might solve the puzzle that troubled her.

Her phone pinged to announce an email. She tapped to open another note from Jules. When she read the short message, she grinned, wishing she could erase the distance between them. The man certainly knew how to make a girl feel loved. Thinking back to her recent time in France brought her thoughts in line with Picasso's brandy and the project that awaited her. Who would have thought the old artist could have hidden so many bottles of brandy for so many years?

Callie thought of the bottle still sitting on the counter of her beautiful cottage in Provence. She decided to save it for her and Jules' wedding toast. There was so much to consider. She'd promised her nephew she'd be the trustee for Picasso's dream and was anxious about the adventure. But she needed to learn to speak Spanish. Her lips turned downward. She'd listened to a language program, but the words wouldn't stay long enough to fill a thimble.

Callie dismissed her wandering thoughts and called Valerie.

Again, no answer.

Now she was feeling less antsy and more worried. A chair pushed against hers in the small space, bringing her thoughts back to Oregon. Where was Valerie? She was now an hour late. Callie knew she wasn't coming. She shoved her iPad into her bag. Then, she tossed her empty coffee cup in the trash and headed for Valerie's office. The rain had intensified. Mistiness had turned into big raindrops.

Ninety minutes later, her legs ached from crossing them so often. She stared out the glass door into the elegant hallway by the elevators. She bit her dry lips and reached for Chapstick. Her mind drifted back to Valerie's voicemail message.

Where was she? Her friend would have called if she could, because it was unlike her not to. That thought was nearly too much to bear. She crossed her legs again, bounced her foot, and narrowly missed the glass table. She grimaced as she tipped the magazines onto the floor and saw the receptionist staring at her.

"I am sorry. Valerie said she'd be here by eleven." She lifted her wrist to stare at her small watch. "She's never late when she gives me a specific time. I don't know what to tell you. I can give her a message when she arrives, if you like."

Callie's stomach thumped beneath her rib cage like a basket of balls. Reaching for her large bag, she pulled it to her chest and stood up. "Yes, please tell her Callie came by."

She couldn't wait any longer.

Mae and Lily were expecting her, and she didn't want to be late. There was a light rain, but the wind had died down. She walked to her car. Just before she pulled out of the lot, her phone rang. Nearly breaking a finger in her haste to dig it out of her bag, she dropped it onto the floorboard. "Dammit." When she fished it off the floor, it stopped ringing. It was from Denis.

She maneuvered the car toward the pay station in the parking lot and asked Siri to call Denis through the Bluetooth connection. Afterward, she paid her fee and edged onto Alder Street toward the river. He picked it up quickly and barked into the phone, "Did you already read the paper about Dom and the girl?"

Her fingers tightened on the wheel. "Yes." The inflection in her voice said it all.

"I suppose Mae has seen it too?"

"Yes. I'm going to their house to talk with her and Lily now. She's invited me to lunch. Mae said Lily's upset and thinks I can help her by letting her talk it out."

"Really? I wonder why. She doesn't know you."

Callie's belly clutched against her backbone. "I have met with them already, and we instantly connected. Maybe it's a woman thing, Denis. Who knows why?" She wiped her forehead as cold sweat seeped into her hairline. When she felt tears clogging her throat because she knew exactly why Mae thought she might be able to help, she stopped talking.

"Will you ask her if I can visit them? They must know how much I've missed both of them. Lily was like a daughter to me, and it's been damned awful not knowing why they erased me from their lives. I'm sure Mae must realize I had nothing to do with Dom. And she must also know how much I'd like to kick him in the...." He sniffed loudly. "Ask Mae if I can call, will you? It's important to me, *mon amie*."

"Of course I will. Right now, this nasty thing seems to be exploding around us, and all I can think about is Lily and another little girl who is hurting just like she did." *And I know exactly how they feel.* "Getting on the bridge now. I'll be in touch afterward, *bon*?"

"Please give her a hug from her old friend, Denis, won't you?"

Callie smiled as she stared at her windshield wipers valiantly kicking off the raindrops. "Yes, I will."

CHAPTER 19

CAllie tapped her dripping umbrella and dropped it into the tall stand under the covered porch. Lily met her at the front door. When Callie opened her arms, Lily flew into her embrace. Mae smiled from the corner of the room. The warmth from the burning fireplace reached Callie's face as Lily led her to an upholstered chair.

"I have lunch ready, so let's eat. And then, Lily wants to talk with you about what happened. Will that be okay, Lily?" She glanced at her daughter, who smiled in return.

Callie was surprised to see the linen-covered table filled with a pasta salad, plump pink shrimp peeking among chilled tortellini shells. Fat slices of French bread were placed beside the three place settings, and sliced lemons floated in a pitcher of water filled with ice cubes. She raised her eyes toward Mae, who motioned for her to sit in the nearest chair.

Lily pulled a cloth napkin onto her lap and lifted the bowl toward Callie. "Guests first, Callie."

Mae's eyes wrinkled into a grin.

As the women ate their lunch, Callie glanced around the small house. Marveling at how Mae had arranged a collection of candle holders and small paintings near the fireplace mantle, she shook her head. With an interior designer's eye, she saw balance and color, noting that everything melded into a pleasing display.

"Do you have an interior design background, Mae?"

Mae smiled. "No, but mother did, and she taught us girls to match colors and balance." She followed Callie's gaze toward the candlesticks. "She always said, 'If you have a collection of anything --- don't put them all over the house. Put them together because that's where a collection belongs, together. So, I've done it automatically over the years."

Her eyes lit up when Callie nodded her approval.

"Bella never enjoyed it like I did. I helped her decorate her first apartment. She chose the ugliest fabric I'd ever seen for her curtains, but that's what she wanted... so we made them up. After we hung them across her living room windows in that little apartment..." Mae couldn't help laughing at the memory. "Afterward, we both sat down, stared at them, and she said, 'Mae, I have to say I...' and I finished the sentence '... hate them.' We both laughed so hard we almost peed our pants." Mae struggled as if she were trying to cling to the once-happy memory.

Callie watched the woman's face crinkle with amusement.

"She always had her head in the clouds, always wanted to live a champagne life on a beer income, but we always had that. Laughter. But that was before..."

"I have met Bella. She's lovely, and you two look so much alike, it's a little eerie. Do you have any other siblings or just...?"

"...Only my twin sister," she answered with a downturned mouth.

Lily quietly chewed her pasta, idly listening to the conversation.

"She thought you lied because she didn't want to believe her husband hurt Lily." Callie's eyes swung toward the girl beside her.

"No, she didn't believe me." Lily's sad voice continued. "I was close to Aunt Bella before that happened. She and Mom always laughed and played around. It was like a silly party most of the time. But I don't miss her. I never want to see her again." Lily bit into her bread and chewed roughly. Her blue eyes resembled deep pools, and her pale skin contrasted with the rosy cheeks that reflected her anger.

Mae touched the back of her daughter's hand as it rested near her plate. Callie watched her mother gently rub it with the tips of her fingers.

When they finished, Mae said, "Lily, why don't you and Callie go talk, and I'll clean this up?" She motioned for Callie to follow her daughter and went to the kitchen.

Lily moved toward the rocking chair. "Callie, I thought about what you said before. When I spoke to the school counselor, she asked who hurt me, but I didn't tell her. You know, there's a law that makes her tell the police if she knows about..." Lily took a breath.

"Yes, I know that, Lily."

"If we tell anyone about Uncle Dom molesting me, the paper Mom signed to avoid court would get us in trouble. We can't do that. We agreed just to stay away from him."

him."

"You would also have to return the money he paid in the settlement, Lily, or face a significant penalty if you discussed it. At least this way, you can attend college. Something positive could come out of the nightmare.

Lily's fingers gripped the wooden arm of the rocker. "How did you ever forget what happened to **you**?"

"You never forget.   However, sometimes facing and discussing it can help you overcome some of it. I was able to enjoy a loving marriage. I wasn't sure if I could ever let a man touch me...you know, in those soft places where you want to hide forever." Callie's belly ached.

When Mae joined them, Lily looked at her mother and made a decision. Callie's brown eyes met blue, and Lily began to speak.

Lily's tongue felt thick, making it difficult to open her mouth and speak. Her voice was a thread at the start, "One night, Mom and Aunt Bella went to a play at the Schnitzer Auditorium in Portland. Uncle Dom said that since they'd return late, I should stay and sleep over. I liked my own bed, but it didn't matter what I wanted...Mom refused to leave me alone, so she left me there...I don't blame her. I blame Uncle Dom!" Her voice broke again.

Callie's heart clenched as she watched Lily struggle with the memories. Her toes curled as the words spilled from the girl's mouth, and she fought to keep her face impassive.

Mae let out a strangled sound beside her.

Lily continued, "By the time Mom and Aunt Bella left, Denis had already gone home to his little house in the vineyard. Uncle Dom said it was a perfect time for me to taste his new Pinot Noir."

laughed and reminded him I wasn't even thirteen yet, but he said European children drank wine from an early age. He poured me more than the usual amount I'd seen at the tasting room, but I drank it. The wine tasted so good...until everything got a bit blurry. When my hands and feet started feeling numb, I wondered why just one glass of wine would do that to me. I felt him catch me when I began to slide off the stool. I didn't remember anything else until..." She sat up straight in the rocking chair and stared at Callie. Her face paled, and she took a big swallow of spit and cleared her throat.

Callie and Lily shared a deep, unspoken bond.

When I woke up, I was sitting on the couch in Uncle Dom's office. Something felt off. Pillows were propped up on either side of me. I felt strange. It took me a few seconds to notice that Uncle Dom was on his knees in front of me." Her eyes flew up to Callie's again, who nodded as she tried to keep her tears from rushing, rushing, and falling all over her.

"His silver head was in front of me, close enough to touch. His face was between my legs, and he was rubbing his nose up and down, making funny sounds. I was so shocked and horrified. My panties were dangling on my knees, and I squealed and tried to push his head away... But I couldn't move his head," she sobbed. "I tried, Mom, but I couldn't move his head away. He slapped my hand away!"

Mae lifted her daughter from the rocking chair and onto her lap, even though she was almost as tall as her mother. She held her tightly and glanced at Callie, asking, ' Why did you make her go through this again?'

Callie shook her head. She hadn't asked Lily to live through the horror, but maybe it had to be done. She knew if she'd had someone to tell, perhaps she wouldn't be stuck in the pause position.

I pushed hard again, but he just kept groaning and groaning as if he was hurt or something. Every time I pushed him, he knocked my hands away from his head. I was crying. I pulled his hair and tried to move my hips away from his face, but he just kept them there, tight, and wouldn't stop. I begged him, 'please, please stop', but he didn't listen. The harder I tried to slide my hips away from him, the more excited he became, and he groaned again and again.

Her words lingered in the air.

"Oh, honey, you don't...." Mae crooned.

Callie was sure she was going to faint, but she still held Lily's hand between both of hers, afraid to let go as the girl cried out her uncle's abuse.

"When I made a final push at his head because I hated him so much, he pulled himself up and smiled an awful smile. And then…. then….I saw it wasn't his nose he'd pushed into my privates…and I think I must have fainted because I don't remember how I got away."

"You got away?" Callie couldn't move. An ache that had been sleeping within Callie rose from the pit of her stomach, filling her chest. *Déjà vu* wrapped a silken shawl of fear around her. She watched Lily's lips move as a loud roaring filled her ears. She heard her own cries, her own anguish.

"I guess I did. When I woke up the next time, I was lying down, covered with a soft blanket. There was a couch pillow under my head. When I remembered what happened, I yanked the blanket up to my chin and stared around the room. I was scared he was coming back, so I got ready to run away…find Denis. But I was alone."

"Oh, my dear girl," Callie whispered brokenly. Lily's words cloaked Callie like a mantle, overwhelming her and dragging her under, especially when the girl lowered her eyes to hide the terror within. She recognized the look and felt the pain. She had blamed herself for a long time, pretending it hadn't happened. It crushed her soul to witness Lily's suffering, and she vowed to help Lily find herself again. But she could only do that if she cleansed her own soul. Mae leaned over and pulled Callie into their embrace, and the three of them held one another.

"You see why I didn't want Lily in court? That night, Lily was hysterical, and she cried all the way home. She didn't want to go to the winery with me the next day. I got angry and told her she couldn't stay home alone. We always went to the winery all summer." She took a deep breath. "But Lily stomped her foot and said no. And then, she broke down and told me what Dominic did to her. I wanted to kill him. I called Bella." Mae exhaled sadly. "That didn't go well," Mae whispered sarcastically. "And then I called my neighbor's lawyer. I'd met him before, and he seemed nice.

"I'd like to talk with him."

"Why? We promised we wouldn't sue Dom. That's why he paid the money. I haven't spoken with Dom or Bella since this happened, except once, when I drove out to confront Dom. Bella was in the tasting room, and Dom was nowhere around. She must have felt my sorrow, because she dropped one of the wine glasses and hugged me as soon as I walked in the door. When she'd stared into my eyes, she must have seen the depth of horror there because she pushed me into a chair as if someone had died. I remember at the time how often Mom told us to stay away from strangers because sometimes they did bad things to little girls." Mae sniffed.

The irony that he was ...not a stranger at all... was so debilitating that I was shaking. Bella listened to every word and pulled away from me. 'No, it can't be true,' she kept saying. When she said it the third time, I slapped her, and we both started crying so hard that we couldn't see one another. It's the twin thing, I think. It was like we slapped ourselves.

Lily sniffed, grabbed a Kleenex, and blew her nose before twisting the used tissue. She stared at her mother and bit her lip.

"When I realized Bella didn't believe Lily, I was stunned. I never forgave her. My girl was saturated with guilt, but she was the victim, not Bella's saint of a husband. Since your François gave us that second check, we've lived without family." Mae dabbed her eyes.

Lily nodded sadly. "François told us there might be a way to fight back...but then he died and we sold the house. I never want to see Uncle Dom or Aunt Bella again, and Mom says I don't have to."

Mae squeezed her daughter's shoulders again. "And we won't, if I have anything to say about it. Now, my legs are asleep, my girl..."

Lily laughed shakily. She rose to sit in the rocking chair again, lifting anguished eyes to Callie.

"Lily, have you spoken with a therapist about this?"

"Oh, no! I can't tell anyone else. The only reason I told you is because it happened to you, and François was so nice... He was furious at Uncle Dom and was going to talk with Denis, but I don't know if he ever did. I don't want to talk to anyone. It's weird, though. I feel a little better just telling you because before now, it was only me and Mom who knew what happened...and Uncle Dom, of course," she spat out.

"Denis misses you very much and wants to see both of you. He didn't know what had happened and is very angry at Dom. He has been very sad to lose you from his life."

Mae turned toward Callie. "And we miss him, too. However, the money will enable Lily to attend college. She still wants to learn viticulture and viniculture. The crazy girl doesn't want to make pinot or merlot. Denis told her about sparkling wine and champagne. He said she should make the wine that bubbles and makes her smile. She wants to learn how to make champagne because it tickles her nose."

Callie smiled faintly and lifted Lily's hand. "I have an idea."

Mae and Lily looked at her quizzically.

"You said you wanted to learn to become a winemaker."

"Yes, but I didn't think about it again after what happened."

"You still want to learn how to make wine?"

Lily smiled.

"Did you know that François's family owns a vineyard in France and that I will be moving there soon?"

Lily looked dismayed. "I will hate to see you go, Callie…"

Callie smiled. "Do you know about foreign exchange student programs?" Her mind had been racing since the idea germinated.

Lily looked interested. "Go to another country for school?"

Mae's face paled.

"Yes. You attend your junior year of high school in another country. I think you'd like France, you could live with my niece and nephew as host parents at the vineyard. I'm sure they'd love having you. You could attend school and find out if it's something you want to pursue. Mae?" Callie looked at Lily's mother.

Her head jerked up.

"Since your mother instilled interior design in you, maybe it's there for Lily too. My stepdaughter recently opened an interior design shop. Lily would have the best of both worlds to determine if either inspires her passion. Would you be open to this idea?"

Lily's eyes met her mother's, and they exchanged a look.

"It's not something you need to decide now. I want to help you get past…well, the past. Don't let it linger inside for years like I did. It needs to get out, stomped to death, and dealt with. Will you think about it?" Callie could see the excitement on Lily's face and the hesitation on Mae's. She knew her niece would love having this beautiful girl for a year.

"And if you like children, Cendrine will have a new baby soon. She has twins already. So, you'd probably be a sort-of nanny too." She smiled when she saw Lily's face dimple shyly.

Mae nodded simply. "Lily can ask the school for information if she wants to investigate the idea. Maybe the timing will help us.

Lily was likely feeling hopeful for the first time in a long while. She hugged Callie goodbye so tightly that her breath woofed out.

After Mae watched them embrace, Callie leaned toward the blonde woman and kissed both cheeks in the French fashion.

Before the door shut behind her, all three women's thoughts were racing in a multitude of directions.

Mae couldn't imagine losing Lily for a year after being without her twin already for three. How would she survive the loneliness? But could she hold Lily back if that's what she wanted? She'd seen the look on her daughter's face, felt her joy about the possibility of France. She was smart, and Mae knew she'd be able to move forward with Callie's help. They had a strange connection that would help them bond and grow. She also surmised the growth wouldn't be for Lily alone. Callie seemed more grounded once she shared her own pain with Lily. Sighing heavily, she shut down her worries and focused on what Lily needed, not her own wishes.

~

The speed of Lily's heartbeat startled her as she lay on her bed after Callie left. She pressed her hands against her chest and closed her eyes. So many thoughts swirled inside her head that they nearly drowned out the anxiety she battled day and night. Excitement and anticipation clashed with fear and anger. The thought of putting distance between herself and her uncle was too incredible to ignore.

Moving to France, so far away from her mother, was a hard thought to swallow. She wouldn't feel so guilty about her excitement if her mother and Aunt Bella weren't angry with each other. Her fingers clutched her bedspread as she thought about her aunt. She had always loved her, but her aunt's last angry retort still rang in Lily's ears.

CHAPTER 20

The lights of the city blinked like stars in the night. Callie angled her way through the crooked streets in the Alameda District toward I-84 and shook her head to push out the stubborn images that refused to go away. She had known talking to Lily would bring it all roaring back in Technicolor, but she had no idea how harshly it would fill her brain, nor how terrible the memories would manifest themselves all over again. The traffic slowed as she swung left toward the I-5 changeover, and she was thankful it kept her mind occupied.

She'd forgotten how terrible the traffic could be in Portland. Swinging the wheel into the next lane reminded her of her desire to move to Pertuis, where the country lanes were quiet and life held new promises. A honking horn served as a quick reminder to stay focused on driving. She raised a hand in apology. The woman glared at her.

Soft violin music filled the car as she eased down to ten miles an hour again. Her shoulders heaved as she tried to compose herself. Attempts to breathe sputtered into short, gasping breaths for air.

Another honking horn forced her to emerge from the mist of anguish. The bridge swung her onto Barbur, and she exited at Hillsdale. "I won't let this beat me, dammit. I must stop being that scared little girl and break Jack's hideous hold on my memories."

Callie looked in the rearview mirror, and her eyes began to clear. After a few minutes of introspection, she merged into the evening traffic. It was time for her to face her demons and toss them into the past where they belonged. She knew the only way to do that was to pull her memories out of the dark closet of her mind to discard them one by one. Alone. Nobody else could help her.

She wondered vaguely why François hadn't told her about Lily as she made her way home. Maybe he noticed that I froze up every time there was something in the media about child predators. Did he see that I clammed up every time I watched a movie or read the news on this issue? If he did, he never questioned me. Not once did he intrude into my private world. Perhaps he knew it was a taboo topic and not open for discussion? And maybe François thought he could help his wife vicariously through Lily?

When Callie drove up the incline of her driveway and turned off her car, she knew her soul searching had lifted away the anger at François. She checked her phone before stepping out of her car, and frowned. There was still no message from Valerie.

Once inside the house, she poured herself a glass of red wine and sat in the dim living room. The couch and two chairs remained with a table and two lamps. It reminded her of a doctor's office, clean and devoid of Callie's cozy décor. The estate sale would begin in this room, where her furniture would go home with strangers.

Tonight, she felt like a stranger.

Procrastination was no longer an option. Her emotions and fears had long belonged to someone else, tucked away in the pocket of lost hurts. But tonight, she had to reclaim them. She wanted peace—moments when she was no longer haunted by terrible dreams or the nagging fear of some hidden danger that her anxious mind imagined. She ached for the stillness she had lost forty years earlier.

When she sipped her wine, her face crumpled as she confronted her past, and the healing began. She set the glass down and wrapped her arms around herself. Her shoulders shook. Dropping her face into her hands, she soaked her fingers with tears. Later, Callie stared into the past for a couple of hours.

Words screamed inside her head from her troubled past to Valerie like a yo-yo. She left more messages on her cell phone, hoping for a return call. She called St. Vincent's and Providence. Valerie was not listed as an inpatient at either hospital. She should have felt relief, but instead, she worried some more.

he woke up with the remnants of a searing headache. The room was dark. She knew she had been asleep for a long time. Raising herself onto her elbow, she tapped her phone awake and saw it was three in the morning. Then, she fell asleep again.

When the peach-colored sky peeked through her kitchen window, casting pink shadows across her face the next morning, she lifted her head from the couch and shook the dark curls from her eyes. Wayward silver bangs fell over her forehead, but she flipped them back with a flick of her wrist. Her neck was stiff from sleeping in an awkward position, and her left shoulder ached from the pillow she had wedged underneath herself sometime during the night. As she swung her legs around to place her feet on the floor, she smiled at the sunrise and the beautiful, snow-capped Mt. Hood.

Callie felt as though a light had turned on to illuminate every corner of the pain box she had hidden for so long. She understood that her desire to help Lily was also aiding the little girl hidden within herself. The headache had disappeared.

Gingerly, she stood up and went to the bathroom.

Jules chose that moment for his phone call. The peace that enveloped her was so profound that her voice conveyed it across the miles to Provence. "My dear man. You caught me in bed, sort of…"

"Just where I wish I was right now, *ma chère*." He chuckled softly. "You sound different today. Is the packing done, then?"

Callie laughed. "Jules --- that is the never-ending story. One day, I will tell you why I am happy at this moment. But not today."

He didn't respond immediately. "…Callie, are you alright?"

"I am, my darling man. I am finally all right."

By ten o'clock, Callie and Alexis had finalized the details of the estate sale. The house echoed around them. Alexis planned to sell items in addition to her own, so they agreed that everything could be brought in the following day.

She declined Olivia's invitation for lunch. Callie was too busy and worried to handle another question-and-answer lunch. It had begun to feel like an interrogation lately, and she wasn't up for it.

When she called Valerie again, she was worried about her friend. "Val, please call me! I know you are busy too, but when you didn't make our coffee date yesterday, I couldn't get you out of my mind. Please let me know you are all right after the scare you had the other day. I'll keep my phone in my pocket. CALL ME."

By noon, the floors were vacuumed and the window sills were cleaned. When the phone vibrated and rang inside the pocket of her jeans, she pulled it out so quickly that she nearly dropped it.

"Val?" She hadn't even glanced at the phone number.

"No, Callie. This is Denis. I need to see you." His voice trembled with anger, and he breathed heavily.

Callie caught her breath. "Of course, what is it?"

I don't want to discuss it on the phone. I can meet you halfway or at Tina's Restaurant here in Dundee.

The urgency in his voice caught Callie off guard, and her desire to find out why far outweighed the cleaning that still required her attention. "I'll leave here in ten minutes, Denis. See you at Tina's."

An hour later, she shared a small table with him inside the quaint green-painted restaurant. It always welcomed travelers passing through Dundee on their way to wine country or the beach. His face was pale, and his fingers jittered against the tabletop.

"Denis? What's happened?" She accepted coffee from the waitress as she grabbed containers of cream. She hadn't had time for makeup, but she'd run a brush through her tangled hair. The day was shifting from peaceful to chaotic since Jules called at dawn.

I saw a photo of the girl.

"The girl? What do you mean?"

The girl who accused Dom is the same girl I saw in the vineyard that day—the one running from someone, crying her eyes out. I had a terrible feeling when you were here before, but damn. I wanted to believe Lily was an isolated incident, even though what happened to Lily was shocking. I didn't want to believe I was making wine for a...pedophile." His lips twisted in disgust.

Callie set the cup down. Her hands shook. Such blinding anger surfaced, and she closed her eyes to contain it. "So, we know the man has hurt two girls." She raised her gaze to Denis and whispered, "Can we assume there are others?"

He nodded, feeling sick. "I saw her photo in the community paper. She was on the yell team at Evergreen Middle School. I recognized her. I've heard rumors since the Oregonian came out, so I already knew her name. Now, I thought about your question last week."

She stared at him over the rim of her cup. "My question?"

"You asked if Dom could have killed François. Perhaps he discovered something about Dom and other girls? I wish he'd told me why he wanted to see me. We know it was about Lily. It makes sense now. If he had told me, he might still be al...." He couldn't finish.

Callie reached for Denis's hand. "Don't be hard on yourself. I have whipped myself to pieces, too. Why didn't I notice this, or why didn't he tell me, or any number of self-blaming questions? François did what he believed was right, and I must believe that. I'm hopeful the police will reopen the investigation into his death. I think we both know his death was not an accident…and by God, I'm going to prove it. If Dominic Jazzy killed François, I'll send him to hell."

This time, it was Denis's turn to squeeze Callie's fingers. He swallowed hard. "Call me if you need help. I may return to France. This is too much for me to stay. But first, I'm going to the police to tell them what I know. I think they'll be very interested to learn Dom was within a few feet of the girl when I heard her screams."

Callie raised an eyebrow. "Excellent!"

As they finished their coffee, there wasn't much left to say, so Callie started to get up when her phone rang. Ever hopeful it was Valerie, she grabbed the phone and answered breathlessly.

She recognized the phone number for the Portland Police and raised a finger toward Denis. "The police! Maybe they found something about François' death."

"Hello. This is Detective Sanders from the Portland Police. Who is this, please?"

Callie snorted. "You called **me**, detective."

"Yes, I'm calling you because we found your phone number in the recent call log and your voicemail messages on a phone that belonged to Valerie Blume. We want to talk to you."

The air rushed from Callie's lungs at the word, belonged—past tense. "Callinda Beauvais. What's happened?" she whispered.

"I'm sorry, ma'am. Ms. Blume was in an accident yesterday morning. She was pronounced dead at the scene, a victim of a hit-and-run driver. We would have called you sooner, but her phone must have been thrown across the street when she was hit. A runner just found it near a storm drain this morning. We hoped you might be able to shed some light on her death since your voicemail messages sounded like she may have been in trouble. And her condo's been ransacked. Would you please come down to the station on 2nd Street sometime this afternoon?"

"Yes, I'll be there." Callie dropped the phone onto the table and covered her mouth with her hands.

"What is it, Callie? What happened?" Denis grabbed Callie.

She stared at him, stunned. Shaking her head and unable to answer, she shrugged off his hand and ran to the restroom at the back of the restaurant. Once inside the stall, vomit spewed into the toilet bowl. She gripped the ceramic wall beside her.

Denis felt bewildered. Within seconds, he rushed after her. Unsure of what to do and reluctant to enter the restroom, he stood by the door, listening to the distinct sounds of vomiting. He ran his fingers through his short, dark hair and exhaled loudly, shifting from one foot to another.

Inside, Callie took a deep, ragged breath before reaching for the toilet paper and blowing her nose to clear away the nastiness. It took a few good blows to get everything out, and sipping water from the tap helped wash the taste from her mouth. When she walked out of the restroom, she was surprised to see Denis leaning against the wall across from the door.

"Bad, huh?" His eyes were warm and sympathetic as he led her back to their table. Her shoulder shook beneath his hand.

"Valerie died; she was François' paralegal. We had lunch a few days ago, went to Saturday Market, and…" Her eyes clouded. "…she was helping me…" She stopped and looked up at the winemaker, unsure of what else to say. "The police have her cell phone, and saw my missed calls. I need to make a statement at the police station. She was scared because she was being followed. Her condo was ransacked. It was a hit-and-run accident. I don't know where she died. He wouldn't tell me much else."

Denis looked pained. "Well, sounds like they told you quite a lot." It's after noon now," he said as he looked at the clock. "Let's have a beer."

Callie ran a hand over her face. "How can the human heart conceive and carry out such a horrific event, running over a person and driving away?!" Her eyes couldn't focus.

When he gave her the glass of microbrewed beer, she took it from him and finished the contents in a few gulps. When she left Tina's, she cried all the way back to Portland.

CHAPTER 21

Dominic Jazzy surveyed the grapevines crawling with pickers. He tipped his finger into his belt loop and felt the rush of ownership. He hadn't talked to Denis about the new Pinot Noir Reserve yet, but he would do that today. He looked for him in the crowd of workers, and frowned when he didn't see him. In fact, he hadn't seen him all morning, and this was a big day. The grapes were being harvested this week, and Denis was usually right in the middle of the activity.

His mind swung from the grapes to his winemaker. As he walked back toward the tasting room, he tried to remember the last time he had seen him. It wasn't yesterday, and today, he was absent from the excitement. His brow furrowed. Maybe he read that damning article in Sunday's paper and believed it?

Dom's eyes cleared. Bryan would take care of it. He always did. So, why should he fret if Bryan worried for him? He snorted, thinking about the money from his dad and grandfather that always got him out of trouble. And he thanked God he found a lawyer with a weakness too. He hunched his shoulders. Nobody was perfect, and he certainly didn't hold Bryan's gambling against him. His own choices weren't always great ones either.

He remembered how soft the girl had felt in his hands. He'd run his fingers through her long, curling hair and told her how beautiful she was. She felt afraid, but he'd whispered his admiration and brushed his lips against her curls. He didn't want the girls to fear him, but they always did. He just wanted to touch them, make them feel his excitement, and respond. But they never did.

A roguish look came into his eyes. Heidi was her name. Sweet Heidi Mason. He'd seen her name on her book bag and tasted the name on his lips. His eyes brimmed with tenderness and passion. He hadn't been able to get her out of his head. He remembered the moment when he was sure she felt the same. The moment when her arm slipped around his neck and he nuzzled her chest. Since that day, he'd savored the memory and massaged the image many times. But he'd imagined the girl's half promises. He'd helped her onto her bike when she'd fallen and gently pulled her into his lap, closer and closer still… And then afterward, when…

His eyes turned icy when he heard her screaming inside his head. Her fingernails scraped across his chest, surprising him with the burning sensation. When he jerked away from her clawing hands, she kneed him in the groin. He lashed out at her; she grabbed her bag and took off running. His dark eyes pierced the distance after her, and his stomach lurched when he noticed Denis a few rows over. He grabbed the snippers from the dirt beside him and began furiously chopping the vines. He wasn't sure if Denis had seen Heidi, but he was certain he heard her stupid wailing.

No, if Bryan fixed gambling problems, he'd fix this, too.

By the time Dom Jazzy walked through the doors of his tasting room a while later, the familiar gentleman's mask descended over his face. When he saw the bar filled with tourists, he grinned. Maybe he'd join the crowd today. They always loved having the owner participate in the wine tasting. He raised his eyebrows at the young woman pouring small portions into stemware, and she pulled another glass from the bar. He lifted his Pinot Noir in a toast, and his chest expanded, knowing he'd brightened up their day.

Callie clutched her large, red purse to her chest as if it held gold. Her heart raced beneath her rib cage; the tears had dried on her cheeks. When she was directed to Detective Sanders, he spoke with the detective she had shown the threatening note to just days earlier. The men noticed her approach, and one pulled out a plastic chair and gestured for her to sit.

"Thank you for coming in, Mrs. Beauvais. I understand Ms. Blume was your friend. I know it's difficult, but we can't find her killer without help. Please tell me why she was afraid. Did she tell you who was following her?"

Callie held her hands up to stop the rapid-fire barrage of questions. Without saying a word, she pulled her cell phone out of her purse and set it on the desk beside her. She couldn't comprehend the reality of Valerie's death or the time and space she found herself in.

After raising her eyebrows, she tapped the voicemail message, relieved that she hadn't erased it. The office was noisy, and people walked back and forth like rabbits. She turned up the volume.

When the policemen listened to the message, Callie covered her mouth to stop the trembling. Hearing Valerie's fearful voice gripped her by the throat. There was a roaring in her ears, and she placed her hands on either side of the chair seat, convinced she was going to fall to the floor. She needed Jules to calm the hysteria bubbling in her head.

The detective took a pen from his pocket. "Again, please?"

Callie stared at him blankly.

He pointed to the cell phone.

She tapped it to hear her friend's frightened voice. Again.

He jotted down the partial license numbers and handed the paper to another officer to research the DMV database.

"There can't be many vehicles with JM and an 8 on a dark SUV, right?" Callie set her chin in a stubborn line. "If this car was following her, you need to find it. She told me she'd been followed a few days earlier but didn't know who it was. I think it might be Dominic Jazzy, the owner of a winery in Dundee."

The detective didn't blink. "Did she tell you this?" His gray eyes studied her shrewdly. "Or are you guessing? He's a pretty important guy in his community. We've heard of him here in Portland for various reasons." The detective didn't share those reasons.

Callie snorted. "I'll bet you have."

The detectives shared a look, watching her.

She didn't repeat it or reiterate her thoughts on Dom Jazzy. Instead, she turned to Detective Goldberg. "Did you investigate the threatening note about my husband?" Her face looked pinched.

The man had the decency to look abashed at the question before answering, "No, not yet, Mrs. Beauvais." He pinched his chin and tapped the pencil on his pad.

"There could be a connection." Callie wouldn't let it rest.

Detective Sanders looked at him with a question on his face.

"Mrs. Beauvais was here last week with a note threatening her husband three years ago. And then he died in a boating accident."

"I am sure it wasn't an accident!" Callie's voice sounded like broken gravel. She wiped moisture from her nose that began to accumulate, and accepted the Kleenex from a box pushed toward her.

"Why would you think these two deaths are related? Is there something you aren't telling us?" Detective Goldberg regarded her with a deliberate squint.

"Valerie was my husband's paralegal. After he died, she was uncomfortable with his law partner's comments, and she left the firm. Maybe Bryan Martos thought she knew who killed François? I don't know. I think you should look into that aspect of her death." Her voice broke. "I still can't believe she's dead." Her whispered comment brought a look of understanding to the men's faces.

"Who is Bryan Martos?" After writing the name on a pad near his elbow, the detective quizzed her.

"He was my husband's law partner."

Detective Sanders looked up from his notes. "Where's the note Mrs. Beauvais gave to you? I'd like to see it."

She watched the detective walk to his desk, pull out his middle drawer, and fish out the wrinkled note. So, it wasn't on a slush pile after all. He knew exactly where it was. Huh. Interesting.

He placed the note on the desk and smoothed it out.

Callie's hope soared when the other detective read it, but his next words shattered that hope.

"Until we can prove otherwise, Valerie Blume's death is a hit-and-run. If we can link her death to someone involved in your husband's death, we will call you. If you wouldn't mind waiting here for a few minutes, I'll get your statement typed up for your signature." He waited for her response, but received only a vacant stare.

Fifteen minutes and a lot of fidgeting later, she lifted her hand to take the two-page statement. After scanning it, she signed her name jerkily and wiped tears from her cheeks. "You have some numbers and one letter. I hope that helps find the car that...the person who..." She stood up, unable to articulate another sentence.

He looked at her with sympathy. "You'd be surprised how many vehicles that could include. But saving that message could bring results. It might not be the vehicle that killed your friend, but it's a good place to begin. I am sorry for your loss, Mrs. Beauvais."

Callie nodded silently and left the precinct. Was Jazzy in that SUV? Was he connected to her death? The police might not inform her if the license plate number came up in the database, but at least she took some action to initiate the process.

She was drenched in guilt. Returning to her car, she pulled off the small parking tag receipt attached to the inside of her window. The rain started falling again as she stood on the curb with her car door open. She lifted her face to the sky, letting the raindrops pelt her face and soak the curl out of her hair. When she slumped into her car seat, she rested her head back. Callie's tears mingled with raindrops and slid from the ends of her dark hair downward between her breasts.

The next day was Wednesday, and Bella was still angry when she joined Bryan Martos for their weekly lovers' tryst, so they skipped lunch, and he whisked her up to their room. He was anxious to relieve his stress with a long love-making session, but Bella had other ideas.

"I could kill Dom." Her teeth chattered as if she were cold. "What can I do?" She sat on the edge of the bed and kicked off her wedge heels. Her fingers began unbuttoning her white lace blouse, and she stepped out of her designer jeans as if on autopilot. Sitting on the bed in her lace bra and panties, she glanced at Bryan, who was still standing by the window. She patted the bed beside her. "Bryan?"

He turned toward the woman he'd loved for several years and wondered how he'd become involved with his client's wife. Then she smiled at him, and he remembered. He hadn't had a chance in hell after she'd given him that smile when Jazzy Cove held the big reception to christen Dundee's fancy, new City Hall. They'd become lovers within a week and met like this every Wednesday for five years. He loved her more than he'd ever loved any other woman, as much as he could love anyone.

She put her thumbs into the waist of her panties, and sauntered toward him. Her eyes told him more than words as he reached for his tie. He knew he had a weakness for gambling on the horses, but that didn't hold a candle to his weakness for Bella Jazzy on Wednesdays.

An hour later, she propped herself up on an elbow and ran her hand across his chest. "You make it all worthwhile." Her fingers danced from one rib to the next on their way downward. "You make my life sing. After you put an end to the scandal of this young girl's accusation and stop Callie Beauvais from talking to Mae, our lives can return to normal." She stretched her hand farther until she found what she had been searching for.

Bryan stopped her questing hand and sat up in the bed. "What's normal, Bella? Your husband is a pedophile. I can't ignore it anymore. I'm sick of saving Dom from the wolves now nipping at his door." Throwing his legs over the side, he reached for his clothes. "You didn't know he likes young girls, did you?"

She stared at him and pulled the blankets up to cover her breasts. "No! But Bryan, but what can I do? What about Jazzy Cove Winery?" She looked like a little girl who'd lost her best friend. Her light hair framed her pretty face and fanned the air beside him. But her pale, blue eyes were flinty.

Bryan turned to look at her. "What about those little girls after Dom teaches them about life in the worst way? How will their parents calm their fears for years afterward? What will **they** do, Bella?" He pushed his feet into his boxer shorts and padded into the bathroom.

He didn't like who he saw in the mirror. He also wanted life to be back to normal, and it hadn't been since François was alive. He'd had his life, and Bryan had his. He was happy. A little gambling, a few horse races, and Las Vegas every three months. Now, he was mired in mud with a man he hated. And the man's wife could only consider keeping her social life intact. He grabbed the soap and swished on the water, scrubbing off every remnant of Bella and the filth in his mind. When he returned to the room, Bella was already dressed. She looked at him with arrogance, something he had never noticed before.

"Bella, you can't share our pillow talk with Dom. He won't trust me. He'll know I've broken client/attorney confidences." He adjusted his blue tie and turned his graying head toward her.

"I don't give a damn what he thinks." She put the second gold hoop into her earlobe and picked up her Coach purse. Walking to the door with swaying hips, she glanced at him. "I guess I'm on my own then, huh?" And then she disappeared down the hallway.

CHAPTER 22

By the time Bella returned home and cooked a light dinner, Dom had already been drinking for several hours. She had seen him enter the tasting room when she'd driven into Portland. When she arrived home four hours later, he was still inside. He stumbled across the lane toward their house as she tossed their salads.

She growled to herself and set the plate in front of him.

He picked at his food and poured more wine. When he refilled her wine glass, the dark red wine spilled over and splashed onto the linen tablecloth. "Uhhh." He dabbed the stain with his napkin.

Bella didn't move, but drank the overfull glass and watched him bumble around. Her face changed when he knocked over the pepper shaker and angrily pushed it and the salt shaker to the floor.

"What now, Dom, taking your anger out on dishes?"

He snapped his head up and glared at her. "I'm just enjoying some wine, and it'd be nice if I had some nice conversation with my little wife. Why are you in such a snit anyway? I told you Bryan would fix everything. He always does." He chugged the remaining wine in his glass and stared at her challengingly.

Throwing caution aside, she said, "Well, maybe Bryan's sick of fixing things. Lawyers can only do so much. You'd think that paying off Lily would have made you stop acting like an ass and..."

"...I said that Lily lied. How many times do I have to tell you that?" He opened the buttons on his shirt as if he were being strangled, hot and angry. His silvery hair shone brightly under the kitchen lights. The gold and brown flecked granite island held a case of wine and a small bowl of peanuts. He stared at it thoughtfully.

She finished her wine. "Really? Well, she certainly has a vivid imagination, then. I'm unsure if Bryan wants to get you out of trouble this time." Bella looked at him smugly, wiped the counter clean, and didn't blink.

He looked confused for a moment. "You seem to know a lot about what Bryan says and thinks. Why is that, I wonder?" He scratched his silver head and narrowed his eyes shrewdly. When he saw her face, he burst into laughter. Then he grabbed a new bottle and opener before disappearing into his office with his empty glass.

Meanwhile, at the Portland Police Station, Detective Jake Sanders tapped a file, staring at Valerie Blume's name. Something didn't fit and yet it did, but he couldn't figure out what he was missing. The Beauvais woman was so sure there was a connection between this woman's death and her husband's, but with the three years and nothing concrete to connect them, how could he justify a link between his death and this hit-and-run? His fingers tapped some more.

His partner walked over, sat on the corner of his desk, and pointed to the file. "We have forty-three DMV hits on those letters and the number eight. How do you want to do this? Do we have the time or manpower to run down every license, or continue walking the streets looking for witnesses?"

Jake Sanders looked up at Ross Goldberg. "There's something about this case that stinks. I'm not sure how the three-year hiatus could bring this woman's murder about…if Beauvais was also murdered. An event of some kind must have triggered a domino effect, and until we find out what that is, I can't connect them except that she was his paralegal." He fingered his short, dark beard.

"That note she found in the bank box makes it pretty clear he was in danger. She probably was, too, but her husband died, and she never knew a thing. She thought it was an accident. Until now, Jake."

"Right. Until now. What changed? Let's talk to her again. She's leaving town, selling her house, so I'm unsure how much time we have. We should tell her not to leave until we get this straight…"

"And just how do you propose to do that? Some of these cases last for weeks or months. Her life has been in chaos for a while now."

"Ross, she may have information she doesn't realize is important. There are too many balls in the air on this one. I say we talk to her again."

"Ok, let's go see her."

Within minutes, Jake Sanders had Callie on the phone.

"Yes, detective. I'm at home but don't know what else I can tell you." Her voice sounded frustrated.

"We'll come to you, Mrs. Beauvais. We can be there in about thirty minutes." When she agreed, they grabbed their coats and headed toward southwest Portland.

Jake drove. Ross flipped open the file, ran his finger down their notes, the DMV list of vehicles with license plates with J, M, and 8, and then snapped it shut again. "François Beauvais opened the safe deposit box a week before he died. Mrs. Beauvais said Valerie Blume was helping him with an investigation. When her boss died, she left the firm immediately. That sounds odd to me."

"Well, it wasn't a large firm. Maybe Martos couldn't pay her."

"True. But what if they had been investigating something that got him killed? The killer must have known they were working closely together. She was his paralegal, for God's sake."

Jake steered the car toward Sunset Highway, grumbling under his breath about the heavy traffic. "So why didn't he kill her too?"

"Right. Unless the killer didn't know she was helping him. And two deaths would have raised a mighty big red flag."

"Mrs. Beauvais focused Dominic Jazzy. Let's shine a light in that corner...very discreetly."

Callie watched the car pull into the driveway and met the detectives at the door before they could ring the doorbell. When she ushered them inside, she offered them coffee, which they accepted. "Make yourselves comfortable, I'll just be a minute." She pulled out three K-Cups and turned on her Keurig. She heard them murmuring and tried to guess what else they wanted from her.

Returning within minutes, she balanced three cups on a tray and set them down on the large ottoman because the room didn't have much furniture. "Milk?"

"Black," both men replied in unison.

Callie took a deep breath and positioned herself in the only chair left in the room. "What do you want from me, gentlemen?"

Jake spoke first. "We want to follow up on the possibility of a connection between your husband and Valerie Blume's deaths. We think something triggered the killer's act since it's been a few years since your husband died. We're moving on a plan and a wish based on the threatening note you found, her mysterious death, and your gut feelings." He lifted the cup of coffee to his lips and looked at Ross.

Callie turned toward the big man. She stared into the brew, taking a moment to answer. "The day I arrived home from France, my house had been ransacked. Everything was tossed around like a tornado, but I haven't found anything significant missing. The police were here. The officers said they doubted they'd catch the vandals. I arrived on a Friday, and my housekeeper was here the previous Wednesday, so they had a two-day window, but nothing has surfaced."

The men gave each other a look.

"I hadn't connected that to Valerie's death, but there's something else."

Both men straightened up. Jake placed the file on his lap and held his pen above the notepad. Ross lifted his eyebrows expectantly

Callie told them about Mae Haydon's note. "I've been told if the reason behind the note is discussed with anyone, the attorney could penalize the person because it involves a cash settlement to keep the case out of the courtroom."

"It could be important. Who was the attorney?"

She bit her lip, and her eyes flew to Jake's. "Bryan Martos, my husband's law partner." Callie ran her fingers through her bangs, digesting the entire picture. Was she not seeing the forest for the trees? Was Bryan involved in something so terrible? No, of course not.

Ross said, "So, we have your husband's death, his paralegal's death, his law partner involved in a private case, and your house trashed." He looked at Jake Sanders, who returned the look with a shake of his head. "That is why you think it's all connected. Tell us why you think Dominic Jazzy has something to do with this." Gray eyes met brown.

By the time Callie had told the detectives everything she thought was ethically correct without breaking her promise to Lily and Mae, three cups of coffee had gone cold. "You see, there's a young girl involved. My husband was trying to help her because he found some papers inside a file showing she wasn't compensated correctly," she finished lamely. Her nervousness and flushed cheeks did not go unnoticed by the men.

Jake took a deep breath. "If you don't tell us everything, Mrs. Beauvais, we can't put all the clues into one box. What aren't you telling us?"

"Please call me Callie."

They both nodded.

She closed her eyes for a moment. "The young girl was a victim of sexual abuse." Her voice shook. "She was only twelve years old at the time this happened, and she's just now barely able to cope. She isn't living a typical teenager's life. She's almost sixteen. My husband managed to fund her future so she will go to college, but until she can mentally face life after…"

Jake's brows came together. "So, doing the math, this girl was victimized three years ago?" His fingers squeezed the folder.

She nodded.

"And your husband died three years ago?" He smacked his leg with the folder, and the papers flew out and onto the floor.

Her eyes met his. "Yes," she whispered.

Jake and Ross looked at each other, nodded, and stood up. They shook Callie's hand and turned at the door.

"Now, we have something to chew on. Take care, we don't want any more victims before we connect the dots." Jake raised his eyebrows at her. "Keep your doors locked and your eyes open."

"Thank you for taking this seriously. If my husband was killed, I want to find his killer. I need answers, whether that is the same person who ran over my friend or not." Her eyes filled with tears.

Ross patted her shoulder. "We'll look for them, Callie."

She mumbled after she closed the door, "And so will I."

~

Valerie Blume's memorial was held at Caldwell's Colonial Chapel across the river on Thursday afternoon. It was across the river from the Pearl District where she'd lived for over ten years. She had no family except her mother, who lived in Salem. Valerie had never married after losing her sweetheart in the military's Desert Storm battle. During the service, Callie had watched Valerie's mother's shaking shoulders, and watched her cry. The sad woman was surrounded by well-wishers and friends that Valerie had accumulated while working at both law firms over the years. She noticed a man who watched over Mrs. Blume closely. She was glad there was someone to comfort her. The memorial had been a testament to her friend's life well-lived.

When Callie saw Valerie's mother walk toward her, the man still at her side, she stopped and held out her arms. Mrs. Blume hugged her and whispered, "Val always thought so much of you, Callie." She sniffed, lifted a handkerchief, and wiped her nose. "She came to see me and took papers with her. She was in a big hurry…she promised to come see me Sunday." Her voice broke, and the man next to her slid an arm around her shoulders.

"I am so very sorry, Mrs. Blume…"

"…And now I'll never see her again." Mrs. Blume burst into tears again, and the man led her toward a bench, whispered to her, and returned to Callie. His wavy brown hair swirled around his ears, and glasses perched on the bridge of his nose. He reached out his hand.

"Hi. My name's Tom Grasse, I'm Valerie's cousin. My mother was Lorraine's sister." Seeing Callie's confusion, he nodded toward his aunt, "Mrs. Blume."

Callie shook his hand. "I'm glad you're here for her. I lost my husband a few years ago, and the empty feeling is hard to carry alone."

Tom leaned in toward Callie. "Do you know if the police have any clues about the driver who blinked out my cousin's life? I heard rumors that you received a message from Val. That she was afraid she was being followed. You and I both know if that's true, her death wasn't a garden-variety hit-and-run, don't we?"

Callie felt tears trying to burst, so she shook her head no. "I spoke with the police, and they don't know anything yet, but they are actively investigating her death. If there's anything I can do to help Mrs. Blume, please tell me. I mean it."

He smiled gently. "Aunt Lorraine's in a state of limbo. We'd hoped they'd have answers before the memorial service. But she's heard nothing at all." He looked at Callie with a sad smile, gave a little salute, and returned to his aunt's side.

Olivia found her there and squeezed her hand.

"Thanks for coming, Livvy." Callie gripped her purse and looked around blankly.

Olivia's blue eyes clouded when she saw Callie's grief. "I know how devastated you are, and I wanted to be here. I barely knew Valerie except through you. I don't have to rush back to the office. Why don't we go to that Albertina Kerr Center nearby for lunch?"
"

The idea had merit, and Callie followed Olivia out the door and across the street without saying a word. The sky had cleared, the rain had stopped, and she smiled as she loosened her coat. It felt good to stop shivering. The weather had been so nasty that she couldn't enjoy the outdoors much at a

The ladies were informed that the tea room had closed, but they remained undeterred. Instead, they walked further and discovered a table inside the cozy, bustling space on 28th and Glisan called Pambiche. It was a trendy Cuban café filled with people. It was one of the wildest buildings the women had ever encountered. It was painted in turquoise, bright yellow, hot pink on the second floor, and royal blue, including the columns on the street below. The east side of the entire building was adorned with vibrant murals depicting Cuban history, people, the Virgin Mary, musicians, and lush green fronds of agriculture.

"Let's sit outside. It's cold, but the heaters warm up the tables." Olivia rolled her eyes, but followed, trusting her instincts.

"I want coffee. That will help keep us warm, too."

"Sitting inside would keep us warm…" Olivia mumbled.

"Ha ha." Callie studied the menu.

"I want the prawns. Bram and I eat them here."

They were ready when a good-looking, dark-haired man came to take their order.

"We both want coffee." She pointed to the menu. "What is *Ajiaco*?"

"A Taíno Indian pepper pot stew influenced over the centuries by Spanish and African cookery, the national dish of Cuba. *Ajiaco* is a one-pot meal brimming with tropical root vegetables such as yuca, malanga, ñame, boniato, yellow plantain, butternut squash, and chunks of adobo-rubbed pork and beef.   This is served with white rice." He grinned.

Callie laughed. "How long did it take you to memorize all that?"

He grinned again, and then he turned to Olivia.

"I'd like the *Camarones al Ajillo*. The prawns are rubbed with fresh garlic and olive oil and sautéed in a sour orange-garlic mojo sauce. I've had it before."

"Very good," he said, "and it is served with white rice, garlic crostini, and cabbage salad. I will bring coffee, ladies."

After they finished eating, commiserated about Valerie's death, and smacked their lips, they left the café and walked back toward the mortuary.

"It's hard to believe she could die like this, and still not know who did it."

"I know. It's so tragic. Why don't you come to dinner this evening? I can cancel my four-thirty meeting and be home by five." She lifted Callie's chin to look into her nutmeg-brown eyes, seeing profound sadness laced with tears.

"I think I'll go home, Livvy. Thanks anyway. I'll call you later."   Callie knew she couldn't face an evening filled with conversation, even with her best friend.

Lorraine Blume's words echoed in her mind as she started her car. Papers. Valerie had driven to Salem and picked up papers from her mother's house. Then her condo had been ransacked before or after she was killed. Now, the papers Valerie wanted to give to Callie were undoubtedly long gone.

CHAPTER 23

After the women split up, Callie drove southeast toward the Morrison Bridge, the busiest connection between east and west Portland. The ninety-foot-wide bridge spans the Willamette River, carrying cyclists, cars, and pedestrians. A steel grating deck made of fiber-reinforced polymer panels provides traction for vehicles.

Callie never liked driving over the bridge; she hated the unstable feeling under her tires. She grimaced as she gripped the wheel, thinking it felt like running on ice without cleats. Her nerves were on edge. The four days between Valerie's death and her memorial had evaporated into thin air. Now, with her mind heavy with worry and grief, she tried to ignore the bridge. It was taking her home, and that was exactly where she wanted to be. Her hand fumbled with the radio. Music always helped her think clearly, transporting her to magical places.

A pearl-colored Buick SUV forced its way into the line of traffic, disregarding the frustrated gestures from other drivers. It slid in behind Callie's Lexus while Michael Allen Harrison's fingers danced over a piano, his soft notes trilling into the warmth of her car. The CD was a gift from Valerie on a past Christmas. The rain had stopped, though the bridge still shimmered with water from the earlier downpour.

The Buick Enclave maintained a safe distance, but no cars could slide between them. Unaware, Callie glanced down at the deep river. She remembered when François pulled her on a slalom ski behind their boat years ago. A bittersweet smile crossed her face as she recalled when she had fallen. He swung their boat around to pick her up and said they would take the boat to the lake and leave it there.

"I don't want to lose you in the river," he'd told her. "It's getting too dangerous on the Willamette…too many boats, too many wakes to knock you down." He had kissed her wet face and teased a smile out of her.

Her mouth turned down. "But you died in the water, not me."

The temperature had warmed a bit after the rain, so she lowered the window an inch to let in a slight breeze. She eased forward when the traffic slowed, and other drivers were leery of the wet deck like she was. As she pulled forward again, she felt a slight tap on her back bumper.

Her eyes flew to the rear-view mirror, but she couldn't see the driver, who wore a hat pulled over his forehead. When she felt the tap again, this time it was harder. She looked around anxiously. The bridge was not a place for a car accident. When she tapped the gas pedal, the Buick pulled out as if it was going to pass her, which wasn't allowed on the bridges. Her clammy hands gripped the steering wheel.

When the big Buick veered toward her rear fender, her car headed for the bridge railing. Her heart raced, now frantic. "What the hell?" She looked around at the other vehicles on the bridge and slammed on her brakes. Did the big car hit a slick spot? Was it hydroplaning?

The Buick swerved deliberately toward her again. This time, the entire right side of her car brushed against the railing, and she heard the crunch of metal on metal. "What are you doing?" she screamed. It wasn't the slick deck; it was something far worse. Surely other drivers saw this maniac guiding her toward the river? Callie pounded a palm against the horn. Hard. She kept it honking with her right hand while she yanked the wheel toward the SUV with her left.

Suddenly, she saw the Buick swing off the bridge at the First Street ramp. She cleared the bridge onto Morrison Street. An empty parking spot was on her right, and she hit the brakes hard. When she jerked into the space, horns honked behind her. Her shoulders heaved as she tried to compose herself, and her attempts to breathe sputtered into short gasps. She laid her forehead on the steering wheel to calm her racing heart. That Buick wanted to push her into the river. Her mind was in turmoil, and her body shook from her head to her curling toes. When she calmed herself down, she knew what she had to do.

Pinpointing her position in the city, she eased out onto Morrison again, turned left at the first stoplight on 3rd Street, and drove south seven blocks. When she saw Madison Street, she quickly returned to 2nd and parked a block from the Portland Police Station.

Since this was her third visit within a week, she knew the drill and took the steps two at a time. She was certain she was onto something, and she wouldn't leave until she spoke to either Jake or Ross again—one more piece to add to their complex puzzle.

Her hand shook as she signed her name to the sheet of paper the officer pushed at her when she arrived. "I'd like to see Detective Goldberg or Sanders, please." Her voice was raspy, but determined.

"Please have a seat, ma'am. I'll see who's available." The young officer's blue shirt was starched so stiffly that Callie wondered how he managed to move his arms. The room was filled with people rushing from desk to desk, answering phones, and tapping keyboards.

The plastic chair was hard, and she was relieved that she didn't have to sit for long. Jake Sanders approached her with a look of surprise. Upon seeing her face, he lifted her up, and they maneuvered around others as he guided her to a softer seat next to his desk.

"What happened? I can see it on your face."

"Someone just tried to kill me." She started shaking again.

His eyes bulged. "Start at the beginning." He wrote as fast as he could, but couldn't keep up with her story. When she finished, he blew noisy air through his lips. "Did you see the license plate?"

She shook her head no. "I was concentrating on keeping my car on the bridge instead of swimming in the river. It happened fast. I know it was a Buick. A light-colored Buick, that pretty pearl color, not white. When it pulled away to take the exit to the left, I went straight, and it was too late to look at a license plate."

He wrote down the car's make. "Don't suppose you recognized the model of the car?"

"An SUV. That's all I remember. This tells us I'm right. You're taking me seriously when I say it's all connected?"

"We sure as hell are, Callie." He was thoughtful for a minute. "Wait here, please."

When Jake walked away, Callie's heartbeat slowed, but her nerves were so frayed that she wondered if sparks were flying from her body. She was afraid now, more than ever. But more than that, she was royally pissed. Anger surged through her as adrenaline shifted from fear to fight mode.

Jake returned with a statement for her to sign. "You'll soon have a file thick with my police statements, right?" She attempted to joke, but she knew he'd missed the humor

"I've ordered a cruiser to follow you home. When you get there, lock the doors and call 911 if anything appears out of the ordinary. We've narrowed the J, M, and 8 license plate to seven cars." He paused with indecision before he began again. "One of them may be the stalker."

Her eyes rounded. "Who is it?!"

Jake Sanders didn't answer immediately. "All I can tell you is, you may be on to something. Where are you parked?"

"One block north on 2nd Street."

"My officer will walk you to your car. A cruiser will be right behind you." He gave her his card and scribbled a number on the back. "Here's my cell phone. Call day or night if you need me."

She sagged with relief and followed the man in blue.

At 6:30 that evening, she received a call from the precinct to tell her a witness had called the station. A woman had seen a Buick SUV ramming into a dark blue Lexus. She hadn't gotten the license number because the traffic was too tight, but she thought it was a large woman. Now, the police believed Valerie's death wasn't a random hit-and-run incident. Combined with her near accident on the bridge, they were now very much involved.

Callie knew this was a warning. She was close to something. What?! Icy fingers skittered up her spine as anger escalated from pissed to even worse.

She couldn't leave a puzzle until all the pieces were in place. Callie replaced the receiver and leaned her head against the arm she'd propped on the back of her couch. She knew something had begun with her return from France. She could feel it. But what was it? Tomorrow, she'd lay it out and connect the dots she'd gathered from the bizarre events. She knew she'd tugged someone's chain. She just had to follow the links.

She shivered. Someone was watching her, and the thought added a new layer of distress, as she admitted she'd never felt quite so threatened before. She wished Jules was on his way. Having Olivia and Bram for moral support was a plus, but they couldn't soothe her like Jules could. He could help her think rationally once she told him someone was coming out of the shadows. She shuddered and closed her back window blinds. Despite the fear of almost being pushed over the side of the Morrison Bridge, she couldn't quit, not now --- she was too close. There was too much at stake. She knew answers were within reach; they had to be.

Two hours later, Callie called Olivia, who informed Bram, who passed it on to Jules in Pertuis, France. The phone lines were buzzing, just like the nerves. Her friends were so anxious that they urged her to move into their home, but what good would that do?

Jules called her as she was hauling her weary body into bed.

"Callie." He spoke softly, and she felt the trickle of intimacy.

She breathed into the phone. "*Halo.*"

He asked her, as nonchalantly as he could, "How was the memorial service for your friend?"

She answered likewise. "Sad and terrible."

"And the rest of your day?" His voice was soft and smooth but threaded with worry.

Hesitating before answering, she finally whispered, "Someone tried to push me into the river today, but it was too cold to swim, so I fought back." Her mind swung back to the moment when she thought she was going to die. "Jules. I'm frightened. Now I know there's a murderer on the loose and by God, I'm going to find him."

"Before he finds you, I hope."

"But, of course."

"Callie. Please do not take chances. Call your police if…"

"Of course, I will. I'm scared, but not stupid, Jules." Her voice came across gruffer than she'd meant it to.

Jules whispered, "Get some sleep, *ma chère*. I am coming to you soon."

After she hung up the phone, his beautiful French voice echoed in her mind. She wrapped a soft robe around her body and walked into the office, where two boxes sat on the now-empty desk. She pulled one open, slipped her hand inside, and felt around for what she was looking for.

When she held the small gun in her hand, she stared at it, feeling its coldness. It was the first time she'd held the .25 caliber pistol since François had shown her how to use it. Its pink handle fit her palm like a glove. Gazing at the small brass lever, she pushed forward and unhitched the slide release. She yanked down the empty magazine and emptied three hollow-point bullets from their box, which were as hard as the determination in her chest. Could she point this at someone and pull the trigger? Possibly. Kill someone with it? She wasn't sure. Uneasiness shook down into her soul. Then she thought of Jack Beaker. Yes, she could use it on the man if she had the chance. She would buy more ammunition soon.

Then she thought of Dominic Jazzy. Lily's sweet face wavered in her mind, as did François' beautiful smile. Her fingers gripped the small handle, and she stared at the gun with deadly intent. Someone had killed two very special people and likely tried to murder her, too.

Hell, yes, if someone tried to kill her again, she could shoot and not regret it. She slipped it back into the small, black holster and took it back to bed with her. When she slid it beneath her pillow, she leaned back and whispered, "I think I could…"

CHAPTER 24

That same night, Dominic Jazzy confronted Bryan Martos in a dim corner of McMenamin's Pub near Main Street in Portland. The candle on the table cast a soft glow over the room that neither man appreciated. A tic twitched in Bryan's cheek when Dom slid into the booth opposite him. His beer was already waiting on the table, as was their usual practice. The first one to arrive typically ordered two beers. This night, he didn't change things up.

Bryan lifted the cold, frothing beer glass to his lips.

"Tell me about Bella."

The beer spluttered out of Bryan's lips. "What do you mean?"

"I think you know exactly what I mean. How long have you been sleeping with my wife?" Dom jabbed his index finger into the tabletop, both knowing he wished it were Bryan's face. "She seems to know a hell of a lot about my business…information that could only have come from you. What, she's your confidant? Who's paying you the money? Your loyalty should be with me, not Bella. So, you think she's good in the sack? Good for you. But from now on, stick it to business instead of my wife, or you'll be sorry you messed with me. I'll make sure you never practice law again."

Bryan glared at Dom, twisting his lips against the rim of his beer glass as he forced the brew down his throat to suppress the angry words bubbling within him. Their eyes smoked as they locked gazes.

"You don't want to threaten me, Dominic." Bryan's face smoldered with angst. He had put up with the man's moods, arrogance, and mistakes far too long and was on the verge of divorcing him and his money.

I threaten anyone I want to--- and I have a couple of ideas that will clear up this mess. I won't tell you because you'd tell your lover!"

"What are you talking about?"

"I want that woman stopped from meddling in my affairs. If you won't stop her, then I will."

Bryan's confusion was apparent. What woman was he talking about? Callie? Mae? Bella? The thoughts were still circling in his head as Dom jerked out of the booth. When Dom shoved the beer glass toward Bryan, he barely caught it before it slid onto the floor.

As the vineyard owner walked out the door, Bryan mumbled, "No, you do not threaten Bryan Martos." He finished his beer and left after he was sure the other man had driven away. When he unlocked his new car, he went home, parked it beside his SUV, and kicked its dented bumper. He'd scrubbed every inch of the vehicle with Mr. Clean. He was towing it to his cottage the next day. Now, he just needed to sell it in Lincoln City, far from Portland, and soon.

Jules Armand leaned backward the next morning and heard a satisfying crack as a muscle stretched noisily. He grimaced, conceding that he had spent too much time in an office over the past few years instead of being outside, a place he had always enjoyed.

The plane trip across the ocean had been uncomfortable. He'd ridden in coach because he had the front row and plenty of legroom. He hadn't counted on the arm space, which was pretty slim. His seatmate had been a young woman about his niece's age, and they'd chatted until they'd both fallen asleep. She had her Bose headphones in her ears, and his Grisham book had slipped off his lap. It had felt good to feel the jet's wheels hit the tarmac.

This was the last day she would sleep in her house. Everything sparkled: the windows were washed, a For Sale sign stood in the yard, boxes were labeled, and tables were filled with everything from dishes to clocks and more. The estate employees had the place looking like a bazaar, a very neat one.

Callie slid out of bed and ripped off the sheets. After pushing them into the basket, she took her shower, and later, the towels joined the unwashed laundry. Her car was packed with personal items, and she'd brewed coffee in the coffee maker she was leaving behind. She hadn't slept well for the past few nights and shrugged. Was it any wonder? Her mind jostled like tiny marbles trying to find the right hole to plunk into, like the old pinball machines. When she found François' killer, the balls would find their way to the finish line.

If only she could quell the spitting anger that overwhelmed her whenever she remembered being hurled toward that bridge railing. She was certain she'd never felt so frightened, so helpless. And that made her angry, too. Whoever was trying to scare her did an excellent job. But it only fueled her determination to find the culprit, not deter her quest to look for him. Or her?

She recalled the conversation she had with the police. The witness on the bridge believed it was a woman behind the wheel. Could Dom Jazzy pass as a woman? Callie let her mind explore other possibilities, other avenues, but she came up empty.

She braced the last box against her knee and shoved it into the back seat. Callie groaned, wishing she had accepted Bram's offer to load the car for her. She didn't want to burden her friends with all her problems, so instead, she broke out in a sweat and strained her back.

"Almost done," she breathed, leaning against the car to catch her breath. The house keys were already in the lock box for the realtor, and Alexis had the spare.

She patted the gun to assure herself it was still there. It was.

The day looked promising. The rain had stopped, and the sun had cleared through the clouds.

Dominic Jazzy watched Callie lean against her navy Lexus on the other side of the cul-de-sac. He was uncertain whether to have a quick chat with her now or wait until she drove away. Surprise her wherever she ends up. She was like a flea that wouldn't go away—an itch he couldn't scratch. And he was tired of it.

He glanced around at her neighbors, wondering who might be watching. Stretching his shoulders until he heard them creak, he hunkered down in the bucket seat. Remembering his confrontation with Bryan left a sour taste in his mouth. If the man couldn't stop the woman from nosing around Mae and Lily and possibly talking them into reneging on their promises, he'd stop her himself

Jules glanced down at the Willamette River as the cab driver crossed the Broadway Bridge. The late afternoon sun cast its glow along the embankment near a grassy park next to the river and a row of condos. He noticed runners pumping their arms along the long boardwalk, and he snorted with amusement.

"That doesn't even look enjoyable," he said when he noticed the driver watching the crowds as they came off the ramp directly onto the 405 interchanges. It had been a long flight, and he was tired, but could rest later. After calculating the time difference in his head, knowing jet lag would soon set in, he could only think of having Callie in his arms again.

He dialed her cell and smiled, anticipating the look on her face when he showed up.

"*Halo*! I have finished packing and am heading for the Canyon Road Storage unit. That's where my boxes will sit until they are on their way to France." He heard the smile in her voice.

"And then?"

"I'm pointing my car toward the ocean after I unload everything. Wish you were here to load these boxes...Bram offered to do it for me, but I reminded him I'm Wonder Woman."

He chuckled. "The ocean sounds delicious. Wish I was there."

"So do I," she responded, the yearning in her voice so palpable that he felt it whisper along his cheek.

"*À bientôt, ma chère.*" See you soon. He leaned across the seat toward the cabbie after he tapped the phone off. "Please change directions and take me to the Canyon Road Storage Units."

"You got it." The cab driver switched lanes and took the Canyon Road Exit. The traffic was thick. Friday took commuters home early, and many headed west for the weekend. Bumper to bumper already, and it was barely noon. When he came off the exit, he saw car dealerships along the highway and moved to the right lane.

Callie stood with her feet spread apart, hands on her hips. Silvery bangs brushed her forehead. She blew a goodbye kiss toward the house for the last time and pulled her keys from her pocket. Tossing the last remnants of her previous life into the back seat, she jumped into the car. She had planned to stop at Starbucks on the way to Canyon, but she decided she wanted to empty the car and be free of it before heading to the cottage. She hadn't been there since her return from France. It was the only haven she had left in America.

She backed up and pointed her heavily laden car north. The mini-storage unit would hold everything until the shipper arrived the following week. She turned up the radio and hummed along with the singer, something she hadn't done in a long time.

She didn't notice the low-slung car following her every inch of the way, threading in and out of light traffic. Lists of items flew through her mind as she thought about Dom Jazzy, wishing she could prove he was more than a pedophile. The attorney for that little girl might be able to do that, but murder? Now that was something else. If the man could hurt little girls, he could hurt adults, too. Her mind swung back and forth between what-ifs all the way to Canyon Road.

When she saw the sign by the tall chain-link fence, she drove through the gates and parked near unit number four. It was small but spacious enough for the boxes and a few pieces of furniture tagged for France. Oblivious and lost in her thoughts, she opened the car door and reached for the first box

Out of the corner of her eye, she spotted a large man walking toward her, prompting her to straighten up for a better look. The sun was in her eyes, obscuring her view of his face. As he approached, her expression darkened. Moments later, a yellow cab pulled up beside her car, and she changed her course; one minute she was alone, and then she wasn't. She gazed into the back seat of the cab as the door opened and Jules emerged with a smile on his face.

She pressed a hand over her heart as it skipped a beat, hardly believing her eyes. Then her face broke into a smile that nearly cracked her face. "What took you so long, *monsieur*?"

He laughed. The cabbie raised an arm in farewell and drove away.

"I can't believe you're really here." She pointed to the boxes inside her car. "And your timing is incredible."

Callie leaned into Jules, allowing his tenderness to soothe her, but she wanted to cry. It wasn't that she was unsure about trying to solve this horrible new puzzle. It was just that the entire, dreadful series of events that had led to Jules drawing her close was exactly what she needed. She rested her cheek against his chest, listened to his heartbeat, and smiled as his love warmed her through his shirt.

When Callie and Jules pulled apart, Dominic Jazzy was gone, and Callie had forgotten that there had been another man present at all.

Forty minutes later, Dom returned to the vineyard, screaming at everyone in the winery who came near him. He avoided the tasting room but directed his anger at the pickers in the vineyard. They were too slow, bruising the fruit, and not careful when emptying their buckets. The man had vanished by the time Denis heard about his employer's antics.

Many disgruntled pickers requested their final paychecks, but Denis calmed them down, promised a bonus, and apologized for the incident they had just encountered. Knowing that the winemaker needed them, they stayed—since he was the man they admired.

When Dom entered the house, he shouted for Bella. "Where are you?!"

She dropped the clothes she was folding as he walked into the room. "What are you yelling about? I could hear you from the back hall." When he didn't answer her, she noticed him moving toward her. His hands twitched as if he wanted to strangle her. She stepped back toward the pile of laundry.

"You probably know that Bryan is negotiating with the Mason family. I don't have to tell you anything since you have a personal pipeline to my attorney." He reached for her and squeezed her upper arm. When she tried to pull away from him, he gripped her tightly.

"Dom, you're hurting me." Bella's voice quivered.

"Of course, I'm hurting you. What did you expect me to do when I found out you're sleeping with another man…and my attorney to boot? Cripes, did you think I would roll over like a well-trained dog? I give you all the money you can spend and all the freedom you expect. I didn't know you decided you wanted to be in someone else's bed, too." He ground out the last few words and shoved her until she fell on the bed.

Seething, she hissed, "And what did you expect me to do when you didn't want sex from me at all? I always wondered why you made such a fuss when we first dated. You couldn't get enough of me then…You even took me on the tasting bar, for god's sakes. But once we were married, it was your time, your decision, and your control. I was sick of it."

He didn't respond to her this time.

"And all the while, you made me feel unattractive. Now I know it wasn't because you had other women. I always wondered what happened to the vibrant man I married. When Lily said you attacked her, I refused to believe it. I chose **you** over my own family. You made me throw away my sister! But not anymore. Any man who hurts little girls isn't a man at all." She'd gone too far, but she couldn't stop herself.

When Dom's beefy hand slapped her across the face, she went down. When she sat up, she covered her stinging cheek with shaking fingers. Surprise siphoned the blood from her face.

Bella swallowed hard and found her voice. "And now you're hurting a defenseless woman, too?" Her voice rose in disbelief. Blonde hair fell across her face as she shook her head in shock. She'd never been hit before, and the weight of it was too overwhelming to accept. She added beating women to his list of crimes. Bella lifted her aching head to glare at him, wondering if he'd shaken her teeth loose.

And then he hit her again. When she twisted out of his way, it only infuriated him. As she clawed her way across their bed, she lost a shoe and pushed herself further with a bare foot.

Dom's expression darkened with an unreadable emotion before his knee jammed into her belly.

She didn't get up again.

He stared at her for a moment before he kicked her foot aside. He bent down, picked up her shoe, threw it toward her, and laughed harshly as it bounced off her hip. "Don't ever dehumanize me again!"

And then he left the room.

Bella opened one eye to ensure he was gone. She couldn't open the other eye at all. Icy fingers of fear seeped into every pore. Swallowing the sob that rose in her throat, she sat, stunned and sickened. She covered her face with trembling hands, then dropped them to the agony in her belly. Her fingers felt the puffiness on her aching face as she swiped at the tears falling from her swollen eye.

Her mind skittered, and she cried, "Mae!" She needed Mae! Time to leave.

Thirty miles east in the city, Mae Haydon dropped the teacup she held. She stared at the broken ceramic shards on the floor. A stabbing pain pierced her stomach, and she reached out to steady herself against the kitchen counter. When she lifted her head to gaze out the window, she felt that something had happened. She didn't know what, where, or when, but she sensed that Bella was in trouble. After hearing her twin's cry echo across the miles in her mind, Mae sank down onto the floor.

Carelessly, she placed her hand on the tile to push herself back up again and felt warm blood gush from her fingers. "Ouch!" She exhaled in short gasps and pulled the ceramic shard from her hand. Then, she wiped the blood on her jeans. But the blood kept coming, and her head blared an undeniable, albeit unexplainable, fear for her twin sister. Grabbing a towel to twist around her hand, she wrapped it quickly and began searching for her phone. The towel soon turned red and started to seep through. She decided to wait for Lily and slid to the floor again. She would be home any minute.

When Lily walked in the door, she slung her backpack onto the floor to reach for the refrigerator door. When she rounded the corner, her eyes widened and she threw herself down beside her mother. "Mom!"

"It's okay, baby. I just cut myself, but it won't stop bleeding. You'll need to drive me up to Providence Hospital for stitches. I thought it would stop bleeding by now, but it must be deeper than I thought. Good thing you passed your driver's permit test, huh?" Mae tried to smile, to tease her daughter into a calmness she didn't feel.

Forcing her mind away from Bella, she got herself into the Mini-Cooper and smiled wearily as Lily ground the gears, trying to pull out of the driveway. "Easy does it, honey. Put your clutch in all the way and let it out slowly as you move the gear shift." Her voice was soothing, but her hand throbbed worse than any toothache she'd ever had. Despite the pain, her mind was far away in Dundee.

CHAPTER 25

B ryan Martos held the phone in his hand long after the Mason's attorney hung up. He'd been so sure they wouldn't want their little girl to face the courtroom drama of telling her story to strangers. His gut clamped tight, and he hung up the phone.

Could he face that girl's parents and a jury while he portrayed Dominic Jazzy as a pillar of the community? Could he erase the girl's stricken face or her parents' eyes when they bored into his? Dreading the thought of going to court, he knew he had no choice, but he'd rather eliminate Dominic Jazzy instead. Enduring the horror of Lily's case while listening to her deposition had been enough to put him in a straitjacket, a straitjacket that Dominic Jazzy should be wearing right now. "Son of a biscuit, I do not want to make this call."

The early winter darkness seeped through his office window as he stacked the Heidi Mason file upright. Her deposition mirrored the one he'd heard from Lily, though she had been caught in the vineyard during the day and assaulted. How could this happen?

The attorney filed with the court before calling Bryan. Could he drop Dom as a client now? Under certain circumstances, Oregon's rules of professional conduct allow an attorney to terminate a client if the breakup won't hurt them, such as at the beginning of a case, or if a suitable replacement is available. However, abandonment may be acceptable even if it harms the client's interests, especially if the client has done something wrong. Since the case was already filed with the court, Bryan Martos needed the judge's approval to withdraw for any of those reasons.

He recognized that withdrawal from representation was a surprisingly vibrant area of legal ethics. This situation created a dilemma, even if Dom informed Bryan that his testimony was filled with lies. Bryan had an obligation to advocate for Dom's interests, a responsibility to report perjury to the court, and a duty to protect Dom's secrets. Since Dom had already placed Bryan in a position where it was impossible to meet all three professional obligations, he could rightfully demand withdrawal.

Unfortunately, Bryan knew it wasn't that simple. He couldn't withdraw in the middle of litigation without the judge's permission, and it's indisputably unethical for an advocate to directly inform the judge that his client is a liar. Could he approach the bench to excuse himself from the case for vague ethical reasons? Knowing exactly what was happening, the judge would usually deny the request because a jury would sense something was off if the lawyer vanished right before the defendant took the stand. The judge would tell me that I met my ethical obligations and must continue.

His pale eyes studied his horse collection before glancing toward the large, framed photograph above the shelving unit. He had been fifteen when it was taken. He remembered the shirt he wore, one of his favorites, and the day vividly. His father had pulled him across the wall into the jockey's domain. Bryan could still smell the earthiness of the horses as they snorted around him. Their small ankles and streamlined bodies had shone in the sun, and the horse his dad groomed arched his neck majestically.

When the winning horse's owner motioned for Daniel Martos to be part of the photograph, bringing his son along with him. Bryan stared at the picture, briefly smiling at his father's proud expression, his arm around his son's shoulder. The racehorse had come in first that day, ribbons hanging from his bridle, and a large wreath of flowers draped around his neck. It had been a day he would never forget. That was also the day Charlie introduced him to the big leagues, when he started betting more than a dollar here and a dollar there. It was the day his life changed forever.

Bryan pulled out the daily horse racing form. Maybe he'd forget the whole thing with Dominic Jazzy and go to the races. It was Friday. Most races took place only on Sunday, Monday, and Tuesday. Today was a celebration race, showcasing the newest race horse from Belgium. He wanted to see both the race and the horse. Nothing would happen with Dom until Monday anyway. Why shouldn't he enjoy the weekend?

He had won last week. Maybe this weekend he'd win again. Next week, he'd be too busy to play. He had a car to get rid of and a brute of a vineyard owner to face down. He lifted the racing form in both hands. No, he wouldn't call Charlie to place the bet this time; he'd do it himself.

Callie aimed her car toward the Pacific Ocean and settled her five-foot-two frame into her leather bucket seat. On each side of Highway 99, flat fields, scattered malls, and service stations yielded to the sweeping view of lavender mountains and forests. She scanned her surroundings. To her left, she noticed signs directing tourists to wine-tasting venues nestled among miles of vineyards. As she veered toward Lincoln City into the forest, her Lexus devoured the miles.

She smiled at the bemused look on Jules' face. He was entranced by the landscape, just as she and François had been years ago when they drove through the old-growth trees along the Salmon River in the Van Duzer Corridor. Douglas firs framed the curved road, and she always marveled at the various shades of green. Once she veered onto Highway 101 south, the road overlooked the golf course on the right, and beyond that, the Pacific Ocean. The views never got old as her brown eyes shifted toward a minor road and spotted the turnoff for Devil's Lake Road. She slowed down and turned toward the quaint residential area and NE John's Loop, where her lake house awaited.

Olivia had given her a bag before she left the city, containing a bottle of wine, which she planned to uncork, and toast Jules' arrival. When Olivia handed it to her, she noticed a bulky envelope inside, but she'd been too focused on stashing the boxes and leaving the house to pull it out. The wine, she thought, could wait until she arrived at the cottage. Of course, she'd imagined herself drinking it alone. The bliss of having Jules beside her still hadn't quite registered.

Ever vigilant since she was nearly tossed off a bridge, her eyes sporadically tracked the cars behind her in the rearview mirror. Traffic wasn't heavy, and she didn't worry about being pushed off the road, but the emotions she relived from the bridge incident were never far from her mind.

Jules noticed her nervous energy, so he reached over to pat her hand while it rested on the gear shift. "I know you are still worried about someone following you, but now there are two of us."

His manner soothed her. She grinned, dimpling her cheeks. Her freckled face beamed as she turned toward Jules again. "Did you see Veronique before you left? She'll miss your monthly dinner date."

"We had dinner together last night. She wants you to hurry back to share the dates with us. She is very excited that you are now her stepmother. I think Aurore is going to act much nicer now, also."

"Hmmmm. I hope so. Yesterday, I received an email from Veronique with photos from her shop. The wall she created for the lavender made me smile. She is talented, and riding the wave of newness with her is exciting. I'm happy she's added the flamenco wall with red and yellow too."

"And she talks about you all the time. She tones it down when Aurore is around us, though. Veronique knows her mother has changed her attitude, but jealousy will always remain. However, she loves her daughter, and I don't think she'll make the mistake of letting her heartache jeopardize their relationship. Maybe one day you will become friends with my sister?"

She tapped his knee. "I'll try."

He wrapped a finger around the dark curls that lay just behind her ear. The magic he brought to her life and the swirling emotions that swept through her when she heard his voice made her feel whole. With his fingers playing a love song in her hair, she felt a giddy anticipation, eager to show him how happy she was to see him again.

"I packed a box for Veronique. Things I won't need now from my old shop. Things I couldn't throw away. I know she'll love them."

"You are amazing. She's lucky to have an expert help her, and she knows it." He pulled the map from the dashboard to study.

Callie's thoughts drifted to Pertuis, far away from her worries and fears. She remembered the grand opening of Veronique's new shop. When she first learned that her husband had fathered a child who was now twenty, she had been devastated. Getting to know the young woman through her Uncle Jules became a beautiful experience. The memories she had created in Provence over the past few months were life-changing, and adventures would soon multiply. But first….

"How much farther to your cottage?" Jules touched Callie's knee and dropped the map. His broad shoulders relaxed into his seat, and the laugh lines around his gray eyes deepened.

"Almost there." She felt a delicious anticipation as her heart lurched madly. When she turned toward him, his eyes looked like silver lightning.

The cottage on Devil's Lake was just as cozy and inviting as she'd left it. After unlocking the side door and bringing in the bags, Jules pulled her toward him. Instinctively, Callie's body arched toward him, leaving no room for misinterpretation.

Callie raised her head. "God, I missed you, Jules." Her eyes, wet and glazed, met his.

He brushed a damp tress of hair from her eyes to sweep it from her forehead. "Touching you is heaven." He spoke in a whisper.

In response, she stroked his lips with her fingers, and a delightful shiver of wanting ran through her. "We need to build a fire, and then I'll show you just exactly how much I missed you..." When her voice died away, she heard his quick intake of breath.

"We can build that fire later. Let's build our own now."

Joy bubbled in her laugh. Nodding toward the back of the cottage, their eyes met with a sheen of purpose.

Some time later, as the sun struggled through the clouds and the fire burned in the grate, Jules stood at the kitchen counter. He was fascinated by the kitchen. Along the west wall by the breakfast table was a colorful mural; a wood-framed window, complete with windowpanes and potted flowers, sat on the sill, painted in bright colors. The cheerful feeling of a warm, sunny spring day came to mind. He was barefoot, with his shirt hanging outside his jeans. He tried to focus on sliding a slice of ham and Swiss cheese between rye bread. Reaching for lettuce was nearly impossible when Callie's hands caressed his bare back and dropped short, sweet kisses along his spine. "Are you hungry or what?" he laughed.

"Or what...?" She grinned up into his face.

"Well, ma chère, your late lunch is served." He kissed her quickly and swung both plates toward her. The cottage was cozy and warm, and they couldn't stop looking at one another as he sat down at the table.

She grabbed the plates and set them beside the chilled water and potato chips. "Sit," she said, belting her robe.

Jules' eyes never left hers as she walked slowly toward him to press herself into his embrace. His arms wrapped around her waist, and his face nestled against her breasts. They held onto each other tightly, swaying gently into one another with their eyes closed.

"Jules, I can't remember feeling so full."

He leaned back to look up at her, his eyes brimming with tenderness. "I love you, Callie Beauvais."

"And I love you, Jules Armand."

He exhaled a long sigh of contentment. "Now, eat."

"*Oui*." She laughed aloud and pulled the plate toward her. With a glint of wonder in her eyes, she watched him bite into his ham sandwich before reaching for her own. Her freckled face glowed as she pushed her silver bangs from her eyes and threaded them into her hair. Not quite believing the man was beside her, the ham sandwich suddenly tasted like ambrosia.

"Wine. You said Olivia gave you wine," he stated between bites.

"Hmm, yes," she managed with a partially filled mouth.

"If I weren't starving, I'd get it now...let's drink it in front of the fire. Maybe it will make me forget just for a few minutes...about Valerie's and François' death and Lily's terrible sadness."

He watched her with a look of pleasure and a touch of concern.

When she lifted her face, he saw the pain still flickering there. He swiveled toward her and placed his hands on her shoulders. She lay her head against him and closed her eyes. "We will find answers, I know we will." His voice was low, urgent.

Callie felt Jules' heart beating fast as he held her. She was grateful he was there. She needed him, required his strength more than she had ever thought. "Then, god help me, let's do it." Her dazzling determination felt like a rock inside her.

CHAPTER 26

Meanwhile, across the lake, while Jules and Callie munched on sandwiches and found Olivia's wine, day turned to night. Bryan Martos pulled into his driveway. Feeling disgruntled since dawn, he left the city behind, along with the unsuccessful horse race. The Belgian horse was a beauty. The numbers he chose were not. Between losing a couple of thousand dollars and knowing Dom would be arrested any time, he figured it was the perfect time to get out of Dodge. He had a lot to do in a short time.

His motion detector dinged when the garage door opened at the touch of a button from the visor. He congratulated himself again for buying this house with cash because, with his recent luck, he might have lost it to the bank. The betting log sat on the seat beside. He flipped it off the seat, where it struck the passenger door with a thud.

He unhitched his SUV from the trailer and parked both cars inside the garage, away from nosy neighbors. He entered the dark house, warmed up the place, and poured himself a whiskey. Standing at the back door, he stared at the dark ripples on the lake. The neighbor's dog started barking and broke the stillness he had imagined during the drive from Portland. He grimaced.

"I'd like to shoot that damn dog." He cursed under his breath. He had enough problems to last a lifetime and didn't need another. When the dog finally quieted, he took a deep breath, sipped, and felt the whiskey burn all the way down his throat.

Something still bothered him about Valerie Blume. She'd been coming out of the Blanchard Building. Why? What could have taken her there at that time of the morning when she hadn't been to her office yet? Meeting someone? No, she hadn't been inside long enough. Something nagged at the back of his mind, but he couldn't quite grasp it, so he threw back the last of his whiskey and headed inside for another splash.

His head and body ached. What a hell of a week, with his worries about Valerie and Callie nosing around. Bella was getting on his nerves, and he'd like to kick Dominic Jazzy where the sun didn't shine. Just when he took care of one problem, another popped up. He wondered what else was waiting to surprise him back in the city.

Slumping in his favorite easy chair, he smiled. Most of the furniture had come with the house, but his La-Z-Boy chair was new, perfect for the room. This was a haven where he forgot everything else. He was sure he had taken care of everything, so he finished his second whiskey, leaned back on the chair, and nodded off to sleep.

~

Callie pulled on a sweatshirt as the sun set and eased open the glass doors. Despite the feeling of François' betrayal lingering in her heart, inching back grudgingly, her anger refused to dissipate completely. She clung to it like a sweet dream. Carefully, she stepped up to the water's edge, bracing herself for the familiar pain that pierced her from memories whenever she gazed across the lake.

Bittersweet—more sweet than bitter—Callie gazed at the lake she loved and hated, filled with memories reflected in the now-gentle, rippling waters. The winter sun began to dip below the horizon behind her, casting a rosy hue on the sandstone brickwork of the cottage.

Jules joined her, and she felt comforted by his presence. Steadying herself, she took a deep, focused breath and gazed into the eerily calm waters. As she allowed that unforgettable, stormy day to replay in her mind, Jules reached for her hand and didn't let go.

She turned toward Jules and leisurely traced the curve of his neck with her fingers. She stood on her tiptoes to trail her lips over his chin and onto his mouth. It was hungry, a kiss filled with promises. He pulled her against him, and within minutes, they thought of nothing else but each other.

Callie felt goosebumps travel up her arms and even as far as her scalp when Jules held her. She glanced at the water and allowed him to lead her back inside the cottage.

The blinds had already been pulled down over the two small windows above the headboard. Callie lit the lamps and glanced at the still-mussed bed before turning to invite Jules forward.

He had already loosened his shirt as he walked slowly toward her, deliberately. It felt like months instead of hours since they had come together, each leaving memories behind and reflecting on the irony of finding one another through François.

Despite having known François since childhood, he'd only met Callie a few times before he and his friend argued and became estranged. He hadn't truly known her until she returned as his widow. He marveled at her directness; her attitude still surprised him. She'd shown vulnerability. He'd worried that she'd turned to him because of that. But now, he knew it wasn't the case at all. He felt her love across the room, and the weight of it nearly knocked him down.

Callie watched the expressions flit across Jules' face and extended her hand. When he reached for her, he pulled her down onto the bed beside him, feeling its softness wrap around them.

In a matter of seconds, their clothes lay in heaps on the floor, and they rested side by side. She turned toward him, and they gazed into each other's eyes. The room was filled with the warmth of their bodies, and they didn't notice the coolness in the air.

When he caressed her hip, she met his lips with a kiss that drowned out other thoughts. Her fingers snagged his neck and pulled him toward her, closer, ever closer. When he traced the edges of her bottom lip with his tongue, she was sure she'd never felt so emotional.

"Oh, my...How I missed you." She breathed near his ear after he pulled his lips away from her mouth and moved to her neck.

"*Oui*...I do not want us to be apart like this again for these weeks. We stay together from now on, agreed?" His words were like spun honey to her ears. She swallowed the words she thought to answer when he touched her with fingers as gentle as butterfly wings.

Her belly tightened. As she entwined her legs with his, the urgency of their love drowned out all other sounds, memories, and thoughts. Only their kisses and touches colliding made sense, and she heard a roaring in her ears as they became one.

Some while later, Jules lifted Olivia's cloth bag from the floor, wedged between his shoulder bag and Callie's large basket of dirty laundry. She had just finished washing the dishes. The warm room beckoned them toward the fire he'd stoked into a roaring inferno. He heard glasses clinking together as she retrieved them from the cupboard. When he reached into the bag to pull out two bottles of Cabernet Sauvignon, he discovered a large envelope stuck at the bottom of the bag. His fingers lifted the corner, revealing Callie's name, c/o Larkspur Insurance/Olivia Phillips.

As Callie placed both wine bottles on the island, she read the labels and handed the wine opener to him with a grin. When he set the envelope beside them, her forehead wrinkled. "What's that?"

"It was in the bag with the wine."

She eyed it for a moment and then picked it up. "What is this?" Apprehension warred with excitement. "It's from Valerie! Oh my god, these are the papers from Valerie." She handed Jules the bottle opener, and he popped the cork while her fingernails ripped open the flap to pull out a stack of papers more than an inch thick. She flipped through several pages, carried everything to the large dining table with trembling fingers, and dumped it there, almost too afraid to go through it. When Jules handed her a glass of red wine, she took it absentmindedly and sat back in the chair. She looked up at him with eyes that said, 'This could be it.'

Jules slid in beside her, tapped her glass, and nodded toward the pile in front of them. Neither said a word as they sipped their wine. The night lights from other houses on the lake had begun to flicker. He'd expected they would share a leisurely evening in front of the fire, but now he knew otherwise. The envelope was just another reminder of Valerie's death, but it might also serve as the catalyst to piece together the remaining puzzle pieces. Then they could go home.

Callie fought to keep her lips from trembling as an overwhelming urge to tear into everything washed over her. Something was in this pile of papers that frightened Valerie—something that could very well have brought about her death. She was sure Jules could hear her heart beating.

Rather than sifting through the papers in front of her, she reached for her phone and dialed Olivia's number.

Callie, how are things going? I hope you're getting drunk on the wine," Olivia snickered.

Callie didn't respond immediately, a sure sign to Olivia that something was on her mind. "Okay, tell me what happened."

Callie said, "First, Jules surprised me, and it was the best part of my day." Her large brown eyes turned toward him, and she smiled warmly, trying to keep the images of their lovemaking from her mind so she could talk coherently. "Secondly, we just opened your wine bag. Thank you again. But…the envelope inside. When did you get it?" Unconsciously, her brows furrowed.

"Three days ago. I forgot to tell you. When Lana brought it to me, I just popped it into the bag. There wasn't a return address, but it looked important. Was it?" Olivia guessed it was.

"Yes, it could be very important. Thank you, Livvy. I'll call again soon." Callie hung up and looked at Jules with misty eyes.

Three days ago, this arrived at Olivia's office. Valerie must have sent it or put it into the postal box the morning she was killed. I'm still torn, wondering if it was a freak accident or something worse. A hit-and-run always comes with questions, in addition to leaving behind a body. Valerie had been afraid. She thought she was being followed. And then she was gone." Callie's eyes filled with tears again, and she swiped them away. She lifted the top piece of paper and pushed the bulk toward Jules. "Let's find out if there's something in here to tell us what she was so afraid of."

"Where do we start?"

He tasted his wine. "We'll go through everything."

Jules pulled half the pile toward him and carried it to the couch, where he studied each page like a doctor preparing to remove an appendix. If a woman was killed over information in this packet, he certainly didn't want to miss anything. He frowned at the paper and glanced across the room to see Callie doing the same thing. He knew her chest must be bursting with the images of François; surely, this information was significant.

When his mind turned to his old friend, his heart ached again. They'd been friends longer than he could remember his childhood without him. They'd done everything together; as adults, they'd been as close as peas in a pod. His hands stilled on the paper he held. The thought that his accidental death might not be an accident at all deepened his grief. And if he could help Callie find the culprit, they could both have a life together that he was sure François would approve of.

He looked at Callie again. Her hands covered her mouth as her brown eyes scanned the words, willing them to reveal answers. Jules couldn't forget for a moment that Valerie had probably been killed by someone seeking this information. He doubted it was a random accident and was sure Callie understood that too. His stomach twisted into a knot, wondering what lay ahead.

Callie lifted the bottle of red wine and filled her glass again. With the threatening note she'd found in the safe deposit box, along with Lily's abuse, these papers might be the final pieces. She sipped her wine and ran her fingers over the documents.

Jules imagined she was praying she could eke out the answers.

When Callie's fingers slipped the stapled pages from the pile, she knew exactly what she was looking at. She saw LILY HAYDON displayed in capital letters. Her deposition, given under oath, took away Callie's breath. She read every word twice. Twice. She stared into her dark backyard and the lake beyond. Her chest ached.

Hopelessness seeped in where it shouldn't. The same depression she'd felt for years, those little words telling her how she should feel and what she should say. Would she ever be able to prove that François' death wasn't an accident? There were so many damn threads, and she felt like she was inside a massive ball of yarn, going round and round. One yank and it would knot up again. Unravel. She squeezed her eyes closed against the heaviness, the knowledge that she'd never, ever find the answers.

So much seemed to indicate that it was at the edge. But could she find it? Could she solve this terrible mystery? Her hands slumped over Lily's terrifying words, the loss of a child's innocence, and a reminder of her own terror.

She knew it was unfair to burden Jules with this, but he was the only person she wanted to confide in about it.

But not yet.

Not yet.

CHAPTER 27

"What were you looking for, François?" he muttered, "And what are we getting involved in?" He lifted his wine glass.

A shout from Callie made him jump.

"Jules! Bryan Martos bought a house here at the lake…and he paid **cash**. This must be important. Why else would François have it buried with this other stuff?" She held the paper aloft.

He got up to read the paper, immediately recognizing a Warranty Deed. His fingers slid down the text, and he noticed that the purchase date was eight days before François's death. When he pointed it out to Callie, her eyes widened.

"This is too much of a coincidence." Rain splashed against the window, in tandem with her heartbeat.

He grimaced and sat down. When Callie saw him run his fingers through his graying hair and shake his head, she sighed heavily again. "No, I don't believe in coincidences when major cash purchases are made simultaneously with a major event and bundled together. It's time we begin listing all these events…where's your iPad? That must be a long list by now, *ma chère.*" He forced a smile.

Now, let's find out precisely what François was investigating. I remember conversations that now make sense. Valerie was nervous sharing information about Bryan when I first met her at Jake's. I think she felt threatened during her time at the firm. I got that impression when I spoke with her." She inhaled deeply at the memory. "And it's probably why she mailed them instead of handing them to me."

Jules nodded.

"Then, when I called Bryan and spoke with him…"

"You spoke with Martos after you met with Valerie?" Jules sat up straight. "When did you do that…and what did he say? What did you say?" He bit his lip and furrowed his brows.

"I called him first…a few days after I found François' note in that book. Bryan was friendly enough at the time. I asked him if he recognized the name, Mae Haydon. He'd paused before answering. I assumed he was thinking about their past clients. Then, he responded with a clear, 'no.' He said he didn't know the name." She shrugged. "He sounded on edge, now that I remember our conversation. In fact, he sounded a bit huffy."

"He obviously lied to you."

"Valerie told me that." A crease formed on her forehead, and she pressed her hand to her heart, feeling tears well up inside her. "Could it really be Bryan instead of Dominic Jazzy who killed François? He was François's friend and partner. Which man had the most to lose? Jazzy has probably bought himself out of trouble for years. But Bryan? François would not do business with a crook."

Jules held his hand tightly across the table and responded, "Unless he didn't know he was a crook…and when he found out, that was the end of François?" His eyes spoke volumes. She noticed a tic race across his jaw, so she lifted his chin to look into his eyes.

Jules sniffed and shook his head. "Let's get to your list and start making connections. Gaps in the puzzle are closing, but we must find out if we're in a guessing game or if it's real."

"He can't get away with this, Jules." Callie pulled her chair closer and started to go through the paperwork again.

Jules gazed at the lone Adirondack chair. Light from the big room illuminated the wet deck as rain pelted the shrubs and water streamed off the slats as if the chair were crying. He turned and leaned against the windowsill. "What do you think François would have done when he saw his firm's bank statement and Martos' cash purchase agreement for a new house here at the lake…hmmmm?"

She looked up. "He would have confronted him."

"Yes, the man I knew definitely would have done that. And how do you think a man like Bryan Martos would have reacted? He was clearly addicted to horse races…there are a lot of racing stubs and gambling chits in that cache of papers. And the man was so low, he protected a man who molested young girls…he had to know if it happened more than once, there was a seed of truth to the accusations. Overall, I agree with you. Bryan Martos may have killed François." He snapped his fist against the window frame as he whispered those words. "The bastard."

Callie couldn't answer and joined him. Pushing her hands into her pockets, she paced the room as her mind raced before she plopped back down with a thump. Her eyes skimmed the text, and her heartbeat quickened. "He's a shrewd lawyer, and he's managed to hide his dealings with…what do you call people who take gambling bets?"

"Bookies."

Her fingers tightened on the tablecloth as the papers painted a darker picture now. She had always been a good judge of character; she thought Bryan was a decent person. François trusted him, and although they weren't best friends, they seemed to have a solid working relationship. They each worked on different types of cases, contributing to the firm's success. She stretched her memory back to those days before the accident and couldn't recall anything that made her think François didn't trust Bryan. He had been moody that day, and she was sure he had something on his mind. She attributed it to a case he was working on, and she had her own problems at her job at Larkspur Insurance. "Bookies," she whispered again.

Gamblers place bets with them, and they pay the gamblers' winnings. If gamblers lose, they settle their debts with the bookies. After seeing this bundle of racing forms and chits, it doesn't take a rocket scientist to see that Bryan Martos is addicted to gambling. And addicts do not want anyone to get in their way," Jules said.

"Okay," said Callie, pinching the bridge of her nose and blinking back her frustration. "This certainly changes things, doesn't it?" She recognized that she had just made an abrupt pivot from her typical color-inside-the-lines character. And she put on the proverbial boxing gloves. It was time to fight.

"Valerie said a man stormed into the firm and demanded to see Bryan Martos? The man with the limp and cigar breath? What do you bet this was his bookie, and Bryan owed him money?"

"Valerie said she was a little frightened of the man when he left Bryan a message. She said the man huffed and puffed like a wolf trying to blow the pig's house down…"

"What? A pig's house…?"

"It's a children's story about three little pigs and a big bad wolf," she said sadly. "The man said to tell Bryan he'd send over his man if Bryan didn't get back to him within twenty-four hours. She thought of that wolf when the man stomped out of the office. When she gave the message to Bryan, he looked upset and didn't respond. She didn't know what to think."

"Well, we know Bryan Martos was in trouble. It was one more thing Valerie knew about him. Too many events point in that man's direction." He steepled his fingers under his chin.

"Exactly. I have to figure out what to do about it." Callie's voice grew stronger, her anger clearly shifting toward bitterness.

Jules gave her a troubled look.

The next morning, the stack of papers seemed to glare at her as she began brewing coffee. Although a fire burned, Callie felt the chill emanating from the wall of windows spanning the back of the house. A smile slowly spread across her face as she wandered to the relative warmth of the kitchen and poured two cups of coffee.

Jules sat at the island bar, munching on a bagel as he flicked through the papers until his eyes landed on the bank statement. He recognized the date: the day after Lily's deposition, a document he'd struggled to comprehend and probably shouldn't have. When Callie placed the coffee before him, he tried to blank out the girl's words.

"There's so much there, Jules, I couldn't make heads or tails of what Valerie wanted me to see. I put the other papers she gave me with that pile." She pointed to the end of the table, slathered marmalade on her bagel, and sat beside him. "Honestly, I didn't know what half his notes meant." She sighed before biting into her bagel. "It's too much…just too much."

"Well, it's a lot of information, but if Valerie was killed over something here, we must find it. We've already found the house and the gambling chits. That's quite a lot." He heard Callie's intake of breath and looked up quickly to see her eyes fill with tears. "I'm so sorry, *ma chère*. I know she was a friend of yours. We won't let her death go the way of François. "You're not alone anymore, but…"

She smiled wanly. "Yes, my dear Jules, and you have no idea how much I need you to remind me…and love me."

He deliberated over his next words. "Callie, sometimes there's more to life than finding answers. I lost a good friend, and I also want those answers. But I love you, and if those damn papers got

François killed and then Valerie... I don't want to lose you, too." He reached toward her. "It's starting to scare me."

"Me too! But I must know why…Just when I think I should give up, I can't! He wouldn't have wanted us to stop, Jules. I'll do it alone if I have to. I know this could be dangerous, but by god, I will not stop now. François was in the middle of something important, and I want to find out what it was." She pushed the papers aside to slide her cup on the table between them.

"How can we learn what happened? It's been three long years. Of course, Valerie's death could be connected, but how do you plan to prove it? This is something for the police, not for us. You can't run around and hope to push an angry killer into the light. Let the police handle it, won't you please?"

"No, Jules. I've told the police everything, and they are investigating; if they've learned anything, they haven't informed me. How can they take it seriously if they don't know where to look? I pointed them toward Dominic Jazzy. But now, with all this," she extended her hand above the papers spread over the table, "we have more clues. I'll call them, but they follow the rules. I don't." Her face turned fierce, and he hid a smile.

She found Jake Sander's card and dialed his cell phone to prove her point. He answered on the second ring.

"Hi Jake. This is Callie Beauvais. I'm at my lake house in Lincoln City, and I have some information that might help your investigation."

"You found something at the lake house?"

"No, I received a large envelope of incriminating papers from Valerie Blume. She mailed it to me the morning she was killed."

Jake Sanders' silence roared in her ears.

"What's significant in the papers? Something to tell us who might have killed her?" His voice rose with each word.

"Martos was in financial trouble. My husband was preparing to open an investigation before he died." Callie stared at Jules.

"I need to see those papers. Would you please go to the Lincoln City Police Station so they can scan it and email it to me? I'll call them. When you get there, they'll be ready for you."

"Why don't I take a photo of each page with my phone and then email it to you?" She and Jules exchanged glances.

"A scan's faster. This could be what we need, Callie. Don't play the hero. Wait for me. Will you do that?"

"I'll get the papers scanned today." Callie carefully worded her reply, and he didn't miss the fact that she didn't answer him.

When she hung up, she told Jules what the detective wanted. "I will not scan Lily's deposition; everything else, but not that."

Jules nodded. "I agree, *ma petite*." As he bit into his bagel, he felt his jaw drop with shock. The reprinted newspaper had been slipped between the bank statements. A thirty-year-old headline read: 'Teenager Accuses Jazzy Cove's Grandson.' He pushed it toward her.

Callie read the article with a racing heart. She stared at Jules before listening to Valerie's voicemail again. Was Jazzy in that SUV? Maybe it was a vanity plate. J for Jazzy? Had he been molesting little girls since he was a teenager... and never been caught in all these years? Jules noticed Callie flinch, and her eyes turned stormy. "He must be stopped from hurting little girls." Her breath hitched.

Jules organized all the papers, stacked them against the table, and grabbed his coat. "Let's go. The sooner your police friend has this, the quicker they can work on it."

After following the tree-lined street, they arrived at the Lincoln City Police Station. True to Jake's word, they were expected. A woman in a stiff blouse and khaki pants scanned the bank statements, the newspaper article, and various notes before emailing the detective at the Portland precinct.

Callie had, true to her promise, retained Lily's deposition. She couldn't shake off her uneasiness and hoped she'd made the right decision by withholding it. Did Jake Sanders need to read this young girl's words that could pull him under? Did he require the information to find François' killer? She'd shared some of it with him; did he need the intimate details too? She couldn't stop the questions from creeping into every corner of her mind. No! She was right, Lily's words were her own, and she'd already had to share the experience with too many people. Since Denis was informing the police about Heidi Mason, maybe they wouldn't need Lily to send the man to prison. She'd keep the deposition private unless it was the only evidence that could make a difference.

When they returned to the cottage, she set the packet next to Lily's statement on the table. She stared at it before leaning against the table to cover her face with both hands. It was almost too much emotion to contain. "Poor Lily."

Jules walked toward her. "I am so sorry you're feeling Lily's pain." Jules reached out and pulled her tightly toward him. When she began to sob, he held her closer and allowed her to cry it out.

"I'm...f...f...feeling more than her pain, Jules." Her face paled before continuing. "Let's sit by the fire. I want to share something with you that I've never shared with anyone before; not my mother and not even François." Her lips trembled as she led him from the kitchen, placing her cup carefully on the counter as if it were a fragile jewel.

Jules was a study in patience as she pulled him across the room. She pushed him into a chair as if she was rearranging furniture. His confusion made her stop. Callie crossed her arms over her chest, backed up to the fire, and sat on the hearth.

She tried to gather her thoughts into one coherent bundle. Callie's voice was low as she began. She didn't stop speaking until she had told him everything. She squeezed both thumbs inside her fists and held them across her chest as the story she had kept inside for so long spilled out. Her eyes widened at the softness on Jules' face.

The burden she hadn't quite rid herself of when she faced her demons a few nights before stunned her. The gushing clarity of her admission pushed away the knot she had carried in her belly like a stone. "I didn't realize its impact on my self-worth. Soon, I didn't see myself as important enough to mention it."

Callie nestled into Jules' arms. When he wrapped his arms around her, he pulled her into a warm embrace. His shoulders shook. "Trusting me with this terrible secret means more to me than you could ever know, my dear woman. No wonder Lily's sadness has driven you to such lengths to help change her life. But I'm unsure what you can do except share your history with her." He pressed his palm to her face and caressed her cheek before running his fingers through the silvery strands that curled loosely over her forehead. He could feel her heart thumping against his own and knew she wasn't done as the words began again.

"It brought fear, anxiety, and shame that I had to overcome as an adult. I used to balance my own experiences against those of others. When I compared it with mine, someone else's heartache seemed to diminish my suffering. But at the same time, I'm still dealing with that past trauma. By comparing my abuse to others, I guess I belittled my reactions, as if I had failed by still struggling, while others, who went through so much worse, seemed to be stronger. I've pretended it happened to someone else for years."

He kissed the top of her head.

"Lily's abuser didn't pay for his evil actions, and I need to make a difference. I didn't tell anyone about my attack, but she did, and it didn't stop him. Except now, Lily has money for a college education. That money didn't help her psyche, though. If I can help by throwing Jazzy under the bus, I'll feel my own redemption."

Jules pulled her onto his lap and wrapped his arms around her to steady his own trembling. *"Je suis tellement désolé, ma chérie."* I am so sorry, my darling. He rested his chin on the top of her head as more tears flowed. She lifted her face when his shirt became wet and gently kissed his lips.

Jules, I need to help this girl. I fell down a rabbit hole and lost my sense of self-worth. I saw myself in that sad face, and her words wrenched my soul. I couldn't speak up because I didn't want to expose myself; I was frightened. When I pretended it didn't happen, I thought silence would make it go away, but it hurt me longer. Lily matters! I am so sorry it happened to her. I want to wash away all the negativity she's told herself… prove to her she's worthy of love. That's what finally helped me. Being loved." She looked at Jules and saw kindness as his hands cradled her face.

He pulled her close again. "Life is messy sometimes, but we need to live it. I'll be here if you want to pursue this, but you may face more than you can imagine." His eyes bored into hers. She brushed a trembling hand across her cheeks. "I will not run away this time, Jules. Whatever it takes, I will not pretend it didn't happen. No more flawed choices."

CHAPTER 28

Bella Jazzy ached from head to toe. Her stomach churned, and her ankle throbbed. When her husband disappeared, she forced herself off the bed, grabbed a small overnight bag, and packed it as quickly as she could manage. Underwear, sweaters, socks, jeans, and a toothbrush. Nothing matched, and she didn't care. She tilted her head to listen for Dom's return. Once satisfied, she quietly opened the door and peeked out. She knew that if she could reach the laundry room, she could slip out the side door and drive away without him noticing. She dragged her bag down the hall and pressed her ear to the door. She silenced her cell phone and stuffed it into her pocket. When she limped to the side door, she was horrified to discover that her purse no longer hung on the hook.

er thoughts were scattered. Where had she left it? Her head throbbed where Dom had hit her, and her memory was hazy. She opened the door quietly. After pushing the bag into her car, next to the stone wall that had been erected nearly a hundred years earlier, she returned to the house. Without her keys, she wasn't going anywhere.

Easing her way into the house and across the hall, she heard the television and hoped that meant Dom was absorbed in the news. Her eyes filled with hatred. She bounced plans around in her mind. What should she do next? As each thought entered her mind, it was just as quickly tossed aside. Ducking through the doorway, she peeked into the large kitchen, which occupied the entire back of the house. Her purse rested on the spacious center island next to her keys. And there sat Dom on the bar stool beside them.

His head was between his hands, braced up by both elbows.

Her heart sank as she backed into the hallway again. The pounding in her head was so loud that she couldn't think. Panic rose within her when she heard him push back the bar stool, unsure whether he was coming her way or heading into the living room. She opened the bathroom door, locked herself in, and sat on the commode for the count of ten.

While she was in there, she pulled down Excedrin and tossed them into her mouth, gagging as the pills turned chalky. Afraid to run the water, she forced spit onto her tongue repeatedly to rush it down her throat. Drops of sweat beaded on her forehead. She needed those keys. When everything remained quiet, she inched open the door and held her breath, but came face to face with the man she now feared.

He dangled her car keys in front of her. "Are these what you're looking for?" His face was so close that she felt his breath on her skin.

She held in a gasp. She knew there was nowhere to hide.

"I'm not going to hurt you again. My anger was out of control and I didn't mean to hit you, but you made me so damned mad."

His eyes revealed that the anger lingered, and she didn't believe him. She stared at his face, feeling bile rise in her throat as it pushed back the aspirin like a geyser.

He placed the key ring into her hand and then gave her the purse with his other hand; she knew he'd been aware of her flight all along. "You can't blame me for trying to leave, Dom." Her jaw ached, and her ankle hurt so badly that she couldn't put all her weight on it.

Dominic Jazzy spun on his heel.

She hurried out the side door to escape him as quickly as she could. It would be too soon if she never returned, but she knew she was fooling herself. How could she leave all of this behind? Yet, she wouldn't let him hurt her again.

She pushed the key into the ignition, but it didn't fit. She tried again, then stared at the key in her hand. It wasn't her key at all. A sinking feeling welled up in the pit of her stomach. She'd been in such a haze that she hadn't realized it was the company's SUV key, not her Volkswagen key. How could she be so stupid? There was no similarity between a Buick and a VW key. She tapped the steering wheel, unsure if she should go back inside.

Taking a deep breath, she stepped out of her car, grabbed her bag, and transferred it to the Buick SUV. Keeping her eye on the house, she didn't want to waste another minute escaping the insanity inside.

Without a second thought, she aimed the car toward her sister's house, the only person who might still love her. Even though they were estranged, Bella knew where her new house was located.

Within minutes, she called Mae but couldn't articulate her thoughts. Her jaw throbbed, and she was sure some of her teeth felt loose. Her swollen eye was bruised, and she couldn't open it wide enough to see the road with both eyes, but she tried—just barely. When her words made no sense, her sister felt exasperated.

"I'm coming and I'll tell you…and then he…we can…"

"…talk when you get here." Mae finished for her.

Mae took a short, sharp breath before unlocking her front door. She had felt disoriented when Bella began babbling incomprehensibly over the phone earlier. Now, as she banged on the door to her home, Mae was still unsure if she would let her in. But of course, she did.

Lily had driven her home from the hospital after they had sewn up her hand. Now, it throbbed like a migraine on steroids, and the bandage was twice the size of her hand. She had finally calmed Lily, who was now at the pharmacy to pick up her prescription.

Her twin looked as if she'd been run over by a Mack truck.

"He's gone over the edge, Mae." Bella's face was so pale, Mae knew she hadn't imagined hearing Bella's call for help.

Bella began speaking through gulps and pauses as Mae listened. As the story went on, Mae handed her a box of Kleenex and watched her sister's blotchy, swollen face. Bella blew her nose repeatedly. She lay on the couch with her foot resting on a pillow, an ice pack over her swollen ankle.

Mae pushed the blonde hair off her sister's forehead and traced her fingers over her purpling cheek. "So, you left him? The man who could do no wrong?" Fury choked her as she stared at her, remembering the betrayal, but feeling so frightened for her that her heartbeat thumped in her head.

Mae's words were uttered with such scorn that they brought Bella's head up, and she stopped sniffling. "I should have believed Lily. I know that now, but…" Bella's face blanched when Mae slapped her unhurt cheek.

The blow knocked Bella into silence.

"Don't you know when you make a statement followed by a 'but' that you don't mean it at all? You've told me that for years. You make me sick, Bella Jazzy! If my husband had sexually abused **your** child, I would have believed her. You just thought about your status and your money and you, you, you." Mae was shaking.

Bella held a hand to her face as she looked reproachfully at her sister. "You've never hit me before," she whispered in shock. "First, Dom slapped me around, and now... Please don't send me away, Mae." She reached for another tissue and caught a sob in her throat.

Mae opened her arms, wishing she could stay angry. Their connection was hard to describe—they felt each other's pain. Mae wondered what had happened between them. Between her pounding hand and her aching head, their lost trust felt far worse—a loss they might never recover from.

One hour later, they each held a cup of hot tea in their hands. Lily walked in and placed her mother's pain pills on the kitchen counter. She halted in her tracks upon entering the living room, arms akimbo. Her eyes darted toward her mother and then swung to her aunt. When she turned to flee the room, Bella hopped up and cradled her niece's face with one hand.

"I was wrong, Lily. Even if you can forgive me, I'll never forgive myself. I'm so sorry." Her hands clutched several wadded-up, damp tissues, and she rubbed them against her nose again.

"You're right, Auntie. I may not be able to forgive you. Why are you here? What happened to your face?" Lily stepped unwillingly toward the woman and stared at the dark, purpling blotches.

Bella dropped her eyes.

Mae intertwined her fingers with her daughter's. Swallowing hard, she reached out her other hand to her sister and joined their hands together. Nobody said a word, but they didn't pull away either.

Lily let her aunt pull her onto the couch beside her, but she doubted their relationship could ever be repaired. Struggling with feelings of love and animosity toward the woman, she sat still and blinked away tears.

"Dominic got angry." She lifted a finger to the purpling bruises and puffiness. "I haven't been the perfect wife, and he noticed.

Ever since the Oregonian printed that article about the girl accusing him…I've been angry and…" She looked at Lily with pleading eyes.

"Nobody's perfect, Auntie. Nobody." Lily's fingers traced down each of her thighs. She nervously bunched the fabric of her jeans in her hands.

Bella and Mae shared a look. She'd told her sister about her affair with Bryan Martos. Heaving a heavy sigh, she whispered, "Can I sleep here tonight? I may drive to the beach tomorrow."

Mae's face was clouded with questions, but she nodded.

"Did you call the police after he hit you? Or did you walk away like you wanted me to walk away and…" Lily's words spilled out.

Lily's question hit Bella like ice water. "I didn't know you would sue Uncle Dom, Lily. Everything was swept under the Jazzy rug. I assumed you were embarrassed for accusing him, so you didn't return to the winery." She looked at Mae. "If we had talked, I would have known long ago that he'd paid you hush money. If Bryan hadn't told me, I'd never have known since we've been estranged, Mae."

Mae and Lily stared at one another in disbelief.

"And I thought you didn't care, that you wanted to keep your fancy place in Dundee society, the money, the clothes, and trinkets."

"Throw you and Lily away? You're worth more to me than all that…" Her chin trembled. "I thought we knew each other better."

"If we'd known each other better, you would have reached out to me long before now, Bella. Don't excuse yourself; I don't buy it."

Bella pressed her lips together and studied her sister. She had no response that could justify an answer. Any words died in her throat.

"I'll get sheets and blankets for you. The couch is the only place we have now since we sold the house in Laurelhurst. That'll have to do." Mae left the room, and Lily stood next to her aunt, still unsure whether she was happy to see her back again.

Bella bit the inside of her lip and patted the small pillow beside her. "The couch is better than sleeping alongside a man who uses others for punching bags...and worse. I need to fix things, and I'm not sure I can."

"What things are you trying to fix?"

Her aunt looked at her and gently touched her chin with her fingers. "I've missed you, little one. The first thing I want to do is earn your friendship back. And your mother's. Sometimes it can be tough when someone faces a shocking challenge. We don't always make the best choices. Humans make mistakes, and mine was a doozy. I thought I loved my husband, and the thought of him doing what your mother told me was more than my brain could handle. Maybe I was just too cowardly to accept it. I am so sorry, Lily." Her eyes turned soft and glazed with tears.

"I'm not sure you can fix it, Auntie. But I met someone last week who told me there is life after being sexually abused."

Bella flinched.

"She is a very nice lady, and I think if any fixing is going to get done, she will do it. She said she met you recently."

"Really? Who is she?"

"Callie Beauvais."

Bella's face brightened. "Oh, yes! The wine connoisseur." She laughed at the look on her niece's face. "Denis brought her to a tasting tour. I liked her. How on earth did you meet her?"

Lily smiled. "It's a pretty long story..."

Bella anticipated her to keep going, but Lily remained silent.

.

Mae returned with an armload of blankets and said, "Lily, please get Aunt Bella another ice pack for her ankle. That one's melting." When Lily left, she dropped the blankets on the couch and grabbed a pillow from the linen closet. "It's not the Taj Mahal..."

"...but close to it." Bella finished.

The sisters laughed. It was a saying they'd heard their mother say for years, and the simple memory eased a tiny piece of hurt away.

Lily lay awake long into the night, listening to her aunt and mother's muted voices. She lifted a finger to her mouth, bit off the short nail that had begun to grow. Spitting it out, she squeezed her eyes shut, pushing aside all the memories that her aunt's appearance generated. She refused to dwell on any of it. Instead, she chose to focus on the brief light Callie had shone into her future if she agreed to the significant change.

She thought about France and Callie's description of what her life might be like living there: a family with children, far from her uncle, and the chance to make wine. Listening to her mother and aunt talk, although she couldn't make out the words, eased the burden of guilt she felt about going. Maybe they'd reconcile, and her mother wouldn't be alone. Her stomach tightened with excitement.

France. She would learn French by immersion, like she'd read about in books. Moonlight speared through her window, outlining her bookshelves. Her favorite book sat among the volumes. Madame Des Jardins had given the French class a six-week project to read the book *Manon des Sources* (Manon of the Spring). She'd read it three times. And she'd seen the movie twice. Taking place in Provence, she could almost feel the soil beneath her feet, see the sky above her, and see *Manon*, the girl whose father died looking for the water that was stolen from them by greedy, evil farmers. Marcel Pangos had written the period drama with such brilliance that Lily had also studied the making of the film from 1986. And loved every piece of it.

The women's voices still buzzed from the living room as Lily lay there, dreaming of France and the possibility of living far away from Oregon. She tried to imagine the twin boy and girl and a new baby. She could run through a vineyard again, feel the grape leaves snap against her bare skin. She could run free without the fear of her uncle waiting on the other side of the vines. Then, she remembered the connection between the Beauvais Vineyard and Denis. He'd described the vineyard in glowing terms. If only he could be in France, too. She learned a lot from him and wished he were still in her life. But Lily had since learned nothing was as it appeared, and her thoughts of France began to waver in her mind.

The jaggedness of her fear seeped in, the silver-haired man who had frightened her and then made her feel like a foolish child afterward. She often lay awake at night, wondering how a man she had trusted could do such a terrible thing and then pretend it hadn't happened. Did he think she would walk away and never tell anyone? Was he so mentally ill that he believed he could hurt anyone anytime he wanted? Knowing her aunt was in the next room with her mother made her heart skip a beat. She wasn't sure if she wanted her back in their lives. Lily and her mother did just fine without Aunt Bella. Didn't they? But a little voice murmured, how could you leave her behind in Oregon and kick up your heels in France if she were all alone? She sniffed and pounded her pillow before lying her head down again.

Lily thought of the money in the bank growing interest, that Uncle Dom thought made everything okay. Blood money, she called it, but her mother made her stop and think about it beyond the why. Now, she could attend a good college and become anything she wanted. She had wanted to be a vintner before. Did she still want to make wine? Or should she go to law school, become a criminal attorney, and eke out the pedophiles of this world, save the children? She started shaking with the enormity of the thought and reminded herself she wasn't yet sixteen years old. With the money and Callie's help, she allowed that minuscule glimpse of light again.

Lily snorted as she recalled what her mother had said when François's partner offered them money for her silence. "I'd like to stuff that money up his…where the sun doesn't shine." Although Lily hadn't been able to laugh then, she now realized with surprise that she found it amusing.

She turned her head to look at the moon and heard Callie's voice in her head, promising hope. Then she dreamed of delicious possibilities.

Hope had been missing for a long time.

CHAPTER 29

Valerie's papers were still spread across the table when Alexis called to confirm her appointment for the following morning. The last thing Callie needed was to think about the estate sale, but the woman was delivering a hefty check, so how could she do otherwise?

Jules brushed the dark curls from her cheek. "I'm feeling overly cautious, Callie, but I'm worried. You were lucky on the bridge. What if there's a next time? And now that we know Bryan Martos has a house nearby, I'm not sure we can handle this alone. I know you're angry at him for cheating Lily, too. God, I wish I had answers."

"Jules." She gestured for him to sit by the fire. Then, she nestled close to him like a kitten in a shoebox. "I feel different for the first time in years because helping Lily made a difference. I can discuss it without feeling anxious or uncomfortable. Talking with her opened the dam for me. Now, it's time for the next step. Bryan Martos."

His arm tightened around her for a moment before he kissed the top of her head and stood up to open a bottle of Malbec wine. "Let's go eat dinner in Lincoln City and talk about France. This crazy talk is putting ice in my veins."

Callie answered cautiously. "Yes, I know a good place not far…but please don't expect me to leave Oregon until Bryan Martos is arrested. Her face darkened, and her knuckles turned white. He **will** confess. And he **will** pay for what he's done."

"It's too dangerous." The look on Callie's face told him she didn't care. "*Ma chère,* please let me handle it then?"

Her face turned stony. "No. This isn't up for debate. I must do this for François. I know he was your best friend, but I won't allow his murder to go unpunished. Stop worrying. I'll be careful. Now that the police are involved in the investigation, neither of us should be in danger. That man is capable of bad things; we already know that. But I must find out what happened. Maybe François never confronted him at all. It was a murky, windy, horrible storm, and he was speeding that boat across the lake like a crazy man. Even if it was an accident, I think Bryan Martos was responsible. I know François chose to get into the boat, but…" Her face closed, and her lips trembled when he handed her the glass of wine.

"Just promise me you won't take stupid risks, Callie."

She looked at him and thought about the small gun she had taken from her glove box. Glancing toward her purse, which was slung over the back of the dining room chair, she battled with herself before answering. "No, I'll be careful, Jules. Promise. But I will make him confess. No way is he going to get away with it." And she meant it. Bryan was lucky that was all she had in mind for him.

As the first signs of dawn appeared in the eastern sky--pink and purple streaks across the lower part of the horizon, fading to lighter blue higher up—a germ of an idea threaded through her mind. She didn't dare share it with Jules. She had to choose her time carefully. She pulled her fanny pack out of her roller bag and stuffed the gun into its black leather pocket.

Alexis called to postpone their meeting, promised to see her the next day, and apologized. "I'll bring your check, Callie. The sale went very well." The woman's voice sounded pleased with herself.

After dinner that night, Callie said, "I'm going for a short walk. I won't be long. I need a little time...to think about everything."

Jules had a towel wrapped around his waist and responded anxiously, "It's almost dark. Wait, and I'll go with you."

Callie laughed, "Naked? The neighbors would love to see you traipsing around St. John Loop nude. I have some thinking to do, and it's best if I do it alone." She saw hurt scamper across his face as she closed the door and turned toward the road.

She pulled the map out of her pocket, where a spot was circled in red. Tightening her fanny pack, she slipped on her tennis shoes, and within minutes, she located his house. No lights were on, but the front drapes were open. She turned her head around the bush where she stood across the narrow street. The lake wasn't far behind the house, and the windows were small and dark. She heard a dog barking nearby. Trees rustled above her, and the wind blew her hair. She shoved her hands into her jacket pocket.

Suppose she could get close enough to see if Bryan was there? Her chest heaved. Really? And then what? She had just eased toward the man's house from the lakeside when her hackles rose. Callie skidded to a shocked halt and slid across the wet grass as the barking dog started raising havoc near Bryan's back door. She hadn't planned for the dog. She started running along the darkened shrubs to stay out of sight from the street light. The dog was now thumping against the door, and she heard a man's voice yelling.

"Who's there?" His anger was palpable.

Callie's heart raced as she crouched behind a van parked across the street, as far from the streetlight as possible. She immediately noticed a man's shadow standing a few feet away from her hiding spot. He didn't move, nor did she. The dog continued to bark, and the man shouted again before heading back to his house.

She counted to twenty before moving away from the side of the van, knowing Jules would be looking at the clock now that darkness had fallen. Quietly, she angled her way back after peeking around to see if Bryan was watching from his front window. Callie was sure he couldn't see her as she picked herself up, lurched across her neighbor's lawn, and followed the lake back to her own house. She could feel her lungs burning as she slid to a halt by her back sliding door and tapped on the glass.

Pulling the door open, Jules yanked her inside and growled, "What have you been doing? You went over there without me, didn't you? Are you crazy?!" He held her tightly against him and turned off the lights, convinced shadows from the lakeside had followed her.

She shook her head, gasping for breath. Leaning down on her knees, Jules placed a hand on her shoulder until she had gathered herself. At last, she steadied her breathing, glanced up at him, and in painful bursts, told him what she had done.

"I know, I know… I just wanted to see if he was there. There was a dog and…"

"Callie." His voice was heated and brusque as he threw himself into the deep armchair beside the fireplace. Without waiting for her to answer, he reached for the bottle of Tempranillo wine and poured two glasses. "You were going to take a little walk while I dressed and poured wine for us? Uh-huh. I should have known better." He didn't offer her a glass, but lifted his own.

Callie breathed a sigh of relief, shifted toward the couch, and picked up her wine. "I've been making decisions for a long time, Jules. Stop expecting me to ask for your permission or approval at every turn. I'm an adult too…I admit that sometimes I am impulsive…"

He snorted. "Sometimes?" His eyes remained dark with anger.

She patted the couch beside her and raised a hand apologetically. "I will keep you in the loop next time…I have to admit, the dog surprised me, and when I began to run as if hellhounds were after me, I **was** frightened."

Jules' eyes softened, accepting her invitation and her sort-of apology. The fire snapped, having been built up to a roar, warming them as they joined hands and enjoyed the stillness.

Callie stared into the flames, mesmerized and calmed by the flickering light. She jumped slightly at a movement in her peripheral vision but relaxed when the neighbor's calico cat brushed against the glass doors with curious eyes. She unfolded herself, lifted her head with a droop of despair, and choked back the tears. She hated to give up, hated feeling weak, but how could she ever hope to prove François died by another's hands? How could she endure mourning again?

Callie thought of all the heroes in the books she'd read over the years, and Harry Potter popped into her mind. What was J.K. Rowling thinking when she created a small boy to fight the evilest tyrant in the land? She had been making some rash decisions, and she wished for just an hour that she could be the boy with all the guts, smarts, and magic. She dropped her head back on the couch and closed her eyes, smiling grimly. Her heart told her Bryan Martos had something to do with François's death, maybe not directly, but indirectly. François must have confronted him, but she knew she could never prove it without getting inside Bryan's head.

Could I confront him myself? Right. A man you think killed your husband, and then you'd stand there and look him in the eye and expect him to say, "Sure, Callie. I did it." Callie snorted at the image. She finally admitted there was no way she could prove it, and the thought made her sag with defeat. If only I had Harry's magic or his cloak of invisibility. She chuckled again. She placed both hands on her forehead and pushed her bangs up and over her head in misery.

Who would know what he did? She'd heard that when a killer did the deed, keeping it all to himself was difficult. A killer was usually proud of the act. If only she could prompt his memory into words. She wondered what Harry Potter would have done. She recalled all the books Rowling had written, all the goofy problems he'd encountered, and how he saved himself afterward. She exhaled loudly. When she glanced over at Jules, she smiled sadly, admitting there was no way to find the answers. But the struggle had lasted so long, she wasn't sure she could let it go. Her head throbbed with an insistent weariness from so many nights of broken sleep.

Jules's eyes closed, finally letting jet lag take over. His hand clutched his wine glass, so Callie gently unfurled his fingers and placed it on the table.

When she returned to her chair, she thought of the magic of Harry Potter once more. If she could enter the man's mind, listen to his thoughts, and eavesdrop on his conversations. She sat up straight, tingling with the possibility of such an experience. If she could get that man to vent to someone, to boast about that day… Anger surged hot through her veins. She would track down Bryan. She would force him to admit what he'd done. Somehow. She would not give up.

As Jules snoozed before the fire, Callie opened her cell phone. She had an idea that couldn't wait until morning.

Her trip into Lincoln City had proved successful, and her stomach tumbled with energy. Mark's Technology was one block off the main street, parallel to the Pacific Ocean. She'd remembered the shop because she'd run in for a camera battery a few years earlier. When she pulled up in front of the small shop, she grinned at the open sign on their glass door.

The girl at the front desk was wiping the glass display case while humming softly to herself. When she heard the bell ring above the door, she gave Callie a slight wave. After Callie explained what she was looking for, the girl looked doubtful but raised a finger in the air. She turned quickly to push aside the curtain hanging in the doorway, and a few seconds later, a man appeared.

Alvin Marks was a short, slender, and nerdy-looking man. His eyes were clear, intelligent, and attentive to Callie's request. He grinned at her as if she had just handed him a puzzle to solve. He pulled something from beneath the counter, dusted it off, and placed it on the glass case.

Callie shifted her gaze from the dusty box to the man's eyes. When she saw him grin, she couldn't help but grin back.

On her way back to the cottage, she heard Alvin Mark's patient instructions echoing in her mind. She glanced at the small black box on the passenger seat of her car, and her heart sped up. He had shown her the app to download onto her phone for the voice-activated listening devices, and she could hardly wait to put them to use.

This would have to be another secret she would keep from Jules because he was watching her closely, wondering what was happening in her mind. She chuckled softly. He knew her well enough by now to guess she wouldn't walk away from this situation.

She was glad he'd taken the empty boxes upstairs to load bed linens and other non-saleable items. By the time she left for town, Jules had boxed up nearly everything in both upstairs bedrooms. They'd decided to donate the rest. Keeping him busy had been her motive. The cottage would be ready for Alexis' people by the end of the week.

Callie's mind flipped from the house to Bryan to Valerie's death and then to Lily. She ached for normalcy. Would this work? Could she prove Bryan killed her husband? And then what? She'd thought for so long it had been a freak accident. Knowing it might have been manipulated to look like it made her determination so strong that she hurt all over. Her fingers squeezed the wheel as she turned off Highway 101 toward the cottage, and she focused on the project ahead. And she was scared spitless.

Callie pulled out pasta, green peppers, tomato sauce, and eggs. Instead of the lazy meat sauce she'd planned, she would make meatballs. Once she had the sauce started and the meatballs rolled into small balls, Jules wandered in with the smell of freshly hewn wood in his hair. He dropped kindling in the box, returned to the kitchen to watch her cook, and continued their earlier argument.

"You are a strong woman. You don't let life beat you down. You fight for what you want." He took a breath.

"Uh huh…" She wondered where he was going with this.

"Those are just a few reasons why I love you, but Callie, these are dangerous people. We know they are ruthless when cornered. We're making progress with our work here, but you need to step back and let me take the lead on this.

Callie raised her eyebrows and held his gaze.

He must have seen the disappointment and simmering anger on her face. Jules tenderly reached out and touched her cheek. "I don't want you to get hurt." She dropped her head, allowing the magic of his fingers to ease some of the stress in her mind before responding. "I remember we had a similar conversation in Pertuis a few weeks ago. You wanted to run the show when I asked you to help me find Olivier. I let you, and I am glad now that I did." Callie looked at Jules from beneath her long lashes.

"Jules, this time, it's on my turf. I can't move forward until I find the answers. I'm glad you're here, but don't put a fence around me." Her eyebrows formed a straight line, and her nutmeg brown eyes challenged his.

"You could end up never finding the answers."

"Okay, fine." She kept stirring the pot. "So what?"

Jules leaned against the kitchen counter and folded his arms over his chest. "I think we should let it lie and keep you safe."

She set the ladle down forcefully, splattering spaghetti sauce on the stovetop. Callie spun around, glaring at him. "What? That's ridiculous!"

He shook his head and returned to watch the fire burn.

They ate in silence.

She observed his eyes grow heavy, and the warm fire seemed to lull them both into a state of lethargy.

As the fire crackled and the gentle popping of embers lulled Jules to sleep after dinner, she tiptoed across the room.

When she was certain he was snoozing deeply, she stuffed the black case into her waist bag and slipped out the side door. She hoped it would only take a few moments to do what she needed to do. Jules wouldn't like it, and she'd have to navigate his anger, but what choice did she have?

She tugged at the scarf around her neck and tucked it into her jacket to protect herself better from the cold wind coming off the lake.

She fingered the small box zipped inside her pocket, assuring herself it was still there. Walking swiftly, she replayed her plan in her mind. The cold wind was forgotten, so she flexed her toes inside her tennis shoes and pushed past shrubs and concrete blocks.

When she reached the second street corner, she ran down to the lake and scooted along its sandy shore. No lights shone in the neighbor's windows. Light pooled from the lakeside, confirming that Bryan was inside. She retraced her earlier steps, this time avoiding the neighbor's dog. Moving stealthily, she walked toward his boat pier and ducked under the window sills until she reached the rear windows.

Callie opened the black case and carefully picked up one of the horse-fly-like micro-receivers between her fingers. It was dark, and she knew that if she dropped one, it would be lost forever. She hoped Bryan wouldn't get suspicious if it sat outside his window for too long. She pushed her hair out of her eyes and grimaced as a breeze whipped it back.

The camouflaged directional microphones must stick to the windows. She peeled the cover off the adhesive strip at the base of the horse fly and inched her body slowly upward alongside the window frame. Splaying her hand into a fist for stability, Callie gingerly lifted the fly-shaped microphone toward the glass. Her hand hesitated. What if Bryan noticed movement on the glass? Crouching in the grass, she grappled with indecision.

Maybe he wasn't even in the room. She closed her eyes. She needed to attach four of these hummers in position. A split second later, the sudden blast of music from inside the room made her jump. The television. She swallowed hard and stood again to peer out the window's corner. Bryan was sitting in a recliner with his back to her.

Extending her hand an inch at a time, she carefully placed the listening device on the glass and then quickly sank into the grass. The music blared again. This time, she knew where he was, so finding the other three should be easier. She held her breath and slipped around to the side of the house. Carefully avoiding the loose gravel that she had slipped on earlier, which framed several small bushes, she approached the next window. A slight breeze ruffled the lake grasses at her feet.

Each transmitter was configured to wirelessly transfer voice-activated recordings to the MICBot app on her smartphone. After placing the fourth horse fly on the bottom corner of Bryan's front window, she retraced her steps. When she was grabbed from behind and pulled back toward the house, she nearly fainted. And when she heard the words, "It's me," hissed in her ear, she swallowed her scream.

It was too dark to see each other's faces. Living on the lake wasn't like living in the city, where streetlights glowed at every corner. He gripped her arm and pulled her behind the large shrub by Bryan's pier, hoping to hide them from view if the man heard anything. The dog began barking, and they squatted low. Neither of them said a word until they were sure it was safe to slink toward the shore and make their way back to the cottage, avoiding the street and the feeble slice of light at the corner.

Jules was too angry to speak.

Callie, however, spun around to face him. "You scared me half to death. I had everything under control." She could see from the expression on his face that nothing she said would make a difference. She felt sorry about that, but she wouldn't apologize. She'd told him she wasn't going to sit still, but he hadn't believed her.

"You had everything under control, did you? Did you see Martos' neighbor when he switched on the porch light? Did you see him attach the lead to his dog's collar? You would have come out from the side of the house right into his hands. And what would you say when he saw you sneaking around there? Even if you'd had a good answer, could you have avoided Martos hearing the commotion or hiding from his motion detector out front? Did you know he even had a motion detector?" His questions snapped at her in staccato bursts.

Callie opened her mouth to make a sharp retort and then closed it again. This was the first time they had ever exchanged harsh words. It occurred to her then that Jules wasn't upset because she'd acted like an impulsive child or against his wishes. He was upset because she'd placed herself in a precarious position, a situation that could have led to a more frightening outcome than it did. What would she have done if he hadn't shown up when he did? The light would have alerted Bryan, and she'd have been caught red-handed?

She turned away from him and pushed her hands into her jeans pockets. Without saying a word, she felt her hands shake as she unbuckled her fanny pack and laid it on the dining room table. When Jules heard the thud, his eyes darted to the bag.

When their eyes met, she didn't say a word. When she reached for it, their fingers touched. He felt the hard object inside, and his face was confused.

"My gun, Jules. I didn't go unprotected, you see?"

rolled his eyes before turning toward the sliding glass doors and stepping outside. She watched him descend the three steps onto the grass and continue until his feet met the small sandy beach.

Callie felt a hodgepodge of interlocking feelings. She knew she should have included Jules, but admitted he would have been in her way. He couldn't protect her from everything; she had to make him understand that. She stood at the glass and watched the movement near the water. Her mind was conflicted, but she loved the man, who deserved her honesty. She knew today's ripples would eventually tumble together. Sliding open the door, she followed his earlier steps toward the lake.

She wanted to clear the air that prickled between them. He turned when he heard her foot on the wood behind him. He offered her a wry smile. As she walked toward him, he opened his arms. He spoke softly into her ear, letting his lips brush against it. She felt a pleasant trickle of intimacy in her core, and a delicious impatience overcame her uneasiness.

They got as far as the living room. Making love by firelight took Callie's mind off horse flies. Jules' hands moved on her like a feather, and she felt the bliss. When she groaned softly into the hollow of his neck, he pulled her close and whispered, "Together. We do this thing together. Promise me."

She made soft sounds of agreement and remained wrapped in his arms, their legs tangled. The fire burned lower, yet they did not move. The last thing she wanted was to confront the hurt in his eyes again. She berated herself for her impulsiveness, but knew it probably wouldn't be the last time.

"Jules, please love me just the way I am."

"Mmmmm," he whispered into her hair.

"I'm willing to change a little, but I cannot allow you to mold me into a woman to fit your design. You must let me be the person I am meant to be."

"I love you the way you are. I want you to be cautious because I have waited a very long time to feel this way. It's difficult for me to stand back and see you jump into situations that could take you away from here...and me."

She chuckled at how his words were strewn together and kissed the end of his nose. "I'll make you angry sometimes, and you will probably do the same for me. You said we'll do things together, and I like that."

"*Oui.*"

She could see the depth in his eyes with the firelight reflecting the silver around each iris. "Sometimes I make snap decisions. I have made decisions based on other people's feelings all my life. I didn't want to hurt my mother by missing my father. I didn't want to tell her about the night I hid from her for so many years because it would upset her.

Jules tightened his arms around her.

There were so many times that I kept my mouth shut to avoid hurting someone else. It was hard to do that, but I don't like hurting others. But I'm over fifty now, and it's time I acted like an adult. I want you in my life, but please understand how important this is to me." Her voice was husky, vibrant, and low. Saying the words aloud she'd whispered inside her head for so long, made it real. She would now listen to her truth meter. It was her turn, and she wasn't budging.

Jules leaned down to touch her cheek and kissed her deeply. "I agree, but when we disagree, we talk, *oui?*"

She felt light-headed. "That's all I ask."

CHAPTER 30

He found her crumpled on the soft carpet when he gave her a mug of steaming coffee the next morning. Their eyes met and they smiled, each remembering their lovemaking the night before. He knew she was pondering something, so he sat in the easy chair and watched a calico cat stretch outside the window. The cat twisted its head around to lick its fur and clean itself before wandering off again.

"I will tell you what I did yesterday, but I want you to listen all the way through before you respond. Do I have your word?" She gazed at him over the rim of her mug, wrapping both hands around it.

He exhaled slowly. "Yes, *ma petite*. Tell me."

She grinned. "We know that the district attorney will not arrest Bryan. Unless we get proof, we are dead in the water." She grimaced at her analogy as it reminded her of François and his watery death.

Jules reached for her ankle as it lay at his feet on the floor.

She began again. "A man in town sold me electronic listening devices shaped like large horse flies." When she saw the surprised look on his face, she continued hesitantly.

"I downloaded the app to hear the voice-activated recordings. He instructed me on placing the little things on Bryan's windows."

Jules' breath let out a noise of disbelief.

She raised both hands. "You promised to wait until I finished..." Her eyes pleaded with him, and he rolled his eyes.

"Before you grabbed me at Bryan's house, I'd already attached four little flies to his windows. Now, I can activate the app and hope to hear something that proves our theory. Maybe he didn't kill François, but I think he did. I've been told that killers often boast about their deeds, and I'm banking on that."

"And how does the app work?"

Callie knew he was finally listening to her. "It turns my phone into a spy device with video, photo, and audio capabilities. He said I should swipe the remote view and then tap to share the viewing link. This sends the link to a computer or other device." She stretched her arm to get the phone hidden beneath the couch.

Jules watched her tap the phone into live mode. "I tap activate and hit the red button here…to start a remote viewing session. Then, I visit the link in the web browser." She nodded toward her laptop on the table. "This is surely something Harry Potter would do, right?"

Jules suppressed a grin. "Harry Potter, huh?"

"The map pinpoints where the recordings take place. I'm unsure if it will work since he's alone, but I had to take the chance." Both hands went to her hair again, as she stared at the phone thoughtfully. "I've checked the program a few times this morning, but there's nothing. Maybe he left."

"How far does the microphone extend so you can listen?"

Callie's eyes grew round. "I don't know."

"Maybe I should download the APP on my phone, too. What's it called?" He tapped the Apple Store on his phone and looked at her.

"MICBot, username is vineyard, and password is Lulu."

He laughed, knowing she named it Lulu after Cendrine's unborn baby. After he downloaded it, he reached for his tennis shoes. "Can I just say this has a bad idea written all over it?"

Callie saw his mouth quirk, trying not to smile.

"I'm going to go for a run and then shower so we can go into town for breakfast. I doubt we'll get a hit immediately, and it'll be a recording, so we can listen later. *Oui?* I saw a French café named Truffles near the beach." When Callie nodded, he pulled on his rain parka and glanced outside where dark clouds hung low over the lake. "I won't be gone long; I just need to get the blood pumping."

~

While Bella showered early that morning, Mae heard her arguing with someone on the phone. Later, she drove away without sharing the conversation. Afterward, Mae and Lily shook their head and prepared breakfast. Lily twirled her cereal spoon and bit into a banana. "When I asked the school counselor about the student exchange program on Friday, she told me it isn't easy." She bit into her banana and chewed thoughtfully.

Mae sipped her mint tea while working the Oregonian's daily crossword. "Do you really want to do this, Lily?"

Lily's blonde head snapped up, and her blue eyes sparkled. It had been a long time since her mother had seen that look on her daughter's face. And her heart melted, realizing her selfishness wanted to keep Lily nearby. "Tell me more, honey."

Lily explained the various non-profits that offered scholarships and the requirements they expected students to meet. "Rotary Club offers the best one. It lasts almost a year, and I'd live with three different families. I'd go to the same school once the town was chosen, but all three families would offer a different perspective on life. I'd be moving three times."

"That sounds good, but also a little uprooting to me, Lily."

"Callie said I could live with her niece or stepdaughter, which sounded better. Can my savings pay for a year in France, instead of jumping through their rules?" She stared at Mae, her lips quivering slightly as she popped the last piece of banana into her mouth.

Mae watched her twirl her spoon again. She could feel her daughter's excitement. Reaching out to calm Lily's twitching fingers, the spoon stilled. "Let's talk with Callie again before we make a decision. There's enough money in that account to do just about anything you want to do, my darling." Her face warmed into a smile, and she squeezed her daughter's fingers before the twirling spoon returned to the bowl of Cheerios.

An hour later, Lily walked toward Grant High School. Her thoughts were miles away, so she didn't hear the large car beside her. When the driver honked and her Uncle Dom climbed out of the car, she was paralyzed. Fear pierced her, and she couldn't move.

"Get in, Lily," Each word punctuated as if he spoke to a child.

~

Bryan Martos glared at the cell phone when it rang for the third time. Frustrated, he answered the call and jerked away when Dominic Jazzy's voice rose an octave with each word he spat out.

"I'm being held in the Yamhill County Jail. They can't prove anything, so this is where you come in. Earn your money, man! I'm in here with two drunks and a kid with more tattoos covering his body than there are fish in the damn ocean."

Bryan stared at the lake behind his house. He knew he was at a crossroads. His disgust with Dom Jazzy was becoming harder to hide. "They are holding you…because?" He knew the answer, but he just wanted Dom to squirm.

"Heidi Mason. Nobody can prove it was me, but they think they have enough to question me. My calls all went to voicemail. Where the hell are you?" Jazzy's voice thundered across the line. "Why aren't you answering the phone?"

"What happened?" Bryan didn't give a fig about him, but running away was impossible. He knew the rules. He knew he might be forced to defend him without a judge's approval at this point.

"I drove home after trying to talk some sense into Lily…"

"What?! You imbecile," Bryan stormed. He paced through his kitchen, into the living room, and back again. His hair stood on end where he'd twisted his fingers through it in agitation.

"I wanted to stop her from talking to the Beauvais widow. Instead, she started running toward the school screaming her bloody head off." Dom's voice sounded panicked.

Bryan took a belabored breath. "You just made it worse for yourself, Dom. Where did the police pick you up?"

"When I returned to the vineyard, they were talking with Denis. Evidently, they asked if he remembered seeing the Mason girl in the vineyard." Dom paused dramatically. "And he said he saw her that day, running through the vineyard crying with snot all over her face. Then he said he saw me snipping nearby vines. The police were interested to hear why I didn't hear her crying when I was nearly on top of her, so to speak." Dom Jazzy chuckled at his small joke.

Bryan's chest squeezed shut. His eyes reflected the anger sweeping through his body. "So, you raped that girl."

Dom Jazzy didn't answer. Instead, he said, "When are you getting me out of here?" His breath was coming in short gasps now.

"I'm not." Bryan heard the sputtering on the other end of the phone, and he hung up.

After Bella Jazzy received the phone call from Denis Sorbets saying the police had taken Dom away in the cruiser, she couldn't believe her ears. Still unsure of her future, she decided to join Denis to figure out how to run a vineyard independently. When she thought of her husband touching those young girls, her stomach heaved.

Once on the highway, she redialed Denis. "I'm on my way. Can you manage the winery with your other work? The vineyard almost takes care of itself with our good employees. If the police have proof to arrest Dom, maybe we can save some little girls a lot of grief and us too." There was a steely silence on the phone.

Denis answered slowly, "Bella, I'll help all I can. But I will be honest with you, it will take a lot more than my deposition to keep Dom in jail. The D.A. will need irrefutable proof before taking this to court. Not only is it sensitive, but it is also political. He won't dirty his hands on this case unless he knows he will win."

Bella and Denis talked from Portland to Tigard before she hung up. Did she want Dom to stay in jail? Yes. Did she want to run the Jazzy Cove Vineyard alone? Maybe. Was this her chance to have a life with Bryan Martos? Could she leave her status in Dundee behind? She wasn't sure. Once she got things organized, she needed to have a long talk with Bryan. No more deception.

While Jules was outside running through the neighborhood, Callie was packing and taping boxes. In between her work, she was checking her new phone app. When it rang in her hands, she nearly dropped it.

Denis Sorbets started talking the second she answered the phone. "The police picked up Dom this morning." His breath hitched.

Callie's heartbeat stumbled for a second. "Because of the Dundee girl's accusation?" She felt like dancing.

"Yes. They were here at the vineyard questioning me when Dom returned from the city. I told them I remembered the day it must have happened and that Dom was very close to the area where it happened. It's not proof, but they took him anyway. I'm not sure how long they can hold him without arresting him. And they won't arrest him unless they're damned sure they have enough to do it."

Callie's voice broke, "Denis...th...thank you so much for calling me. If there is a god, Jazzy will be in prison. We found something in an old Oregonian newspaper that my friend gave to me." She swallowed hard. "Dominic Jazzy was accused of sexually abusing a child when he was sixteen years old. His parents must have paid money to shut it up, and he got away with it. I have a feeling this will make a difference when the D.A. finds out the man has a muddy history." Her voice rattled in her throat.

"And, Callie... What if they also find other girls who have been too afraid to come out of the woodwork about him? He's lived in this area all his life with too much money and too little accountability. There are bound to be others who might speak up to seal the man's fate."

"I hope so," she breathed. "What will you do?"

"Bella asked me to manage the winery, and I'll do that until she finds someone else. Like I told you before, I'm thinking of returning to France. Maybe old Andres Frenot can find a place for me at Beauvais Vineyard." His voice sounded hopeful.

Callie laughed. "He probably will. But first, let's keep this evil man where he belongs, and you keep making wine. Thanks for calling me, Denis." She couldn't hide her excitement. Dominic Jazzy is in prison. She knew it would be a lengthy legal process, but hoped in the end, he wouldn't be able to hurt anyone else like he hurt Lily or the way Jack hurt her.

When Jules opened the door, he grabbed the towel he'd left near the back door to swing around his neck. His face was flushed, and his breath came in short, gasping bursts. "I am so out of shape!" After he wiped off the sweat that dripped from his forehead and neckline, he noticed the look on Callie's face.

Tears streamed down her cheeks. Although a silent testament to her sadness, she wore a smile while he looked confused. She attempted to speak, but her words got lost somewhere between her brain sending signals and the hard swallows stuck in her throat.

He rushed toward her. "What now?!"

She threw herself into his arms, indifferent to the damp sweat covering his shirt and skin. When she began to cry in earnest, he simply held her, having no idea what else to do. After several minutes, she looked at him with such a peaceful expression that he guided her to a chair and helped her onto the cushion.

"Tell me," he said, kneeling down in front of her. He didn't let go of her hands as his eyes urged her to talk to him.

"I think it might be over at last, Jules."

"Over?"

"Dominic Jazzy was just thrown into jail."

Jules' shocked face made her laugh.

~

Lily shivered even though her mother had wrapped a blanket around her shoulders. When Mae tucked it into the crevice of the couch beside her, Lily said, "He tried to make me get in his car, Mom." Her face was as pale as the creamy paint on the wall beside them.

"Oh, Lily," Mae crooned, pushing the blonde curls off Lily's forehead and smoothing them back repeatedly to quiet the girl.

"I don't know if I will ever find peace, Mom." The girl's voice quivered and broke. "I started running away, down the sidewalk toward the school. And I couldn't stop screaming. When I heard his tires squeal away, I just kept running--- and screaming. I hid in the school. When he was gone, I told the secretary I was sick. And I ran all the way home."

Mae's chest tightened with the pain she saw on her daughter's face. Her hands trembled, and the torrent of emotion washing over her was building. After Bella's surprise visit and her quick departure that morning, plus this --- Mae wasn't sure what to do.

"Nobody can stop him..." Lily's blue eyes brimmed with tears. She blew her nose with a handkerchief clenched in her fist and wiped her cheek with it afterward.

Before Mae could respond, her phone rang. Torn between comforting Lily and answering the phone, she stayed put. When Lily jerked her head toward the ringing, Mae reluctantly picked up the call.

"Mae? This is Callie."

"Callie, it's been wild around here… Dom tried to get Lily into his car this morning. He said she should remember all the good things he did for her instead of just that one night. She ran down the sidewalk all the way to school, screaming her little head off."

Callie was shocked. "I have news to stop her screaming."

"It would take something mighty big, Callie. With a restraining order on him, how could he think of approaching her, especially so close to school grounds? The man is insane, an imbecile." She was sputtering.

Callie couldn't help the chuckle that escaped her. "Dominic Jazzy was picked up by the police a little while ago. Denis more or less turned him over to them. He put the man within a few feet of that young girl who was attacked in the vineyard. Dom Jazzy's now sitting in the county jail."

Stunned disbelief etched Mae's features. "I'm speechless."

Callie responded, "Our Lily can finally rest a little easier, *oui*?"

Lily sat up at the look on Mae's face. "What happened?"

Mae held a finger to her lips. "The timing is incredible. Bella came over late Friday afternoon. Dom had beaten her. She's purple, swollen and half crippled. She left this morning, but we talked and we've sorta made up." Mae laughed.

"Sorta? I hope so. I know you've missed her. With Dom in jail, she will have a lot to think about. I had to share the good news."

"Thanks so much." When she hung up the phone, Mae reached for Lily's hand. When she burst into tears and grabbed the Kleenex box, Lily felt her heart swell with anxiety. When her mother started laughing until tears streamed down her cheeks, Lily was confused. But somehow, she knew it was a good thing, and she couldn't help herself. The atmosphere shifted, and their laughter intertwined until Mae could speak coherently.

CHAPTER 31

Dominic Jazzy's unrepentant and arrogant behavior didn't win him any friends on East Fifth Street at the Yamhill County Jail in McMinnville. He came in swearing and didn't shut up until they showed him the fingerprint pad of ink. He stared at it with denial written across his features. "You can't make me do this."

When the officer told him to empty his pockets, he jerked around and glared at the man. "Do you know who I am?"

"Yes, I know who you are, Dominic Jazzy. Owner and operator of Jazzy Cove Vineyard and Winery. Second-generation Italian whose grandfather built a dynasty for our community. Alleged," he said under his breath, "child molester."

Dom Jazzy spun around but was yanked back into place when two officers grabbed him by his elbows. One raised his hand to the pad, pressing each finger and thumb into the ink, rocking it back and forth like a seesaw.

"You can't do this to me."

"We just did." The taller officer smirked.

"I want to call my lawyer. I know my rights." Dom felt a fluttering in his chest. He needed to call Bryan again. He couldn't have been serious when he said he wouldn't get him released. He'd make these bozos stop treating him like a common criminal. He looked around furtively, expecting them to lead him to a phone. Instead, they took him to a concrete bench, pushed him down to sit, and made him wait. He waited.

For two hours.

When he was finally led down a long, white corridor, he started to breathe easier. Now, he would call Bryan. When he was pushed into a room, he was marched to a plastic chair and told to sit. He sat. His bushy eyebrows rose in anger, and the hairspray began to lose its stranglehold on his silver hair.

"I'm Sgt. Martin. Make yourself comfortable, Mr. Jazzy." He pushed a telephone toward him. "Make your call."

Dom lunged for the phone, picked up the receiver, and dialed Bryan Martos. On the third ring, his stomach sank. Voicemail. "Bryan! This is Dom Jazzy. I'm at the Yamhill County Jail. Come get me out." His voice felt out of control, just like his spiraling thoughts. He couldn't believe he was in this position, and he didn't like it. "It went to voicemail. Can I call again?"

"Yes, sir. Ten minutes. In the meantime, we have some questions for you." Cel Martin's eyes communicated that he didn't give a damn how uncomfortable his prisoner was, nor did he care if he managed to contact his lawyer. He pulled up another chair and a tablet, and a pencil poked through his curly gray hair, nestled between his head and ear.

"You can't question me before my lawyer arrives, can you?"

"Sgt. Martin read you your Miranda Rights before he put you in the cruiser, Mr. Jazzy. The questions we have for you should be easy. Just tell us the truth." Clive Danner didn't like the man, and Dom felt it to his bones.

Danner took a deep breath and pulled out the second chair across from Dom. His eyes lifted toward Cel Martin and nodded.

The tablet's cover flipped up and over, and the pencil was poised on the page. "Let's begin with Heidi Mason, Mr. Jazzy. Tell us again that you have no idea who this young girl is, won't you?"

Dom Jazzy's eyes narrowed, and he gripped each pant leg. "Never heard of her." He heard his heart pounding; surely the cops could too. He stared at both of them.

A dozen questions later, Dom felt the sweat pouring down his temples. He wiped his forehead, lifted tissues from the box on the table, and swabbed his sweaty skin. He was sure Bryan would arrive as soon as he learned the police had fingerprinted him, for God's sake. He could hardly wait to sue their asses off.

Sgt. Martin pushed the phone toward Dom Jazzy again.

He redialed Bryan. This time, it went straight to voicemail without ringing at all. His face turned as red as a new beet. His fingers cramped around the phone. Where in hell was he? He always answered his cell phone before, always fixed things, and always took care of him. Maybe he was still angry because he had confronted him about sleeping with Bella? No, this was business. Bryan was a professional. And he paid him enough to answer the damn phone. Maybe he should call Bella. She had an inside track with Bryan. Yes, she'd find him. His stormy eyes stared at his folded hands as they rested on the dented and scratched table. If he hadn't slapped her around, she would have come to save him with bells on. Damn. And he only had one call. He'd better save it for Bryan.

Later, in his cramped cell, he sat on a cot and cursed the three-inch mattress. His eyes followed the white PVC piping running across the wall toward the white ceramic sink, the commode, and the short wall that concealed a shower. What in the hell had he gotten himself into? His head throbbed, so he pushed the thin blanket aside and rested his head on the pillow. It flattened as soon as he pressed down on the thin mattress.

He felt cold. It was noisy. Glancing toward the foot of his bed, the steel bars seemed to dance in front of him: tall, hard, locked. They had taken his clothes, his watch, rings, and even the St. Christopher medal his father had given him at his first communion. Looking down at the light blue cotton pants and V-neck shirt, he grimaced. They could have at least given him a long-sleeved shirt. This reminded him that the man who handed him his new clothes was an inmate. Dom noticed his eyes narrow when he read the charges on the intake paperwork. He'd sue their asses for libel.

Where was Bryan? He must have heard his voicemail message by now. Dom looked out the small window above him to gauge the light, trying to estimate the time. Midday. When he'd found Lily, it was around eight thirty. When the idiot girl tore off, screaming her lungs out, he'd left the city, which took about an hour. He'd pulled into the vineyard lot next to the tasting room, surprised to see a squad car parked near the old stone wall. He was even more surprised to see Denis Sorbets and three of his employees deep in conversation with the officers when he walked in the door.

When he reached the group, he had asked, "What's happened?"

Both officers turned toward him and Denis' face flushed a deep red. He'd been angry, upset about something, and stared at Dom as if he were a fly on the wall. That's when he'd turned toward the other employees. They'd separated and left out the door he'd just walked through.

"Dominic Jazzy?" The first officer's brown eyes had shown a distinct distaste, and his face was so serious, Dom had stepped back to figure out what he'd missed.

"Yes, I'm Dominic Jazzy. What's going on here?" He was sure Bella must have called the police and told them he was a wife beater. He smiled because he would just tell them she was sleeping around, and he didn't like it. They were men. They'd understand, and that would be that. He was Dominic Jazzy, by God.

The second officer reached behind him, pulled handcuffs from his belt, and stepped toward Dom. Sgt. Cel Martin said, "Dominic Jazzy, you're under arrest for child molestation and the rape of Heidi Mason."

Dom felt the floor try to rise up and meet him, but he fought to remain calm. He turned toward Denis and realized that his winemaker wasn't just upset about the Oregonian article, but also recalled when Heidi caused all the noise in the vineyard. He'd fire him when this was over. Feeling a bit more in control after making that decision, he allowed the officers to pull his arms behind his back, manacle his wrists, and lead him toward the police car.

He knew Bryan would get him out, and then Denis would be very sorry he second-guessed Dominic Jazzy. They had nothing on him, no proof, and who'd listen to a kid anyway?

Now, he figured he'd have to wait a while longer before Bryan got his sorry butt to McMinnville to talk his legal way into the system. He'd get Dom out, they'd have a beer, share a few laughs about it, and then he'd head home to kick Denis out of the vineyard.

"Hey, Jazzy. You can try that call to your lawyer once more and that's it." He heard the steel wall of bars click and open against the wall. The guard stood beside the door and motioned with his head. "Move!"

"You don't have to treat me like dirt, officer," Dom said with fake temerity. "My taxes pay your salary, put food on your table. Once my lawyer arrives and gets me released, you might see things a little differently."

When the guard laughed and poked him in the small of the back to make him walk faster, he felt shaken. His hands clenched, and his belly coiled tighter than a rattlesnake. If he could pounce on the man and inject him with venom, he would do it. But first, he needed to get out onto the street.

Ten minutes later, his heart thudded in his chest. Bryan wasn't answering his cell phone, and Dom knew why. He wasn't going to get him out at all. How could he ignore his client like this? The money would stop as soon as he was free again. Words tumbled around in his head. When the guard led him back to the small cell, Dom realized he might have to spend the night there. And he didn't like that thought.

This was Denis Sorbets' fault. And Bryan's. If he'd paid Lily the money without stealing part of it, François Beauvais would have left him alone. Lily would have been richer. Denis shouldn't have been in that part of the vineyard at all. Denis. His fault.

"Hey, Jazzy. Your lawyer is here to see you."

Dom's eyes flew open. How could he have fallen asleep? "Well, it's about damn time." He followed the guard past the clanking door. He didn't dawdle this time to avoid a shove from behind.

He was led into a room where the guard pointed toward a door. "Go into door number four. You have fifteen minutes."

Dom scowled at him.

When he walked into the small cubicle, he saw a glass window with a round metal speaker embedded in it. On the other side sat a man he'd never seen before. He craned his neck to look past him before shifting his gaze back again. "Who the hell are you?"

The stranger nodded toward the phone on the wall. When he picked up the phone on his side, Dom did the same. "My name is Michael Torrey. I've been assigned as your lawyer from the public defender's office since you can't connect with yours." He opened the file in front of him, and his eyes rose to Dom again.

"This can't be right. How did you know I needed a lawyer? I've never heard of you. And besides, I have plenty of money to pay a lawyer. I don't want a public defender."

Torrey stared hard through the glass. "Your arraignment should be within forty-eight hours. The prosecutor will formally charge you in a written statement. You will be listed as a defendant and asked how you plead. You will, of course, plead not guilty. Do you understand, Mr. Jazzy?"

"Well, of course, I'll plead not guilty. Can you get me out?"

"No, sir. I cannot."

Jazzy looked at the man who stared with slightly narrowed eyes. He pressed his hand to his chest to steady his heartbeat. When he wanted to demand something further, the expression on the man's face didn't seem open to debate. His thoughts slammed shut again.

"Mr. Sorbets, who is under your employ, stated that he saw you within a few feet of this young girl after she ran past him, crying and hysterical. What can you tell me about this?"

Dom's face flushed pink and he felt his blood pressure spike a few more notches than he could count. "I was snipping canes that day. I heard the girl crying, too. But I didn't see her. It's just circumstantial evidence and nobody can put me there hurting that girl."

The attorney didn't answer him. Instead, he stated, "And I have spoken with Ms. Mason's attorney. He said she will state, in court, that you are the man who accosted her. She remembers your silver hair," he continued. He gazed at Dom's head and shook his head as if to say, 'there's that.'

"She was obviously hysterical and thinks it was me. Well, it wasn't!" Dom tried to recall that day. The vines were thick in that area. Even though Denis had already snipped some of the canes, he made sure nobody was around. His eyes returned to the at

"Find Bryan Martos. I have him on retainer. He knows me. He can help you." His eyes stared blindly through the glass.

Michael Torrey raised his brows. "One more thing, Mr. Jazzy."

Dom's face swung back to the man across the glass. "What?"

"The judge assigned to your case is Loren Sampson. This judge has severe problems tempering mercy with justice with charges of this type. He also has a 98% conviction rate on person-to-person crimes." Michael Torrey banked the file on the small counter, and gave Dom another hard look. "See you in the morning."

Dominic Jazzy was stunned into silence. Before he could think of a rejoinder, a guard pulled him up from his chair. He was led back to his housing unit. When he stepped into his pod, steel bars clunked behind him, and he stood staring into the darkness.

CHAPTER 32

Callie's fingers were beginning to turn numb from tapping into the app so often. She pushed the last box into the pantry for Jules to stack on top of the others. The only room left was the master bedroom and a few kitchen items. God, she was sick of all the packing, and the turmoil in her head wasn't making it any easier.

She checked the audio feed again. When she saw the red blinking light, her finger froze mid-air. Alvin Marks had explained that meant a recording was available. Her hands shook as she tapped the button and listened. Callie's heart skipped a beat. She pressed the phone to her ear so hard it felt like it was inside her skin.

"If François had kept his nose out of my business, this wouldn't have happened......No, I'm not going to get him released from jail. I don't give a damn that he's paying me. He can't pay me enough to.... No, don't come here. Dammit." Callie heard a harsh sound as if he'd slammed his fist against something. And then everything went silent.

Jules stacked the boxes near the washer and came back into the kitchen in time to see Callie spin around and stare at him. She started to stutter and point to the phone.

"It...he.... someone...."

Jules struggled to understand her, so he took the phone from her hand. She pressed the red button again, and they both listened to Bryan's conversation together, with their heads pressed together.

"We need to call the police."

"What? Jules, you aren't making sense. It's illegal to record his conversations, and there's still no proof he killed François. That's all I want to do at this point. Prove. He. Killed. François."

"So, you are putting this personal vendetta before your safety?"

"That isn't it and you know it, Jules. Until I can shut the door to this, I can't open another one."

He whispered, "He was my best friend, and you know I want his killer caught, if he was killed." Sweat still ran down his temple and his shirt hung loosely around his waist.

Callie's eyes filled with tears, and she turned away from him.

"Maybe you're right. I'll probably never know if François's death wasn't an accident. How could I ever prove such a thing?" Failure cloaked her like a mantle. "I just wanted to ..."

He pulled her toward him and pushed her dark head onto his shoulder. "*Ma chère*, I am sorry."

She hiccupped, and the weight of defeat held her there. "I should just finish up here, get my money from Alexis, and walk away. I really thought I could..." She didn't finish her sentence.

"But you did make a big difference. Look how you were able to get past all those horrible memories when you helped Lily. Your idea for her to come to France is a good one. Can't you concentrate on that and put away the rest?" His voice was soothing, and she was drawn into his argument.

She couldn't speak because no words would come.

"I'm going to take a shower. When I was out running, a large vehicle nearly ran over me. I had to jump into a mud hole to avoid her. Crazy drivers. And she was going very fast." He mumbled something further and left her side.

Callie didn't think she wanted to move or talk to anyone. Her phone was still in her hand, and she tossed it on the cushion beside her. "So much for flies on the wall...or windows for that matter." She said sadly.

When Callie heard Jules' shower start, she settled down on the couch and reflected on the past couple of weeks. She couldn't remember the last time her emotions had been on such a roller coaster ride. She recalled the list on her iPad that she'd begun with such high hopes, and now her lips drooped in a frown. She just wanted to have it all over with. She sighed deeply and rested her head back on the couch. When her phone pinged, she lethargically lifted it from where she'd tossed it aside, and her breath caught.

The red button on her phone was blinking again. She wasn't sure if she wanted to listen to another one-sided conversation, so her finger paused over the off button. But, of course, her curiosity got the better of her, and she tapped it instead, bringing the screen to life.

Bryan was unhappy to see Bella knocking on his door. "I told you not to come here, Bella." His dense eyebrows rose as he stared at her. He didn't want her to see his indecision, his anger at Dom.

"I know that. Dom is in jail. Are you going to get him out? Denis is managing the vineyard, and I can stay here with you for a while... When are you going back to the city?" Her dark blonde hair flew into her face as she followed him inside after he opened the door wide enough for her to slip through.

"I don't plan to get him released." He walked toward the kitchen, where a large window framed the lake like a picture postcard.

She spun around. "But Dom pays you a retainer. Can you ignore him just like that?" Her voice sounded hopeful.

"Are you worried about him staying in jail or my getting him out? I'm sick of Dom hurting little girls, and I'm not going to help him this time. I may have a fight on my hands with the court since the Masons have already filed, but I'm standing my ground. Period." He turned toward his coffee pot and pulled down another cup.

She sat in the chair next to his table, crossing her black-clad legs. Covering her cheek, she turned away and maneuvered the strands of hair to hide the telltale bruise.

He poured their coffee. "Look at it this way," he said. "If they're focusing on Dom, they won't be listening to the little widow asking questions about François." His sweater was bunched up beneath his arm and caught on the edge of the table. When he dribbled a bit of coffee, he yanked the yarn loose and sat down.

"What are you talking about?" The color flushed her cheeks. When she leaned toward him, her bangs brushed across one eye, and she pushed them aside impatiently.

'm talking about Callie Beauvais and Valerie Blume coming together. You don't think Dominic and I were angry only about Lily's issue, do you?" He paused for a minute, then glanced at her for the first time and wrinkled his forehead.

She was confused. "Yes, I did. What are you hiding from me?"

"First of all," he said as he lifted a hand to her chin and turned her face toward the window to stare at the bruise, "What the hell happened to your face?" His eyes were inches from hers.

She looked down at her hands before reaching for the black coffee at her elbow. "Dom wasn't happy to learn about our affair." She sniffed angrily. "When he hit me, I was too shocked to think straight. I yelled something stupid at him, and then he really gave it to me." She snorted. "I'm glad he's in jail!" She opened a package of macaroons that sat beside her on the table and pulled one out.

"Shit. I should have known he would do something stupid."

"Did you tell him?" She sounded surprised.

A muscle in Bryan's face twitched. "He guessed. When I met him at McMenamin's last night, he knew. I didn't deny it. You know I love you, and now he does too."

Bella's eyes warmed for a heartbeat. "What did you mean about Callie Beauvais and the other woman?" She wouldn't let him change the subject this time, and tried to think of anything she'd heard about it before. Her mind was blank. She'd believed all along that Dom and Bryan feared Mae and Lily would discuss that time at the winery. Her head felt clouded as she stared at Bryan.

He watched her face, and knew he might as well come clean. "I think Valerie Blume gave Callie something that François found--- something that could hurt me."

She gaped at him, and shoved a second cookie into her mouth.

"Horse racing, gambling and paying off my bookie with the firm's money. François found out and I think Valerie was helping him prove it." He lifted his coffee mug and swallowed the contents, and lifted a hand. She placed a macaroon into his palm.

Bella blanched. "What?! François Beauvais was investigating you **and** Dominic?" The cookie stuck in her throat and she coughed. He patted her back, and she glared at him with tears in her eyes.

He laughed. "Yes, my darling. I had to stop his meddling three years ago and now I'll have to stop his wife too. I threatened him and his little wife, but he ignored it." Bryan turned toward the window to stare at the lake; a view he'd paid a hefty price to enjoy. With money that didn't belong to him. His eyes narrowed at the memories that slipped into his head.

Bella sat down abruptly. "Tell me the rest, Bryan. I know I won't like it, but I want to know everything."

Bryan Martos was well into the story now. His eyes gleamed as he turned toward her. "I was on my way back to Portland the day François died on the lake during a terrible storm. When I saw the boat heading toward my pier, I was stunned because the trees were wild, and the sky was dark. I had a bad feeling." He placed the cup down on the table and fingered its edge with his thumb.

"No kidding." Her voice dripped with sarcasm.

He scowled at her and continued his story.

"His boat hit your pier, and you couldn't help him." She urged him to confirm their old conversation.

"Well, part of that is true." He leaned back in his chair, tipping the front wooden legs off the floor a few inches, and his eyes gleamed.

"What part isn't?" Bella yanked her hair behind her ears. Loosening the gray scarf she had laced around her shoulders, she lifted it and draped it on the chair. And she waited.

"You aren't going to let me out of this, are you?" When he saw her shake her head, he said, "When François jumped out of the boat on my pier, he saw me packing my trunk. When I had one foot in the car and one still on the ground, he yanked me out and tackled me like a damn high school football player. He was a straight arrow and when he found out I'd used the firm's money to pay off those gambling debts, well.... he wanted answers. But what made him even angrier was about Lily…"

Bella's head came up. "What's Lily got to do with this?"

He groaned. "…When Mae accepted Dom's money for Lily to settle her claim out of court, he gave me $300,000. I gave Lily $50,000. I figured that was plenty for a kid. **That's** why François was so angry. He told me he was going to the police."

Bella swallowed hard, and every muscle quivered. "Damn you both to hell." She stood up quickly.

"Well, I couldn't let him go to the police, could I? I followed him back to his boat. The storm water was churning everything crazy. Trees were bent nearly in half. The storm jerked and rocked his boat toward my pier so hard, that he fell down on the pier. When he grabbed at me again, I shoved him and he fell between his boat and the pier. He screamed for help, but he looked bashed up; his head was bleeding and his arm was limp. I knew he would have died anyway, so I walked away. The storm finished him off. I drove to Portland."

"Oh my god, Bryan. Oh my god. No." She lifted her cup with a shaking hand. Wrinkling her nose at the now-cold coffee, her eyes told him she'd heard enough. But she couldn't make her legs work.

Callie drew in the little breath she could through the tightness in her chest and felt the ground shift. Dropping the phone, she pressed her temples. She felt like a fox that had chased something down a hole and discovered that the thing she had cornered was a venomous snake. She massaged her head to erase the voices from her memory. She raced to hug the commode in the laundry room and vomited. She felt as if she'd lost François all over again, only this time she knew what happened. She blew her nose to get the gunk out of her nose and throat and then laid her cheek on the cold rim of the toilet. "Oh god, oh god, oh god."

Callie weighed her options and chose action over self-preservation. Her heart was beating fast and her whole body tensed to fight. Tossing the mucked-up towel onto the floor, she squeezed her feet into both tennis shoes. She grabbed her bag with the gun inside and buckled it to her waist. She twisted the knob on the bathroom door, and yelled into the steamy room. "Jules! I just heard Bryan Martos admit he killed François. Call the police!! I'm going over there right now."

"No! Wait, Callie!" He heard the back door slam.

Callie pushed her arms into her coat as she ran through the streets toward Bryan's house. She was oblivious to every sane thought she should have had in her head. Her chest hurt so badly, she felt the pain all the way into her throat. Anger fueled her feet as she ran over the grass and onto the road.

Jules fought to turn off the water, his heartbeat accelerating to fever pitch. He reached for a towel, put one foot on the tiled floor and slipped backward. When his head hit the tiled wall, he fought the blackness that promised to envelope him by reaching for the towel rack. He blinked hard. And then he slid to the floor.

CHAPTER 33

When Bella saw a woman zigzagging across the lawn toward her car, she accelerated. The road was pot holed and uneven where she had nearly hit a man jogging earlier. Her wheels churned up loose gravel, splattering the side of the Buick Enclave with mud and sending small stones rattling beneath her floorboards.

Callie's heartbeat sped up and adrenaline pushed her forward. As the road curled gradually to the left, she panted the words out loud, "You aren't going anywhere, lady." The bag bounced against her belly, and Callie held it with a hand as she ran.

She ran toward Bella's car, and crouched to jump as the car neared, but she slipped in the mud. With one final burst, Callie sprinted, and threw herself at the moving metal. Hands, feet, face, and body smashed onto the unforgiving hood. Pain shot through her body. But she grabbed the windshield wiper blades and held on as the driver slowed at the sharp corner.

As Bella slowed down to bank into the turn in front of a white house built for the glorious view of Devil's Lake, their eyes met through the glass and she hit the stone embankment. The air bag exploded and her body slid into the pillow.

Callie was shocked loose; she lost traction and slid off the car's hood. But she didn't let go of the side mirror. Pulling the woman's door open, her hands reached in and jerked Bella from the airbag. "Now get out!"

Callie suddenly lost her thread of reason. When Bella fell to her knees, she began slapping her face as frustrated tears fought with anger. Each time she hit her, she saw the railing of the bridge coming up to meet her.

"You're crazy. Stop it!" Bella whipped her head away and used her feet to push herself away from the onslaught, but Callie moved with her. When Bella's head came up against the open-door frame, the edge of the floorboard punched into her back.

"It was you on the bridge! Why did you try to kill me?" Callie was yelling at her from an unknown well of anger. "And you stayed with that man after he hurt Lily…and …I'd like to beat you senseless."

Bella shook her head and fear filled her blue eyes. When she tried to respond, Bryan came around the back of the car and pulled the women apart. He yanked Callie from Bella and tossed her into a tall hedge of blackberry vines.

When he tried to help Bella up, she hissed, "Get back, Bryan."

His dark eyes widened and he pulled his hand back as if he'd been burned. Straightening up with surprise, he heard a steely voice behind him, "You better listen to your girlfriend, Bryan."

He sneered and snapped around. He came to a shocked halt when he saw the small gun pointed at him. His face showed not only surprise, but a brief, uneasy fear before he replaced it with a look of contempt. He gave her a cod-liver oil stare and chuckled.

Callie's arm didn't waver. She shifted her feet, thinking that Jules and the police were taking their sweet time. Now that she had the man in front of her, she didn't think the gun was such a good idea. She watched Bryan, and remembered the conversation she heard just moments earlier. Her fingers tightened on the gun.

"Oh, come on Callie, you know you aren't going to shoot me. Didn't François tell you not to point a gun unless you plan to use it?"

"Make a move and I will use it, Bryan."

He lunged toward her, but she was quicker.

Callie twisted out of his reach, but knew she'd made a mistake as she became wedged among sharp blackberry thorns. She yelped as their vicious points stabbed her. Warm blood trickled down her neck. Her curling hair wrapped around the thorns tight as a drum. She rocked her head back and forth, but she was trapped. Fear curled in her belly as she saw Bryan smirk.

Bryan pushed her back into the brambles to restrain her and laughed as he reached for her curly hair.

That was all it took for her to break loose, not what he intended. Callie abruptly shifted her feet, steadied her body and lifted her gun again. She stared at him with such venom he stumbled. "When I found the missing piece of the puzzle, I knew it was you, Bryan. I only had to prove it. Don't expect to lawyer your way out of this one."

She held her small, pink-handled gun firmly in both hands. *Where in the hell is Jules and the posse?*

They stared at one another a heartbeat before Callie straightened up. "I should just shoot you dead right now for killing François, Bryan, but I'd rather visualize you in a cement room filled with other killers, eating rotten soup and feeling afraid."

Bryan's mouth turned sour. "You can't prove it. The police ruled François's death an accident."

Callie ignored him and kept her gun pointed at his chest. She continued in a hoarse whisper, "And for all those little girls you threw under the bus for Dominic Jazzy, I want to visualize your new friends in jail using you for their sex toy." Her eyes teared up. "You are as bad as he is, Bryan."

Callie's face snapped toward Bella. "And you were part of all this..." Her voice was soaked in dislike.

Bella's eyes darted between Bryan and Callie. "I wasn't involved in any of this." Her voice shook. She hadn't moved during the exchange, but decided it was time to get away from the crazy woman. "Let me go. I didn't do anything." She stared at her flattened tire wedged against the stone abutment and slammed her palm against the fender before sliding down onto the road with a defeated groan.

Callie didn't flinch at the woman's moaning beside her. She kept her gun leveled on Bryan and answered her, "Shut up. I recognized your car. I know you tried to push me off the bridge and the police have a witness, so they'll figure it out soon anyway."

Her sharp intake of breath brought Bryan's head around. "Bella?"

"What? No!" She lifted her head and her shaking fist twisted it over her forehead. "This isn't my car. It's the vineyard's car...It must have been...and..."

"Don't say anything that can be held against you," he barked at her. He glanced between Bella on the ground and Callie's gun.

Bella's head jerked upward. "So, what...you think you'll get out of this mess and be my lawyer now?" She laughed cynically and got up from the ground. Leaning against her broken car, she brushed the mud from her slacks in angry jabs.

Bryan suddenly grabbed Bella, who was now whimpering, and dragged her to a position in front of him. Using her as a shield, he started backing toward his house. She jabbed him with an elbow at the same time Callie reached out a foot to trip him. Feet tangling, they both fell, Bella's head missing her bumper by an inch. Bryan jumped up and started to run.

Callie's safety was still on her gun, knowing full well she wasn't going to shoot anyone. Quickly stuffing the small gun into her jacket pocket, she ran after him and butted herself into his back. The momentum crashed him to the ground. When he tried to throw her off, Bella joined Callie and they gave each other a look. He wasn't going anywhere.

Moments earlier, Jules's disoriented gray eyes had gazed up at the bathroom ceiling. When reality swooped down like a sledgehammer, he jumped off the ceramic tile floor and flew toward his phone. Impervious to his nakedness, he dialed 911 and craned his neck to look out the back glass doors.

"No, I don't know how long ago she left. I fell and knocked myself out getting out of…it doesn't matter! She's going to confront a murderer." Jules held the phone in one hand and grabbed clothes from his bag with the other. Jumping around on one foot, he tried to slide his leg into a pair of jeans and talk to the emergency operator at the same time. Devil's Lake. We're south once you turn at the Neotsu Post Office off road Highway 101."

"What's the address, sir?"

Jules yelled into the phone. "I don't know the address. It's two blocks southeast from us. I'm at 3297 NE John's Loop at the lake. Hurry!" Jules stuffed his bare feet into tennis shoes at the exact moment his phone went dead. He looked at it in the palm if his hand, his heart hammering in his chest. His hand shot out toward the handle on the sliding door.

CHAPTER 34

Two police cars screamed toward them and careened around the corner. Blue and red lights flashed through the mist. Neighbors were coming out of the adjacent houses, now fully alert to the skirmish, the noise and police. They hadn't had that much excitement since two cows ran amok the previous year.

Callie took a deep, thankful breath when she saw Jules. He darted between the nearest houses and ran straight toward her. His face was a map of fear as he dashed at a fast clip with his shirt tails flapping behind him.

He grabbed her in a fierce hug and she burrowed into his chest, wild with relief. Her body shook, but she didn't have time to allow herself another moment of warmth.

Bryan Martos was trying to sweet talk himself out of assault and Bella was acting the victim. Callie wasn't having any of it. She marched over to them and slapped Bryan's face so hard, his neck snapped. When he lunged toward her, the officer jerked his arm and glared at Callie with a question on his face.

She meekly lifted her cell phone, tapped her phone and turned up the volume. When the voices emerged, Bryan's face froze. The recording ended in silence for a moment before Bryan turned toward Callie again.

"You can't use that in court. No judge would allow it because you recorded it illegally." He stopped a moment on that thought. "How in the hell did you record me? He looked at her with hatred.

"I didn't know he did it. I'm innocent of all that." Bella cried.

Callie turned toward her and said, "Someone tried to kill me on the bridge driving that car. Tell that to the police if you're innocent." Callie dared her to deny it. She saw truth in in Bella's face. So, that was Dominic Jazzy too? Well, let the police figure it out. She hoped, for Mae's sake, Bella **was** innocent.

Both officers rolled their eyes, and handcuffed Bryan Martos and Bella Jazzy. They read the couple their Miranda rights and Callie smiled when they shoved Bryan into the cruiser. She wasn't smiling when Bella turned to her before the officer put her inside the car.

She shook her head at Callie as if to say she was sorry, but Callie didn't think it was a look of guilt, but a look of sincere sadness. The woman had been through a lot; she saw the bruises on her face to prove it. Was that Jazzy too? And then Bryan using her as a shield. She spit out a curse.

One of the policemen returned to Callie and Jules. When he lifted his hand toward her, Callie looked at him quizzically. He nodded toward the gun and she placed it in his hand. "I suppose you have a concealed weapon permit to carry this, Annie Oakley?"

Callie smirked before shaking her head. "Yes, sir."

"It sounds to me like there's a lot of history going on between all of you. I'll need you to come down to the police station to make a statement. The bridge you were talking about…in Portland? Was this guy part of the case involving all those papers we sent off to Jake Sanders in Portland?"

"Yes, the Morrison Bridge above the Willamette River in the city. I reported it to Portland Police the same day and there was a witness who thought it was a woman. Now, I'm not so sure. The papers involved Bryan Martos, the man you have in the car. I think he may have also killed my friend in a hit and run early last week." Her voice shook. Callie's white-knuckled memory on the bridge wouldn't go away.

"And François. Who was he? I seem to remember a boat accident a few years ago here at the lake." The officer tipped his hat to keep the sun off his face, just peeping out of the clouds.

"My husband. And it wasn't an accident." She stared at the blue-uniformed officer. "I know the motive behind it now and I believe those papers will prove it."

"We'll need statements. Please come down after one o'clock."

Callie and Jules nodded.

"And which house belongs to Martos? We'll get a search warrant to look at his car. If he ran down your friend, the car should show some signs of damage. I'd send them in right now, but since the man's an attorney, we better follow all the rules on this one." He winked at her.

Suddenly, Callie felt as though she was underwater as he spoke. When Jules slid his arms around her, she leaned in and didn't let go. They walked in tandem back to the cottage.

"It was amazing, Jules. I knew the man was sick, but Mae told me Dom Jazzy actually thought Lily would listen to him. And his wife? She's a piece of work, but I think she's innocent. She looked too surprised when I accused her of nudging me on the bridge. If that's a company car, it was probably Dom Jazzy behind the wheel." Callie heaved a heavy sigh.

"My head feels like a tank rolled over me." He lifted his hand to the back of his head and Callie saw the knot. She reached up to touch his hair and he jerked away.

"What happened??

"It's a long story. I'll tell you later. Didn't you wonder what took me so long to run after you when you shot out of the house?"

She nodded as if she'd forgotten. "But the police are listening to me now. I am glad I found the car that was on the bridge that day. Even though the police wouldn't tell me where the car was registered, I recognized it. When I saw her car pull out of Bryan's driveway, everything clicked." She ran her hands through her curly hair, letting her fingers linger in the silver strands on her forehead.

Sitting down on the arm of the sofa, she turned toward him, loving the way the light shone on his finely sculpted face. Her body felt years lighter, without frantic thoughts running through her mind.

He pushed up the cuff on his sweater and looked at his watch. "The police said after lunch. Let's eat."

She saw Jules' gray eyes soften. "You said you'd do it and you did."

Callie's shoulders dropped as she let the final pieces of anger fall away. "Let's go into town then, *oui?*"

They drove south on Highway 101 through tourist traffic. Even in February, the small seaside town stayed busy. It took them thirty minutes to reach Moe's Chowder House in the south of Lincoln City, located in the Taft area of the beach town on the Siletz Bay and the Pacific Ocean. The view was one Callie often thought about, one of her favorite places. When she ordered them each a bowl of hot clam chowder, Jules pointed to the fish tacos. The waitress placed large glass jars in front of them filled with water and lemon slices.

Callie wasn't sure how to make the words in her head stop screaming at each other. How long had it been when she could sit like this without worrying, fidgeting, and planning? She took a deep breath, and Jules's warm hands covered hers as they tapped the table.

Gray and white seagulls squawked outside the wall of windows beside them before they spiraled down to land on the sand. Jules was mesmerized with the large birds and smiled at their antics. When he saw a small blonde girl running between the sand primroses, he grinned. "She reminds me of Veronique when she was a child." He smiled in memory.

Callie wished she'd known her stepdaughter at that age. A beautiful child she would be part of, a life François should have shared.

"I would have loved being part of her life. I miss her."

"Ah, so we can make plans to leave now?" Jules whispered.

"In a heartbeat," she teased.

"Like in a plane reservation to Marseille?"

"Yes," she agreed. "Exactly like that. But first, we stop by the police station and then our life is our own." She slurped her lemon water through its straw.

When Jules laughed at the noise, he thought how lucky he was to be in that place, at that time, with the woman across from him. The clam chowder was hot and when it touched his tongue, he groaned. "Yes, it is just as you promised."

When she reached for one of his fish tacos, he pretended to jab her fingers with his fork. She raised her eyebrows, blew him a kiss and lifted it to her mouth. Eating at the beach had always been a high point when she'd spent time there. Now, sharing this experience with Jules pushed it higher on the scale. The fish tasted better, the sky was bluer and she was happier than she'd felt in far too long.

When they were directed to the Investigations Division just after one, Jules held her hand tightly. They were placed in a small room to answer the detective's questions.

"Bryan Martos has been booked on attempted murder, alleged murder and embezzlement. I'm sure there will be a list of other charges, but for now, it's enough to hold him awhile."

"And Bella Jazzy?" Callie visualized Mae's face and didn't like the image.

"She seems to be an innocent bystander and we cannot hold her on anything. The bridge incident was bad, but she says she has an alibi for the day someone tried to push you against the railing." He pulled a notepad across the table. "A man named Denis Sorbets was with her and he's corroborated her alibi."

Callie sighed with relief, not realizing she'd held her breath.

The officer's face turned serious again. "Tell me how you recorded that conversation, Ms. Beauvais." He bent his head and looked at her through half-closed eyelids.

Jules snorted softly next to her.

"It's an app on my phone called MICBot. I stuck recording devices onto the man's windows last night."

The officer's eyebrows rose. "Really...?" He glanced at Jules, who nodded and rolled his eyes skyward.

She didn't care a toot when the detective frowned while she told him about the horse flies and recording Bryan's conversation. "I was determined to prove he killed my husband. Sometimes a woman has to take chances."

He tried to keep from smiling as he typed up her statement.

When he handed her a pen, she signed her name in large swirling letters. "What next?" she asked.

"It will be a long procedure, Ms. Beauvais, but I've already called the Portland Police and spoken with Detective Sanders. Bryan Martos will be lodged in the Multnomah County Jail and he will take it from there. The detective told me that one of his clients is in the Yamhill County Jail and he's been yelling for Bryan Martos. I imagine they'll be able to talk about both of their arrests when they're arraigned and moved to more permanent lodgings."

Callie smiled at the image. "And what about Mrs. Jazzy? Did Jake Sanders mention the car that pushed me on the Morrison Bridge? She was driving that Buick today. I imagine Dom Jazzy was angry because I was getting nosy. He wanted to stop me from talking to one of his victims…and…" Her eyes filled up with tears and she reached for a tissue on the officer's desk. Jules' fingers gently squeezed the back of her neck.

"Yes, Ms. Beauvais, he told me about that too. In fact, he said something at the end of our conversation to lighten your mood."

Her eyes lifted to his.

"Detectives Goldberg and Sanders both said they should hire you because you're the best investigator they have had in quite some time."

Everyone laughed.

"Will the recorded conversation keep Bryan Martos in jail for killing my husband?" Her words stuck in her throat.

The officer shook his dark head thoughtfully. When he lifted a hand to squeeze his bottom lip, he said, "Probably not, but the betting records and bank statements show a powerful motive. Remember…even if your husband's death can't be proven, we will undoubtedly find proof of paint and damage to the man's car that proves he ran down Valerie Blume." Sympathy crossed his face.

Callie was stumped. "How would anyone know that?"

He shuffled some more papers. "Detective Sanders told me he suspected Martos after he spoke with you the last time. It must have been something you said, because he began investigating him that day. We're sending a man to look in his garage once the judge signs the order. I don't think Martos will avoid a jail cell."

"And to think none of this would have come out if I hadn't found that note from Mae Haydon lost between the pages of a book." She shook her head sadly before putting it onto Jules' shoulder. When he put his arm around her, the policeman continued talking.

"When I asked the detective about Dominic Jazzy--- It appears that the D.A. has enough not only for an arrest, but to prove the man guilty of rape of a minor and sexual assault. They've dug up old records showing this man has been abusing girls since he was sixteen years old. He'll definitely spend a long time in jail. And rest assured, he will be a registered sex offender for the rest of his life. As far as his fancy vineyard is concerned, I'm not sure of its future, but I hope the wife can keep it going. My friend in Dundee says it's a landmark there and it'd be a rotten shame to lose it. They make the best Pinot Noir in the area."

Her eyes rounded. She looked at Jules, and she couldn't speak.

~

Callie had a $16,000 check in her purse and the promise of another one that would be electronically deposited into her Chase Bank account. The boxes were stacked neatly, the cottage was clean and her head was clear. Jules was locking the outdoor area with the stash of kindling when Callie's phone rang.

Her stomach knotted. It was Cendrine and she hoped it was the call she'd been waiting for. When she tapped the photo of her smiling face, she was surprised to hear Olivier's voice instead of her niece's. "She's in the hospital and we should know if Lulu is a girl or a boy in a few hours. And, another thing I needed to tell you…"

"Exciting news! I've had her on my mind every day. I've also been thinking about something else…I wanted to ask you both for a very big favor."

"Oh?"

"Would you and Cendrine consider being host parents for a sixteen-year-old girl to go to school in Pertuis so she can also learn to make wine? Would this be too much for you?" Callie held her breath.

"Eh? I will speak with Cendrine about it…once this baby is born. Who is she?" His curiosity mingled with his excitement over becoming a father again.

"It's a long story and I will tell you another time, but I just wanted to run it by you first…" Callie's face was wreathed in smiles.

"Run it by me?"

Callie laughed. "It means that I wanted to ask you before I invite her to be part of our lives for a year."

"*Oui*…ok. Life with this teenager and Veronique and the new baby… The days will be full, but of course we should love it. I promise anything for you, especially since you are coming back to live near us."

"Thank you." Callie was so happy, she almost missed his next sentence. "What was that, Olivier?" The phone made chirping noises and the words sounded far away.

"There is a little issue about the brandy sale in Spain. There is a lot of news on Spanish television about Pablo Picasso's wish to build that flamenco guitar art colony in Algodonales."

Callie drew a breath. "How did that happen?"

"Picasso news travels fast. The Alonso people who are related to Picasso's partner who produced the brandy, want the money from the brandy sales. They say it belongs to them instead of a flamenco guitar school. We will work it out because we have Picasso's letter, but I'll be glad when you get home. It will add excitement to your life besides packing boxes."

Olivier heard his aunt's laughter on the other end of the phone. He wasn't sure what he'd said that was so funny, but he promised to call again when the newest Benoit was born.

The day before, Callie and Jules watched the police go through Bryan Martos's house. When the tow truck pulled his black Cadillac SUV down the road, they'd smiled sadly.

The cottage door was locked. The rain had stopped and the lake was smooth as glass. As Callie walked toward the packed car, she touched the wooden For Sale sign with a melancholy look on her face. Her fingers lingered over the post and she had one last look behind her. Veronique's scarf was triple wrapped around her neck and she hugged her jacket tightly to keep out the cool breeze.

She turned brown eyes toward Jules when he tapped his fingers on the top of the car to hurry her along. "Are you ready for your first Spanish lesson? It sounds like you will need to...as you Americans say, hit the ground running."

He joined her inside the car and rested his hand on the gear shift. The car was packed from front to back, and he was a little apprehensive about being the driver back to Portland. He'd thought of this day for weeks, and now that it was here, he didn't want to waste another minute. He couldn't stop grinning when he turned toward the woman he wanted to spend the rest of his life with.

She reached over, pressed her lips against his, and ran her fingers through his graying hair. "Mmmmm, *si, señor.*"

The End

If you enjoyed this book...

One of the most powerful gifts a reader can give an author is recommending a writer's work to a friend. So, if you have friends who might enjoy reading about Callie and her escapades, please tell them.

I don't have shelf space in airports or many bookstores, so your reviews help more readers discover my work. When you have a moment or two and would like to spread the word, please write down your thoughts and reactions in an honest review. I would greatly appreciate it. Just visit the website where you purchased the book, click on the cover image, and scroll down to "leave a customer review."

About the Author

Genealogist, family historian, and fiction author Patricia Steele was born in Woodland, California, and moved to Oregon when her mother remarried nine years later. She then became a nomad as an adult, living in eight cities, five states, and eleven houses before settling in Arizona, closer to her roots. She speaks English and a bit of Spanish. Her hobbies include gardening in pots of every color, traveling, being a grandmother to her six grandchildren, and enjoying wine. She includes recipes that use wine in the pages of her cookbook, Cooking DRUNK.

You can find her books at www.patriciabbsteele.com.
Stop by and say hello at www.facebook.com/patriciabbsteele

If you missed books one and two of this series, please read excerpts on the following pages…

Excerpt – Book 1

Shoot the Moon: Book One of the Callinda Beauvais Series

"Callie. I think I just shot Hunter."

"You *think* you shot him? Oh, my God!!" Callie heard Olivia crying and Hunter yelling in the background. Her mind froze only a second before she screamed into the phone. "I'm not far away. Stay away from him if you can." She blew her nose loudly, stunned as curiosity married fear.

"Yes, hurry! He's so angry, I have a bad feeling. He is a little bit crazy, Cal. He is ranting about our new prescription drug contract to upgrade Larkspur's health insurance policies. He sounds serious, as if his life depended on it. He is angry that we want to use another company for the drug coverage. We can save our policyholders money with the new contract! But he isn't focusing on the people we insure at all. Here he comes again, Callie."

"Oh God, Olivia…I'm coming!" She tossed the phone onto the seat and heard a sharp blast. Horrified, her brain went into overdrive, knowing her car was not backfiring. Her foot slipped off the accelerator and then quickly adjusted as she tromped downward and sped toward the Milwaukie exit. She raced a few blocks, turned onto Carlyle, and left on 13th. Her little car careened into Olivia's driveway at 40 mph, bumping the edge of the curb, jerking her body like a rag doll, and banging her head into the headliner. Oblivious, she downshifted, turned off the engine, ripped the door open as the Audi rocked wildly on its tires, and slammed the door before making a beeline for Olivia's front door.

Skipping up the condo's sixteen cedar steps, the tantalizing perfume of lilacs bombarded her. She reached the door but was dismayed when it wouldn't open. Everything was silent. Rushing around the large deck to the bay window, she looked into the living room, shading her eyes with her hand. Now what? Call 911. That's it. Why didn't I do that first? Dammit!! Blindly, she rushed back to her car and reached for her cell phone on the passenger seat. Her fingers didn't want to work, but she eventually thumbed the button and frantically dialed 911.

Callie's voice shook so severely that she barely spoke in complete sentences at the sound of a woman's voice. "I'm sure she's in danger; please send the police because I am outside her house right now, afraid to go inside. Just a few minutes ago, she called and told me Hunter Roget had threatened her…" Callie glanced at the house again.

"What is your name, ma'am?"

"Callinda Beauvais. Can't you ask me that later?"

"What is the address, Ms. Beauvais?"

Callie reeled off the house number and rubbed the stinging tears from her eyes. "Is there a police cruiser nearby? We may need an ambulance too. I don't know what to do!" Callie sniffed before leaning against the door. She pressed her head against the cold steel before slumping onto the car seat.

"Please remain in your car, ma'am. I will send the police and an ambulance right away." The woman hung up.

Ok. The ambulance and police. That's good. That's good. Her hand jerked the car door open a few seconds later, and she bolted for the house again. Remain in my car? Hell **no.**

Lunging toward the front door a second time, she rammed herself against it, pushing hard with the palm of her hand. The heavy, leaded glass door lurched open, stunning her momentarily. She grabbed the knob before it banged against the wall, fearing the noise, damage and broken glass. She was so sure it had been locked.

Callie heard a whimpering sound and realized it was her own. ~

Excerpt – Book 2

Wine, Vines and Picasso: Book Two of the Callinda Beauvais Series

The following morning, a warm glow flowed through Callie in Portland as she sat in her best friend's office at Larkspur Insurance. "Cendrine left another message. I should fly to Pertuis. I can help and just......."

"...run away?" Olivia struggled with irritation.

"I don't need to run away, Livvy. We're trading phone calls, and frankly, I'm worried."

"Well, take Nate with you...after my wedding." Olivia's diamond earrings glimmered as the sun shifted through her office window. Her green eyes stared at Callie with a question.

"No, François' ghost would be between us. Of course it would."

Olivia Phillips bit her lip and heaved a heavy sigh.

Callie grinned. "Nate and I had a long talk last night after I'd falsely accused him of...well. You know why. We spent time under the stars..."

"You mean, in your hot tub?" Olivia perked up.

"He is a lovely man, Livvy. Now back to work," she teased without answering. With a small wave, she left the office.

***

The phone woke Callie from a deep sleep at dawn the next day. Her eyelashes fluttered, and she jerked awake with a gasp. Twisting both hands beneath her pillow, she nuzzled deeper into its folds. The phone jangled again. Callie's tousled head lifted off the pillow a few inches, a swath of chestnut and silver bangs covered one eye.

"François? François, are you awake?" An eerie silence met her question as December's morning sun streamed through the bedroom window. Space met her questing fingers. And then her eyes popped open, and reality swooped down like a hammer. She heaved herself onto her back. "Of course, François can't answer the damn phone." She was sick with the struggle within her. *I'm a widow. Say it!*

Flipping the covers off her satin-clad body, she jerked the coverlet upward. Goose bumps rose on her arms; she swore she saw the indentation of François's head on the other pillow. Would she ever adapt to widowhood? The morning's slip confused her. *Cendrine's phone messages have taken me back to Provence and, of course, to François.*

A niggle of alarm wormed its way through her mind when ringing split the air again. Making a mad dash for the phone, her niece's words crashed together like a racing freight train. Listening intently to the garbled story, Callie's chin sank to her chest. "Slowly, *ma chérie*. And please, in English. My French needs some practice."

"Callie...I cannot tell *grand-mère* and *grand-père*. Olivier took money from the vineyard's account. I do not know why. I'm scared and do not know what to do, and he...has disappeared. Please come help me."